MW01489510

Moonbaby

Moonbaby

the legend of the changelings

Best Wishes!
Kate Mallinger

KATE MALLINGER

To my Aunt Joyce, my sister Cindy, my nieces Grace and Julia, and my brother Don who showed their support and gave their honest opinions during this endeavor.

Contents

Prologue: Two Weeks Earlier   1

Chapter One: Maren Malone   11

Chapter Two: A New Adventure   17

Chapter Three: A New Pet   25

Chapter Four: Dr. Don Minnetonka   31

Chapter Five: Big Silver   41

Chapter Six: The Changelings   50

Chapter Seven: First Revelation   57

Chapter Eight: Letting Go   67

Chapter Nine: Unexpected Hero   80

Chapter Ten: Kenny Shane   90

Chapter Eleven: Second Revelation   100

Chapter Twelve: Damien Jon   115

Chapter Thirteen: The Human Life   119

Chapter Fourteen: Human Hypocrisies   132

Chapter Fifteen: Starr   143

Chapter Sixteen: Wolves in the Closet   151

Chapter Seventeen: Free As a Wolf   167

Chapter Eighteen: Herbs and Silver   175

Chapter Nineteen: Yuletide-Christmas   181

Chapter Twenty: New Year's Eve   189

Chapter Twenty One: Wolf Moon   202

Chapter Twenty Two: Three Moons   229

Epilogue: Two Months Later   236

Prologue

Two Weeks Earlier

Julian James tracked the black female wolf to the edge of a dense growth of trees. He shook his head, dumbfounded. For ten years she had evaded every hunter on the reservation, becoming somewhat of a legend. They called her the moon-bitch, or the "Moon." She had a thick, silver ruff that reflected the moonlight on a clear night, the only time anyone could catch a glimpse of her. The elders on White Earth Reservation respected her. The younger ones blamed her for missing family pets and livestock. Now here she was standing in plain sight—even looking back at him.

Something was off. Julian looked back toward the rocky ledge where he had spotted her tracks the previous week. He couldn't believe the lucky break, yet it was strange. Her tracks were rarely seen by anyone. They said she knew how to cover them.

Now here she was, taunting him—giving him the shot he had dreamt about for years. He raised his .270 Winchester rifle to his shoulder and pulled the trigger. The crackle echoed across the open field.

Julian ran toward the black pile of fur at the tree line. He couldn't believe it. She had just stood there and let him take the shot. He inhaled sharply. She was huge—coal black with that infamous, silver shawl of fur at the shoulder. She reached out with her front paw, moving it painfully in the dirt. Julian stepped back. Piercing, copper-yellow eyes shifted toward him. She tried to lift her head but couldn't. Her jaw moved slowly with her labored breathing.

Julian grabbed at his chest. His throat tightened; he coughed to get air. He couldn't turn his eyes from hers. She didn't growl or snarl. There was only that softly undulating paw, and those wild, glowing eyes that searched his face. Julian looked away, hoping she would hurry up and die. It was taking too long.

He couldn't stand it. He knelt down next to her and placed his hand on her moving paw, marveling at its sleek power. He didn't know why he did it, why the urge to caress her came over him. He squeezed her paw, rubbing the webbing in-between her toes. He had never done anything like it before. He never gave a second thought to the animals he hunted, or their death throes, some of which were downright awful.

Julian struggled to regain control. The flame in her eyes, now an emerald-yellow color, mesmerized him. Julian winced. He felt her pain himself, but still couldn't turn his head. Then the flame softened; the glow dissolved. The jewel-toned irises grayed into the lifeless color of death. She was gone.

The black she-wolf that had been hunted for over ten years lay in a heap of pine needles, her empty eyes staring into nothingness. Julian shut his own eyes. He squeezed her paw, feeling the roughness of the pads and strength of the claws, now limp in his hand. He dropped the paw and jumped up. He was dizzy. *What just happened?* His heart pounded and his neck stiffened with repressed anger.

He walked a few feet from her body, pulled his pack of cigarettes from his shirt pocket, and lit one. *Gotta get my shit together.* He paced back in forth in front of her body while he smoked one cigarette and then another.

Julian squashed the fourth butt in the dirt, and then yanked his Rambo-style knife out of its sheath on his belt. He clenched his teeth, knelt down, and began the ugly business of retrieving his trophy head and hide. It took longer than usual. His watering eyes kept blurring his vision. There was something about her … he couldn't shake it. He hadn't cried in years.

Julian slammed his blade into the dirt to clean it off. He had now recovered from his bout of emotion—or insanity, as he saw it. After all, there was a $5000 reward for the wolf that was raising havoc on the rez. He threw the heavily stuffed duffle bag over his shoulder, flinching under the weight. He fumed. The guilt kept creeping up, whirling in his stomach, leaving him nauseous.

He headed over to the rocky ledge area where he had first spotted her tracks. *Damn weird her leading me off to the woods, then just standing there.* The hair on his arms stood up and his neck tingled. Her tracks were all over the place, heading in different directions and back again, trying to confuse him. *She was smart all right.* Julian sat the heavy duffle down. He felt for his rifle and maneuvered into position and waited. All was quiet around him.

After a good five minutes, Julian squatted down to get a better view of the indentation of the rock ledge behind him. The large outcrop was called "the hook" by the locals. It was a marker for the dead center of reservation land. A flat surface of limestone stood out like an overhang, and then bent back around on itself, giving the impression of a hook. Outsiders were spooked by it. It was eerie looking, like it wasn't nature-made.

The locals took full advantage of this. They told the bothersome tourists it was an ancient, Indian holy site and that people who snooped around it never came back. It worked. The Ojibwe locals kept their reservation to themselves … at least most of it.

Surrounding the hook were little nooks in the rock walls which usually housed some small animal. It took Julian only a minute longer to note the pile of fresh, broken rocks and dirt lying just left of the ledge. *Had there been a landslide?* He shouldered his gun and crept closer. *God, she has her tracks covered here.* He looked around as he took a step back. Then he knelt down and stirred through the rubble, just a pile of rocks and some partial wolf prints. There was something behind it. *By god, it's been dug out!*

Julian twisted his rifle into his armpit. He glanced over his shoulder as the thought occurred to him of a mate or pack nearby. Yet, he doubted it. A pack or mate would have made itself known by now. Either would have sensed the recent kill. Besides, she'd been traveling alone as far as anyone knew. Still wary of his vulnerable position, Julian turned his head to peer in, then crawled slowly through the rubble pile and froze. *Damn, it's a den. That she-wolf dug this out with paws. Unbelievable!* Julian let out a soft whistle, forgetting he had his head in a wolf den. Then he heard it. A whimper … then another, then full harmony. She had pups.

Julian backed out, jumped up, and dug through his duffle to get the flashlight he always carried. He shivered as his hand grazed the still-warm head of the pups' mother. His heart pounding, he looked around again, then dropped to his knees and scrambled back in. *I can probably get another $1000 off these pups, if I play my cards right.* He smiled and shined the flashlight into the small cave. Huddled in the back corner were three wolf pups. *Couldn't be more than a week old.*

Julian worked his way out of his flannel outer jacket in the cramped quarters, trying not to further frighten the wolf babies. He wasn't sure how deep the den went or how far he would be able to reach. His hand felt for the fur balls. He grabbed the first one and pulled it into the light. *Nice and healthy … a girl.* He laid out his jacket and placed her in the center. He grabbed another. It was also a female with the same color and markings—silver with some black. *They're definitely twins.* The last one was feisty, growling and snapping all the way. Julian looked it over and whistled. *What a beauty*

… a little boy, too. He was coal black with a little spot of silver on his miniature ruff—a spitting image of his mother.

Julian stared at the little guy's face. *Cute for a wolf,* he couldn't help but think. Just then the pup opened his eyes, made his mouth into a little "O," and howled as hard as he could. *God, those yellow eyes!* He dropped the little male into the pile of his sisters, rolled up the edges of the shirt, and tied it like a bandana. Then he dragged the bundle and himself back out into the light. The pups were strangely quiet. *A little unnerving, they should be freaking out by now.* Julian looped the bundle over his arm, picked up his pack and hiked the mile to his parked jeep, all the while staring at his boots. They moved forward on their own.

It was about 6:30 pm when Julian arrived back in White Earth's little downtown area. He grabbed his parcel, which had remained remarkably quiet after the drive, and threw his backpack over his shoulder. He flinched under the weight. He walked down the sidewalk to Redwing Tavern which doubled as the local bounty office for nuisance animal rewards. His uncle, Jesse James, owned it.

"Wait till you see what I got." Julian had a northern Minnesota accent with a touch of the slow, quiet Indian drawl. He laid his jacket bundle on the top of the bar and untied it.

"I'll be goddamned," Dr. Don Minnetonka said. He was sitting at the bar enjoying his evening beer. He was the only customer. Jesse came out from the back kitchen and stopped dead in his tracks.

"What you got there, Jules?" Jesse always called him "Jules." It was a nickname that had stuck from better times. The pups woke from the commotion and started whimpering. Jesse hurried over to them, wiping his hands on a towel he was carrying.

"Damn, Jules. You aren't supposed to bring in litters, or touch them or anything like that. What is this? You want to get a fine?" Jesse kept wiping his hands although they were long dry.

"I didn't have a choice, Jess. Look at this." Julian grimaced as he lifted the heavy pack off his shoulder. It hit the floor with a dull thud. He fumbled with the straps and reached in, trying to get ahold of his prize. Then in one smooth movement, he swung the huge, black head of the she-wolf out of the bag and plopped it onto the bar. Dr. Don's stool screeched as it shot backwards across the wood floor. Julian bent down and splayed open the pack so that the famous black hide with the silver ruff was visible, folded in a wet mass of hair and blood.

Dr. Don's beer glass hit the floor and shattered. He leapt off his stool and stood frozen, a look of pure horror on his face. "It's her, it's the Moon." He was oblivious to his beer-soaked pants and broken glass everywhere.

"Damn right," Julian boasted. "Now's the time, Jess," he said, turning to face his uncle. "Roll out the five big ones."

Jesse stood transfixed near the bar. He didn't speak. His eyes were locked on the wolf head. Two trickles of water ran down his cheeks. Julian looked back and forth from Dr. Don to Jesse, and then back again.

"What the hell is the matter with all of you? This is her, the Moon bitch. Took *me* to get her. Now where is my money?"

Jesse cleared his throat and wiped his face with the towel he was still holding. "Well, now," he said, his voice raspy sounding, "We got to take care of these pups first off. I'm calling Blackhawk. He'd want to know. I know he'll take the pups."

"Damn, Jess! What's the big deal? I want my money. Take the pups. Should have known you'd act like this. I'll take a beer, thank you. And I'll be outta here before old Blackhawk Malone gets here. What's the buddy-buddy between you two, anyway? He's not one of us, Jess. He's not a James." Julian dropped onto a nearby bar stool. He slapped his hand on the bar.

Jesse walked around the bar and automatically poured the beer. He turned without looking at Julian and started back toward the kitchen. "Pack up that carnage before I get back," he said, his voice a hoarse whisper.

Julian gathered up the Moon's remains and pushed them back into the pack on the floor, wiping his hands on the outside of the well-used pack. It wasn't the first time his backpack had seen blood. There were several old streaks of a dark brown color all over it.

"Why'd you do it, Jules?" Dr. Don had pushed his stool back up near Julian and the pups. He wrapped them back up in the jacket, looking anxious as he moved them away from their mother's death smell. He paused a moment, only to look hard at the black male.

Julian took a big swig of his beer and slammed the glass down. "Cause I hate those fucking wolves, Doc, and you know it. Nothing but a menace. And that damn she-wolf was breeding? God, man, more of *her kind*." He looked directly at Dr. Don with his last two words.

"You don't know that for sure, Jules. You just don't know that." Dr. Don cradled the bundle in his arms. He stared off in deep thought.

Jesse appeared from the back of the tavern. "Blackhawk's on his way. Wasn't too happy, Jules."

"When is he ever happy with anything I do? I know a lot of other folks that will be relieved. She was a killer. Should 'a stayed deeper in the woods," Julian said. "No one would of known 'bout her but me, of course." He gave them a cocky grin.

The James's' and Malones' didn't get along. Some old feud is what Julian heard. Even the death of Blackhawk's son, Jonny Malone, hadn't smoothed things out. Jonny had taken a header off a beam at a construction site in Wisconsin. The talk at White Earth whispered suicide. Julian assumed old Blackhawk held it against him. After all, *he* was alive when Blackhawk's own son Jonny, was dead. *Jonny—nothing but a self-pitying drunk.* Whatever the case, Uncle Jesse liked Blackhawk, and that really pissed him off. He rubbed it in whenever he could. Today Julian didn't give a damn. Today he just didn't relish the idea of running into the old man.

Jesse walked over to Dr. Don. He pulled back the corner of the jacket. "Take a look at that black one. Looks just like her," Jesse said, as he picked up the pup.

Dr. Don nodded in agreement.

"Let's take them in the back," Jesse said. "Got a box back there and some towels. Give Jules his jacket back, if you would."

Dr. Don tossed the jacket across the bar, not looking to see where it landed. He and Jesse started toward the back room with the pups gathered in their arms.

Dr. Don stopped halfway and turned back to Jules. "Julian, put your jacket back on or get it out of here. I can't stand the smell. Something all wrong with this."

Julian shrugged as he pushed his arms back into the wrinkled mess of the flannel shirt. He sat back down and finished his beer. No one called him Julian unless they were really pissed off. *What the hell is his problem?*

"Bring my money while you're at it," Julian yelled out to Jesse. "I gotta go." He knew he was throwing gas on the fire but the whole thing was irritating. He could hear some mumbling, and then the slamming of the safe door.

"There you go, Jules." Jesse came back with a stack of hundreds and other bills wrapped in tape. He held the bundle up to Julian's face.

"Part of it is the town donation; the other is what the Council donated. Sure you want to keep it all? Not sure if it's the right thing, Jules." Jesse grabbed his spit cup with his other hand and sent a wad of chew into it as if it tasted really bad.

"Damn sure I do," Julian said, as he yanked the wad of bills from Jesse's hand and laid it out on the bar. The blood on his hands smeared onto the bills as he moved them around, doing a once over count. *Guess blood money is blood money,* he thought, letting out a little snicker. Then he took the flannel shirt back off and wrapped the bills. The new bundle smelt eerily like death, wolf pups and money.

He jerked the packed shirt tighter, retied it, and looped it over his shoulder. *Money instead of more dirty wolves—not a bad exchange.* He was feeling more like his old self. He bent down and hoisted the pack with the wolf remains from the floor and headed for the door.

Julian paused with his two parcels, his hand on the doorknob. He could barely hear Dr. Don and his Uncle Jesse talking. It was the unusually low tone that stopped him at the door. "I'm staying till Blackhawk comes," Dr. Don whispered. "We got to talk. This is serious."

Chapter One

Maren Malone

Maren held her long, auburn hair behind her as she examined what she felt was a hideous roll of fat around her middle. She had promised herself that she would get over the weight thing yesterday. After all, she could only squeeze half an inch. *I don't care what Mom thinks, I still feel fat.* She stuck two fingers down her throat and gagged. Her stomach convulsed as it pushed out part of a cheese sandwich. She grimaced as she reached for toilet paper to wipe her face and hands. Maren slammed the toilet seat down and flushed. "That's it," she said out loud. "Disgusting."

The girls at school were always starving themselves. Or taking laxatives, or throwing up. *Pretty pathetic,* she'd thought when they told her. Now here she was trying it herself. *Could never get used to that—gross.* A wave of guilt swept over her. She thought about how fat she was, although she was a size six, how much she missed her father, how much she hated her father, and what was she going to do now?

She had just graduated from Black Water High School, located right in the middle of the Lac Courte Oreilles Reservation in Wisconsin. It didn't seem much like a reservation because she didn't hang around with the Native Americans. There were a lot of non-Indians living there, something about owning land or property there. She knew it was a big mess. Her father had talked about it often. She never paid attention. And now he was just gone. She didn't date and she didn't even have a best friend. She wiped her face with a wet cloth. No way did she want her mother to know what she had just done.

Maren walked out of the bathroom, brushing her hair. It was waist-length now and sometimes she just wanted to chop it all off.

"You OK, honey?"

Laken Malone was sitting in their living room with a stack of papers in her lap. Maren assumed they were related to her father's death. The insurance company was trying to say his fall was suicide so they didn't have to pay. It wasn't a lot, but her mother wanted her to have the money for college.

"Fine, Mom."

Maren walked over to her mom to kiss her on the cheek. She hoped she didn't smell like vomit.

"You don't look fine," Laken said, as she pulled back and wrinkled her nose. "And you're not cutting your hair. You father would just die."

"He already did, Mom. And I already told you I wouldn't do anything until I picked out a hairstyle I want. No one has plain, long hair in college anymore. I don't want to look like a backwoods' hick."

"Oh, honey. You could never look like that. Look at yourself! You're beautiful. That hair is special. Thick like your father's. But that color looks like his and mine mixed together. You've got your father's eyes, though, Maren. Completely. I loved his eyes. Coppery-green that glow golden when you're angry. Just like Jonny's." Laken looked down suddenly at her papers.

Maren knew her mom was fighting hard not to cry. After all, her father had only been gone two weeks. One thing she knew for sure about her parents. They had been crazy about each other.

"I'm sorry, Mom. I miss him too. I'm sorry."

Maren leaned back over her mother and held her head against her. She really did miss her father. She was sick with guilt about how she had treated him. She hadn't been strong enough to handle the whole alcoholic thing—so humiliating. Too bad throwing up didn't help anything.

"Ok, honey, you're right. I shouldn't be doing this anymore." Her mother patted her face. "Can you sit for a minute? I have to talk to you."

"Sure, Mom."

Maren grimaced. She would make it up to her mom. She wouldn't cut her hair—for now. It was that old traditional thinking. *The Indian way.* Although her mother was Irish, she had taken to the culture immediately. After all, she had married a full-blooded, Ojibwe Native American.

Maren sat on the brown, leather couch close to her mother's chair. A hand-made, cherry end table separated them. Her father had made it. He had made a lot of the furniture. Just constant reminders of him.

"Your grandfather called this morning. You remember him, don't you honey? Blackhawk? I think you were ten years old when we visited the Minnesota rez. You know you could have gone to your father's burial service. Blackhawk really wanted to see you."

"I know, Mom. I don't believe in all that Indian stuff, and it was right in the middle of finals! I did my own grieving at the church here. Don't make me feel bad about that now." Maren threw her hands down hard onto her lap.

"I'm not. Your father *wanted* to be buried in White Earth. That's not the point. Blackhawk wants you to come for a visit. Just a couple weeks. He sounded really desperate about it. I'm not sure what's up. He's an old man, Maren. And he loves you." Her mother paused to gauge her reaction.

"He was attached to you from the time you were born. You'd have your own room. Jonny's—your father's old room. And he just got a dish antenna so you can watch movies and use your computer there." She waited patiently for an answer.

Maren felt she could throw up for real. She knew she owed her mother this. She shouldn't have made her go to the rez alone. She just hated the idea of some Indian burial ceremony with all those traditional weirdoes. That was one thing she regretted about her relationship with her father. She never gave him an inch when he tried to talk to her about her bloodlines, where she came from, the old Ojibwe traditions—everything *Indian*. She felt he had been leading up to something that she never let him go to. "I'm only half!" she would scream at him. "Half is plenty," he'd say back. Then she'd storm out and he would get drunk. *How many times had that happened*, Maren thought.

"Ok. I'll go."

Maren looked at her mother who now had tears running down her face. *Shit. Don't really want to though.*

"I'm so happy, Maren. Thank you. I'll call Blackhawk back right now. You can leave this weekend. You can even take your car. You'll have more freedom that way. Oh, I'm so glad."

"Whatever, Mom. Don't make such a big deal over it. I'm going to bed." She gave her mother a quick smile, which dissolved as soon as she turned her head.

Maren walked to her bedroom and shut the door. *Well, that's done. I can handle a week or two.* Maren took her jeans and t-shirt off. She was tired. She just wanted to turn on the TV, lie down in bed, and forget everything for the rest of the night. She stood in front of her dresser mirror, pulling her hair down both sides of her face. *Guess I do look sort of Indian. If this were black, I'd really be there.* Her mother was right. Her hair was pretty special. Shiny and thick. Never touched by artificial color or highlighting. She did wash it with that concoction her mother made. All those herbs and oils from the reservation. Her mother had taken her salon shampoo from her and replaced it with her own version about five years ago. "Just try it," she said. "You can have this back if you insist." Maren had never wanted it back.

Maren got out her father's old t-shirt for sleeping in. It was worn and soft with some faded Harley Davidson decal on it. She started to turn her bra around to unhook it and stopped. She did like her breasts, from this view, anyway. The other girls at school were always complaining about theirs— too big, too small. She wasn't the type that needed a lot of male attention, although she got her share of stares. It just wasn't about her breasts.

Thank god I don't get the jokes and leers that Chelsea gets. Maren smiled, thinking about the only girl she talked to at school. Chelsea was always laughing, always telling her how beautiful she was. She was the only unselfish girl in high school. And she definitely knew how to draw attention away from her oversized breasts. Maren admired her. *Guess I could learn a thing or two from her. But no one has really seen mine … .*

Maren stood in front of her dresser mirror. She ran her fingers over the extra wide band of her bra. It was a sports bra with three inches of width along the band. She would only wear that type and had to special order them. She was narrow in the middle with softly, rounded hips and long legs. Willowy, she often heard. *Could be a little skinnier,* she thought, momentarily distracted. Sometimes she felt she looked really good, then her mood would change and she was disgusted with herself. Her mother said it was a "teenage thing," that she'd get over it. *Yeah, right.*

She turned her bra around and unhooked it. She let it drop to the floor. She turned side to side in the mirror, studying her body. *Can't really see them when my breasts are out of that contraption.* She slowly lifted the rounded bottom of her left breast.

There it was—the extra nipple. Then the right breast—another nipple. They were completely symmetrical. Maren had four breasts. Two were undeveloped.

The doctors had told her and her mother years ago that she could have the nipples removed after she reached puberty. Until then, it hadn't even occurred to Maren that she wasn't normal. Then she turned fourteen, and insisted on their removal. The specialist told her that she had actual breast tissue underlying the extra nipples; they were mammary glands capable of producing milk. He said the surgery could be complicated. And there would be scars.

Her mother had been against it from the beginning, chewing nervously on her lip during the entire consultation. The doctor did say that since they had not developed into breasts so far, even with her hormones in full swing—they might never do so. Maren had heard her mother and father talking about it in hushed whispers. Of course they knew from the beginning, she was born that way, but they never brought it up to her. She had caught her father looking at her after that last doctor's appointment. He had looked really sad. *Yup, I'm a freak after all*, she had thought.

Maren threw the big t-shirt over her head, letting it fall to her thighs. She threw herself onto the feather mattress. Her father had made it too. *So many things to remind me of him every day! Maybe it will be good to get away. Even to the northern rez. That's really the least of my problems.* Maren ran her hand up under her shirt and closed her watering eyes. *Two completely normal breasts—and then these things. I will never have a boyfriend.* She turned her face into the pillow and fell asleep.

Chapter Two

A New Adventure

Maren looked at the GPS on the dashboard. She had about twenty miles to go before she reached White Earth Reservation. It was time to stop and stretch her legs again. It was about 700 miles total from her home in Wisconsin to the northern Minnesota Ojibwe reservation—White Earth. It was eight years since she had been there—with both her mother and father. She hadn't liked it. Her grandfather Blackhawk was real nice, but weird. At least that was how she had seen it as a ten year old. All the people had long, black hair and talked funny. Kind of slow and mumbly. Blackhawk had the long, black and gray braid. He was quiet but always watching her. They were all whispering all the time—even her mom right in there with them. She remembered she had just wanted to come back home. The night was dark and scary and wolves were always howling somewhere. *Then again, I was just a kid, what did I know.*

Maren pulled over at a little convenience store to gas up and get a drink. It was her last stop before getting to the rez. She had to prepare herself. She paid for her gas and Diet Coke and went into the bathroom. There she took her brown-red hair out of the ponytail and brushed it out. She redid her lipstick and mascara.

She had on her best, tight-fitting designer jeans and a t-shirt Blackhawk had sent her for Christmas. It was a yellow-green dusty color with "From Where I Came I Will Return" written on it over an eagle feather. Maren thought it was corny but wore it at her mother's insistence. Her mother said the color made her hair look glorious. Maren had rolled her eyes. Then her mother whispered that the shirt was the same color as her eyes when she was mad. Maren had playfully slapped at her mother's arm at that comment and they both laughed. Now Maren was wondering if she could quick change into something better. She decided against it. After all, they were all weird up there and no one would even know "cool clothes" if they saw them.

Maren headed out of the bathroom and past the attendant toward the front door. Half way there she heard a long, loud "wolf whistle." She stopped in her tracks and whipped her head around to face the attendant—a young, blonde-haired man at the cash register.

"Was that supposed to be for me," Maren stated, more than asked. Her face got hot. She glanced around. There was no one else in the store. She focused her eyes on the young man behind the counter. At first she was angry, then just plain embarrassed.

"Hell, yeah. Wow. At least *that* got your attention." He was in his twenties, tall and lean. "Where you from and where are you going, is all I can say. Great shirt."

Maren had her hand at her mouth. He did have a nice smile. She took a breath.

"Well, I'm from Wisconsin and I'm going to White Earth," she said, getting her composure back. Then she broke out into laughter. *This has never happened to me. And he is awfully good-looking.* She stood there in the aisle, awkwardly trying to look cool.

"I thought so. White Earth, I mean. You look like one of them. But better … I mean I can tell you're Native American, but mixed." Maren could see he was getting flustered. He must have thought he wasn't being "politically correct."

Maren smiled. The blonde hunk was blushing. *So this is what it's like being on the other end. Maybe this trip is OK after all.* She walked up to the counter.

"I'm Maren. And you?" She reached out her hand. She was still trying to figure out why she hadn't noticed him when she came in. *Guess I'm still used to high school and the same old people … or just terribly inobservant.*

"And 'Indian' is Ok," she added, smiling. "We are a proud people." She couldn't believe what was coming out of her mouth.

"Kenny. Super wonderful to meet you." He grinned showing perfect white teeth, his blue eyes locked on hers. "My mother is doing some kind of doctoral fellowship up here," he continued. "To do with the 'unique culture.' She's really into the wolf stories. But. *I* would love to go to a movie or anything. Gets kinda boring." He touched her hand, letting the contact linger.

"Well, Kenny. I just might take you up on that." Maren pulled her hand from his, laughing. She then grabbed one of the store business cards sitting on the counter. "I'll keep this handy."

"Please do."

Maren purposely slid the card into her back jean's pocket and patted her butt, knowing Kenny was watching. *I can't believe I'm acting like this.* She stopped suddenly. "What wolf stories?"

"Oh, you know. The super-intelligent ones that are supposed to live up on the rez."

"Really? I haven't heard a thing about that." Maren cringed at the thought. Her only memory of wolves was that eerie howling.

"Yeah. My mom, Cindy Shane, stays up there at a resort. Writes on her report for days on end." Kenny rolled his eyes. "I go up on my days off and visit. It's pretty cool, though. Weird legends. Mom said the 'smart ones' wolves protected good people from the 'Wendigo,' some kind of man-eating monster. She insists it's still around." Kenny laughed, and then his face went blank. "But I don't know anything about it, really. Have you heard of all that?"

"Wendigo … . Yes." Maren shivered. "I'd totally forgotten that name. My father talked about it. He'd make dreamcatchers and hang them above my bed to protect me." Maren stood perfectly still. *God. Forgot all about that. How could I? Dad was so weird about it. He scared me.*

"Well, anyway, maybe I'll run into your mom. I'll let you know," Maren said, changing the subject.

"You probably will. She likes to get into the middle of everything." Kenny smiled.

"Ok, then. Got your work number." Maren patted her back pocket again. This time it felt more natural.

"Hey, wait. Let me put my cell number down. Just in case." Kenny smiled when she dug the card back out and gave it to him. *Oh, what can this hurt. I didn't give him mine. Just might want to talk to someone.*

Maren gave him a last smile and wave, got into her car, and headed back onto the two-lane highway to White Earth. *Well, that was fun. I guess I am missing a lot being the shy introvert.* Maren felt a surge of pleasure, and maybe a little sense of power. She blamed it on the trip. *Wow,* was all she could think … *wolves and all. Wendigo? What was it?*

She reached White Earth and then pulled over to read the instructions to Blackhawk's place. Her GPS didn't read the roads past the main highway. She leaned back in her seat for a moment and looked around.

Maren's eyes widened as they took in the view. Magnificent, emerald-colored pine trees that shot straight to the clouds. They were taller than any she had seen before. *And this is second growth forest*, she thought, remembering all the logging that had pretty much cut down everything in the last century. And the lakes—they were a dark, navy-blue with ripples of silver. The one nearby looked as if it were a huge Indian rug, woven of blacks, blues, and silvers—then just unrolled out over the green grass—like you could walk from green to navy-blue in one step.

It was late June in the north woods and spring had just turned to summer. A huge, jet-black raven flew by. It glistened as if its feathers were dipped in oil. The massive black bird had to have a wingspan of six feet across. Maren shivered. *I don't remember it being this beautiful—not even close. This is astounding.* A jolt of electricity zipped down her spine. She felt renewed, like she got her second wind. For the first time since she left Wisconsin, she was looking forward to the whole adventure.

She had about a mile of gravel road before she arrived. She checked herself out in the rearview mirror. *Ok, here goes nothing.*

Maren pulled up in front of the three-bedroom, log cabin. It was extraordinary for reservation property. Her mother had reminded her because she had no recollection of it. Blackhawk and her father had built it. They had cut the pines and milled all the lumber themselves. Some of the logs still had shreds of bark on them. The place fit perfectly in the middle of the wild woods and nearby lakes. No real lawn, just flattened-down prairie grass. A stone walk and a great front porch.

To the side, she could see an old, rusted trailer home—overgrown with trees and shrubs—almost hidden. Her father had told her about the original trailer that he had grown up in. *That must be it.* He and her grandfather Blackhawk had pushed it aside and built the cabin piece by piece. *Wow.* Blackhawk had taught her father Jonny everything about construction. Maren knew Jonny had a faultless reputation as a builder in Wisconsin. That was before he started showing up drunk, or didn't make it in to work at all. She shook her head. *It was all so horribly embarrassing. Not thinking about that now.*

She opened her car door and paused. There in the doorway was Blackhawk.

His hair was a lot grayer, but still in that long braid she remembered. Traditional. Tall and thin. A little hunched over, but not too much. She suddenly felt sad, and a little guilty. *Damn,* she thought, as she walked up to the door.

"Maren, Maren." Blackhawk put both hands on her shoulders. His intense, coppery-brown eyes fixed on hers. His weathered skin was ruddy, but healthy-looking.

"Hi, Grandpa." Maren reached up and hugged him. She was surprised at her reaction. He felt familiar and well, safe. It was a good feeling.

"You are stunning. Of course you know that. A lot like your mother—but Jonny's in there too. It's too good to see you, my girl. You'll give this old man a heart attack. Or heartbreak. Think I'd prefer the former... ."

"Oh, Grandpa. I *was* a little worried about coming up here alone. I don't remember a whole lot. I remember everyone is kinda private?

Blackhawk chuckled. "Private is an understatement. Well, come on in. It will be fine. We'll get your things in a minute. There's someone who wants to meet you."

Blackhawk guided her through the doorway. All wood and rugs. The rugs were old and woven. A simple, colorful floral design. *Probably real Indian stuff, she thought. Real cozy.*

He motioned her into the living room area. Maren looked around, taking the place in. It was wonderful. She stopped at a painting on the wall. It was an Indian man. Young, good-looking—even defiant.

"Is that *Dad*?" Maren walked up closer. She had never seen her father like that. He looked strong and confident, like nothing could bring him down.

"Yes it is. Those were the best days. I will never forget my Jonny." Blackhawk's face showed no expression, but his voice wavered.

Maren could barely turn her face away from the picture of her father. But Blackhawk seemed anxious to show her something.

He stood in front of what looked like a bedroom door. She walked over and stopped next to him, curious. He smiled at her as he turned the knob. The room was a bedroom, but was currently used as a storage area. No bed or furniture, only boxes of stuff. In the near corner, there was a small pen built out of chicken wire and wood. The sides were about three feet high.

Maren could see doggy pee pads lying on the floor in one corner of the pen, and a closed, wooden box in another corner. The box had a ten-inch hole cut out of its side. She stared at it, trying to figure out what was living in a pen in the house.

Blackhawk went over to the pen and stepped over the chicken wire, easily, with his long legs. He made a short whistle sound. A twitching, wet, black nose poked out of the hole in the box. It sniffed the air. Then Blackhawk whistled again, louder. Next came a floppy, black paw with thick claws, and then another. Finally—a blackish, furry, doglike creature stepped out of the box. It turned its larger-than-a-dog's head, and looked directly at Maren. Its brassy, yellow eyes pierced hers.

Maren sucked in her breath. Her eyes moved over the rest of the creature, stopping at the silver streak of longer hair running down the back of its head—a dramatic contrast against the coal black of its body. *What a gorgeous creature!*

"Grandpa, who and what is this?" Maren said, taking a tiny step forward.

"He's yours. He's a wolf baby from the smartest stock in this area. His mother was killed. He had two sisters, who are now at the reserve. Couldn't give this one up. He's special. You can come over. Don't be afraid."

Maren stood frozen in place. *A wolf baby? Now this is going to be interesting ... .*

Chapter Three

A New Pet

"Maren?"

"Oh, sorry, Grandpa. I've never seen anything like this." Maren took a small step. *The little creature must be friendly or Blackhawk wouldn't be pushing me.* "It's a he, then?"

"Yup. And mighty healthy. Huge for his age. He's about three weeks old, I'd guess."

Maren took another step and knelt down. "I've always been afraid of wolves. I've watched Discovery Channel. I hate the way they take down their prey. It's so vicious. I can't even watch it."

"Maren. I know. But it's nature. Wolves do bite the neck as quickly as they can. You know they never toy with their food—like a cat would. Have you ever seen your friendly household cat torture a mouse?"

"Oh, god, yes. You do have a point, Grandpa. Wolves just seem scarier."

"Have you seen a big cat? Like a mountain lion? Now they're scary. And vicious killers. Of course, I'm prejudiced. I love wolves." Blackhawk smiled.

Maren laughed. "OK, come here little one," she said as she held out her hand, palm down.

"I see you know how to approach a strange animal. You don't know how many times I've tried to tell people that an open hand is aggressive. Good job."

"Guess I never thought about it," Maren said. She was totally fixated on the wolf pup. "He's staring at me, Grandpa. Straight in the eye. It's a little unnerving. His eyes are so yellow!"

"That's what wolves do, Maren. Don't look down or away. You have to establish your dominance right now. You are the alpha female, my girl. Wolves have a strict hierarchy."

The furry, black pup took slow steps toward her, his shoulders up and head out in front of him. His silver ruff was standing straight up.

"Is he mad? Will he bite me?" Maren felt a twinge of fear sweep through her. She had never seen an animal like this one.

"What do you think? Work it out. Show your confidence."

Maren kept her eyes locked with the baby wolf's. *Easy for you to say*. When the little guy was about a foot from her, he crouched down and crawled to her hand. He smelled it and then licked it. Maren moved her hand to the top of his head and petted him several times. Then he was in her lap, licking her face. Maren laughed.

"That's it! He's being submissive now. That's good. You will have to earn his trust. Wolves aren't like dogs. They don't have that innate nature to please. They are instinctual and quite smart. Well, I'll be damned … ."

Maren was rolling around on the floor with the wolf pup. They were all over each other.

"He's great, Grandpa. Is he really mine? To keep? He's adorable!"

Blackhawk's smile disappeared. "Yes, he's yours. But, you understand, he has to stay on the rez. It's his home. He wouldn't fit in anywhere else." Blackhawk took a deep breath, waiting for her reply.

"Oh, yes, of course. We could build a pen, or whatever he needs. Oh, thank you, Grandpa!"

"Well, Ok then." Blackhawk exhaled sharply. "Let's take him outside. He needs a collar for now. Until we know he'll be OK." He picked up a dog collar that was lying by the pen.

Maren spotted a retractable leash that hung on a nearby hook. Obviously, Blackhawk had done this before. She snapped it on and they headed out the back door. The pup's head already reached her knee. She figured he weighed about thirty-five pounds. He was about the same size as her neighbor's adult cocker spaniel back in Wisconsin.

"They grow a lot faster than dogs, don't they?" Maren rubbed her knee against the pup's head.

"Ohhh, yes. And we need a name for him. Got any ideas?" Blackhawk motioned toward the huge porch that wrapped around most of the cabin.

"Hmmm," Maren said, as she led the little wolf up the wooden steps nearby. "I'm thinking … ."

The wolf pup's claws tip-tapped across the wood planks to a wrought iron and wood bench, located at the front of the house. Maren collapsed onto it with the pup immediately doing the same—on her feet. It was a cool night and the stars covered the night sky. It was unusually light out and then Maren realized why. A full moon. *Wow. I don't remember a moon being so huge and glowing.*

Just then the little wolf popped up, stretched out his head and neck, closed his eyes, and let out a howl that made her spring forward on the bench.

"Oh, my god!" Maren said, as she stared at the wild wolf pup. She looked over at Blackhawk and laughed. He had jumped too. He readjusted his rocking chair and sat back down, smiling.

"He sounds like a full-grown wolf. Just a little squeakier," she added, between giggles. The little wolf was oblivious to it all. He started another long, mournful wail.

"He's howling at the moon! Right to it, like it's his mother," Maren said, sitting forward. "That's it. That's his name. Moonbaby. I love it. Moonbaby."

Blackhawk was back rocking at a slow, leisurely pace in his chair. He had his eyes closed. "You don't know how right you are," he said softly. "Moonbaby it is."

Moonbaby lay back down. Maren leaned back against the smooth, wooden slats of the bench and shut her eyes. *It's so easy to relax here—I don't think I've ever felt like this. Just a few moments in time when everything is perfect. Wow.*

It was quiet for a long time; there was only the peaceful lull of the rocking chair's rhythm against the wooden porch floor. Moonbaby slept soundly on Maren's feet which were starting to fall asleep themselves. She wiggled her squished toes to keep the circulation going. One was actually numb.

"Why do they call you Blackhawk, Grandpa? I assume that's not your real name." She spoke as gently as she could. The noise of her voice cut through the peaceful aura that enveloped them. She didn't have a choice; she *had* to move her numb foot out from under Moonbaby's weight. He made a little growl noise in his sleep.

"You're right," Blackhawk replied, his rocker coming to a halt." Would you believe it's Hawkins?"

Maren giggled. "I'm sorry. I just never heard that before."

"Well, no one has used it in decades. Actually, when I was young they called me Hawk. Then with the black hair, it became Blackhawk. That stuck. Guess it's not black anymore, though." He smiled.

"I like Blackhawk. It's a great name." Maren's stomach was rumbling.

"Guess it's time to get you some food," Blackhawk said, rocking one more time to launch himself out of the chair. He stretched his body. "I'm not sure what you ate on the road, but we have real food here. Some great fry bread and roast. Time to go in and put Mr. Moonbaby to bed."

Maren yawned. She couldn't wait to go to bed, but she was starving. She hadn't eaten anything but a Snickers and a Diet Coke.

"What's fry bread, anyway?" Normally, she would eat little or nothing, worrying about gaining weight. Now it was the last thing on her mind. Her stomach was so empty it felt like she had swallowed ground glass.

"You'll see." Blackhawk took Moonbaby's leash and put him back in his pen. The tired pup went without an argument. Then he sat Maren down at the dining room table and fussed around in the kitchen for a while.

"Here you go. I make the best fry bread around. Since Marina died, anyway. I'm sorry you didn't get to know her, Maren. Your grandmother. She would have loved you." Blackhawk's face saddened for a moment.

"I'm sorry, Grandpa," Maren said. "Mom told me about her … all good stuff." She stared at the plate in front of her. It looked like a big piece of deep-fried dough shaped like a Honey Bun and some kind of sliced meat. *Maybe beef? Who knows what they cook up here, and my god, this must be a million calories!* She slowly picked up the conglomeration and took a small bite. *Wow, this is good.* She ate everything on the plate, barely taking time to breathe.

"That was a real surprise. I don't usually eat stuff like that. Too fattening." Maren snickered at her grandfather's expression. It was the same as her mother's. The eye roll.

"I get it. You're right," she said. "But I'm totally whipped. Can't keep my eyes open. Is this the way?" She pointed to a room that was next to Moonbaby's room, hoping it would be the one.

"Yup. It's your father's old room. Sleep well. We've got a lot to do tomorrow."

Maren headed toward the bedroom door, then stopped and turned around.

"Thank you for everything, Grandpa."

"No problem, my girl. Now get to bed before you topple over."

Maren barely got her shoes and jeans off. Then she climbed into bed under a big, flannel quilt. *And I don't even want to throw up.* She literally passed out.

Chapter Four

Dr. Don Minnetonka

Maren woke suddenly. She thought she heard a crash in the room next to her. Next there was a mad scratching sound at the door. *Moonbaby!* She jumped up, threw on the same jeans she had on the day before, and opened the door. Moonbaby bounded into her bedroom and jumped all over her.

"I think he needs to go outside, Maren. And I'm not sure what he did to his room," Blackhawk yelled from outside her door. "I'm going to let you handle it."

Maren noted the humor in Blackhawk's voice. She looked into the room and started laughing. "Oh, no. Moonbaby, you trashed it."

She grabbed his leash and hurried out the door barefoot. Moonbaby immediately took care of business. When she came back in, Blackhawk had scrambled eggs and toast waiting for her.

"I really can't eat that much, Grandpa." She sat down at the table anyway. It all smelled good and she was surprised at her appetite—once again. Blackhawk had filled a bowl of dog food for Moonbaby. He was just as hungry.

"We will stick to dog food for now. Don't want to get his hunt instinct going just yet. It will happen soon enough. And don't worry about that little terror's room right now. I knew he'd find a way through that chicken wire. It's time to take it down." Blackhawk grabbed some keys and his jacket hanging nearby.

"We're going to see Dr. Don Minnetonka this morning at his clinic. He's a real doc, but is glad to help out and give Moonbaby his first exam. You can shower or whatever and we'll leave after that. Oh, and just call him Dr. Don. That's what everyone calls him here."

Maren finished her breakfast. *Yes, definitely a shower and clean clothes*, she thought, wondering why Blackhawk didn't go to a regular vet. *Well, he's a wolf, after all. Don't know how many wolf pets they have around here. Dr. Don? Wonder what he's all about.*

Blackhawk had pulled his old pickup truck in front of the cabin. Maren guided Moonbaby toward the middle of the bench seat. He jumped right in. It was easy to see his curiosity would go far.

"Keep an eye on him, Maren. First car ride for him."

Maren took turns watching the road and Moonbaby, who seemed to be doing the exact same thing. Dr. Don's office was right on the main downtown road. *If you could call it that.* Just a few small businesses and a tavern.

Maren hooked on Moonbaby's leash and they got out of the truck. He stood right by her side, one paw on her foot. A tall, black-haired man stood on the steps of the cabin-like building. He had his long hair pulled back in a ponytail, no braid. Hardly any gray, just a little at his temples. His skin was dark and weathered with deep crows-feet around his dark-brown eyes. He was fairly good-looking. Maren wondered how old he was. He looked to be about the same age as her father was when he died. He had on Levi jeans and a flannel shirt with the sleeves rolled up. He seemed like a regular Indian guy.

There was one sign hanging over the door that said simply, CLINIC. Blackhawk was already walking up to greet the doctor. Dr. Don was almost as tall as Blackhawk, who was over six feet. They immediately started a conversation. Both of their faces looked serious and Maren strained to hear their low voices. She could only make out a couple words—wolf, moon, dangerous. No one was smiling.

"Come on up here, Maren. Meet the best doc in town—oh yeah, and the *only* doc in town." Blackhawk's expression had magically changed. He was now smiling. The eerie seriousness had vanished.

Dr. Don Minnetonka stepped forward to greet Maren. His eyes shifted back and forth from her to the wolf pup. He put on a quick smile. "Really glad to meet you. Your Pops' been talking about you nonstop. Glad you're finally here. Now he can calm down."

Maren reached her hand out. "Nice to meet you." An aroma of alcohol on his breath startled her. *Oh, no. A drunk doctor.* Maren shivered and flinched from the smell.

Dr. Don cleared his throat, but the smile remained fixed on his face. His expression didn't change much while he shook her hand—except for the little quiver at the corner of his mouth. She felt sick that she had shown her repulsion.

"Well, look at this guy!" Dr. Don immediately knelt down in front of the black and silver wolf pup.

"His name is Moonbaby," Maren said, politely. Blackhawk looked over at her and nodded. *Well, I guess he smelled it too, or he's just glad I didn't say anything nasty.* She smiled weakly back.

"He's the greatest," Maren added, relieved that she hadn't disappointed Blackhawk with her bad manners.

Moonbaby had his nose in the air, taking in the scents. He looked at Dr. Don and apparently decided that the doctor was OK—alcohol and all. Dr. Don patted him on the shoulders.

"Let's take him inside and have a look. Go on in, Maren. First room on the left. I'll be right in." Blackhawk nodded to her to go ahead.

Maren opened the glass door and walked into the office. It was nice for a little wood building. The waiting room had a sofa and several comfortable-looking chairs. A flat screen TV sat on a small table in the corner. There was a small receptionist desk, but no one occupied the chair. Maren walked into the left room which was a small examination room. There was one stainless steel examination table in the middle of the room with a leather top. Paper had been placed on top of it. *Pretty much regular doctor's office. Some things look expensive and other equipment like hand-me-downs.*

Dr. Don and Blackhawk appeared after ten minutes. Dr. Don's face was red and Maren noticed he had a mug in his hand. She could smell coffee. *Humpff … nice try.*

Blackhawk lifted Moonbaby onto the table. Dr. Don put a muzzle on him. Moonbaby made a low growling noise. "Just in case," Dr. Don said. "This is all new to him."

Dr. Don did all the normal things vets do when they examine a dog. Moonbaby didn't do much but glare with his yellow eyes. His silver ruff was standing on end. Maren was sure he knew exactly what the muzzle was for. *He's being real good so we won't put that contraption on him again. Really smart.*

"I'm going to give him his shots now. Rabies is especially important. But you have to know, that if he bites anyone, they may order him to be put down. Rabies vaccine isn't recognized as effective in wolves. Pretty silly, actually, but they have no testing results to back it up. Just want you and Blackhawk here to be extra careful. He's quite special." Dr. Don administered the shots while glancing at Blackhawk. Moonbaby only jumped a little. He kept looking around the room, taking it all in.

"What do you mean, 'put down?' " Maren's chest tightened. "Why even bother with the shot then?" Putting Moonbaby down was not an option in her mind.

"Because rabies is a very real problem in the woods. I'm convinced it will protect him. You just need to protect others from him. He's a wolf, Maren. Albeit, a smart one."

Maren exhaled. She did wonder how an Indian that lived up in northern Minnesota would use words like, "albeit." *And why does everyone keep assuming Moonbaby is so smart? Especially Dr. Don. He doesn't even know the pup.*

Blackhawk lifted Moonbaby off the table and took off the muzzle. He went right back to Maren and sat on her foot.

"Oh, by the way, that's a 'possession' thing he's doing," Dr. Don said. "Sitting on your foot. He's claimed you as his own." He smiled and turned to Blackhawk. "Tell her now, my friend."

Maren looked back and forth at Dr. Don and Blackhawk. *What's going on?* She sat down in a nearby chair, dragging Moonbaby with her.

"There are some things you need to know, Maren. About Moonbaby. About some of the wolves on this reservation. Uhmm, well, he's a different breed, a different gene pool, you might say. He's, ahhh ..." Blackhawk was stammering.

Maren couldn't stand it anymore. "*What?*" she blurted out.

Dr. Don moved closer to her. Blackhawk just shook his head. *What could be so difficult for him?*

"This is hard for your pops, Maren. He's involved with this deeply, as I am. Let's just start out by saying Moonbaby's mother was killed by a local here. Her name was Moon. By the way, you couldn't have picked a better name for your guy there. Anyway, Moon was an old-timer here. She's from the oldest bloodlines of these special wolves. We were pretty sure she was the last one, and then Jules brought in the pups—*her* pups. Moonbaby is a spittin' image of her, the Moon. We all respected that old girl. Would have left her be." Dr. Don tapped his foot as he talked.

"Then some of the people here blamed her for killing a couple calves and some dogs. We know it wasn't her, but they put up a bounty anyway. It's all pretty sad. Me and Blackhawk, well, we were downright heartbroken when he brought her in."

Maren stiffened in her chair. *Wow. That's what Kenny at the convenience store was talking about. The smart wolves.*

After a moment she said, "Who would kill this Moon? Why?"

Blackhawk kicked at the table with his toe. "One of the James' boys' sees himself a big hunter. Thinks the 'smart ones' killed his sister years back."

He and Dr. Don shot each other a quick look.

"Julian James," Blackhawk continued. "He wanted the money, Maren. I took the pups. Moonbaby has two sisters. They're at the wolf reserve in Ely. Had to pick one. He was different, special. Had that look about him."

"What look?" Maren asked. She was watching Moonbaby. *Did he just get agitated when they said his name? Or was it when Grandpa said "sisters"? No, he doesn't know that many words.* Maren frowned.

Dr. Don responded. Her grandfather just stared at the floor.

"The look ... well, it's hard to explain. Let's just say we know it. We knew Moon. We had both seen her several times through the years. As smart as a human, Maren. I'm not kidding. The legend says she was a strange and wonderful creature of nature, of ancient times before we all took our different genetic paths. It's all based on physics and the ability to rearrange matter because it's not truly solid. I know, pretty heavy, but has a lot to do with quantum physics. I can go into that more but," Dr. Don took a deep breath.

"Let's just say that some of us, or wolves, I mean—have never lost the ability to evolve, at a phenomenally accelerated speed—to another form. Scientifically, we all evolved from simple bacteria, each taking a slightly different road—to what we are today. Throw a couple genes in here and the understanding that matter can be rearranged quite easily—very unusual things can happen."

Dr. Don poured himself a glass of water and returned.

"Pretty weird, huh? I know. I was a surgeon in Minneapolis before I ended up here. I struggle with a lot of things, Maren. But my devotion to protecting 'the smart ones,' as we call them, is total. I'm sure Moonbaby is one of them. Take care of him with your life, Maren. There are some on the rez that don't feel that way. They see them as 'freaks.' Would like to see him dead, if they knew. I'm sorry to be telling you this, but me and Blackhawk talked long and hard about this."

Maren didn't know what to say. *All that ancient Indian stuff. Evolving to another form? Quantum physics? Wow, that's pretty far out. Hope his brain isn't damaged from alcohol … .*

"That's a lot to take in," Maren replied. She was trying to repress a smile, then noticed Dr. Don's disappointed look. "I really need to know more about this. The only legend thing I remember Dad talking about was the Wendigo—that the wolves protected the good people from its evil.'"

Maren was relieved that she had something to offer to the "over the top" conversation, that she had actually remembered something her father had said. *I have to ask Mom … see if she remembers anything like this.*

Both Blackhawk and Dr. Don locked eyes.

"We were waiting for the right time. You're connected to this. You'll see," Dr. Don said, looking a little relieved.

"Ok. How am *I* connected to this wolf? This 'Moon'?"

"You're right. I've thrown a lot at you right off the bat. The old man here can answer any other questions." He looked directly at Blackhawk with a whimsical look on his face.

He's dumping this back off on Grandpa. And Grandpa's not happy.

"This is our life here," Dr. Don continued, after giving Blackhawk a "you chicken" look. "And I'm glad to finally meet you. You and Moonbaby are very special. I hope you will decide to stay with us for a long time."

"Thank you. So far, I'm really liking it here." Maren said, thankful for the subject change. She'd ask more about Moon later. She had enough to think about. "I *have* to call Mom tonight though. Let her know everything's Ok and well—about him." Maren looked down at Moonbaby. His eyes were fixed on her face.

"Oh, yes." Blackhawk said, visibly relieved. "And time to get back to the ranch."

With those words, Moonbaby bolted toward the door, and scratched at the knob.

"See what I mean?" Dr. Don stood there watching with his arms crossed. After a brief pause, everyone laughed.

Maren and Blackhawk waved to Dr. Don as they drove off, Moonbaby now asleep between them.

"Looks like all that commotion wore him out too," Blackhawk said, looking over his shoulder at Moonbaby.

Maren turned to Blackhawk. "I know you both believe all that stuff so I am not just putting it down like I used to do with Dad." She looked down at her hands. "Dad and I weren't so close at the end. I wish I could take it back."

Blackhawk kept driving, his eyes on the road.

"He tried to tell me things about myself, and other Indian things I wouldn't listen to. Some of it just seemed like silly stories. And scary stuff like the Wendigo."

She took a deep breath. "You know he drank all the time, Grandpa. It was awful. I smelled it on Dr. Don. He seems like a nice guy but that reminded me of … ." She stopped. She wasn't ready to reveal everything about her father's alcoholism.

Blackhawk sighed. "Doc has his problems, Maren. Just like Jonny, your father, did. It had to be tough on you, but there was nothing you could have done. He never held a thing against you. Never. And that topic, my girl, is for another day."

Chapter Five

Big Silver

Several weeks had passed since Maren talked with Blackhawk and Dr. Don. It was August and the leaves were starting to turn. Colder nights and cool mornings took over the north woods. That morning she lay in bed a little longer than usual. Now that Moonbaby had a nice pen outside she didn't have to get up at 6:00AM to take him out.

Moonbaby was already the size of a large German Shepard. Maren was amazed at how fast he grew. His size and spectacular learning ability weren't the only things she lay there thinking about. It was all the weird stuff Blackhawk and Dr. Don had told her that day. The "smart ones" thing, the way they seemed to hover over Moonbaby like he was gold. She just didn't get it.

And the new pen—Maren couldn't believe how much work Blackhawk had put into it. It was about fifty by one hundred feet, and all expensive chain link fencing. She felt a little guilty about how much he must have spent on materials. When she asked why he was going through so much trouble, he just replied, "We need to make it as acceptable to him as possible for as long as possible. It won't be long before he won't stay in it."

Maren dragged herself out of bed. She rubbed at her lower belly and squeezed her head between the palms of her hands. *Owww. Must be that time of the month coming.* She grimaced and stretched while pushing against the hollow of her back with both hands. She sat on the edge of the bed while she put on jeans and a long-sleeve, t-shirt, then threw herself back down on the mattress.

Maren had been sleeping in her camisole/bra the last few nights. The support felt good. Her breasts were really sore. It wasn't uncommon when her period was coming, but it was worse this time. She would have to go into town for some supplies. Hopefully, Blackhawk would let her go alone. Maybe she would bring Moonbaby along for the ride.

Maren jumped up, revived at the thought of her wolf, then brushed her long hair and tied it back in a ponytail. She heard the phone ringing in the kitchen as she hurried from her room.

Blackhawk picked up the receiver. He still had an old-fashioned land line; it was a necessity out in the wilderness where cellphone signals were totally unpredictable. He did carry a simple cellphone, which he rarely used. Maren slowed to a walk and stopped at the counter next to him. She grabbed the loaf of bread and dug for a piece in the middle of the package.

"You're kidding." Blackhawk said into the phone. His face looked unusually worn and old. He sounded stressed.

Maren stopped. A piece of bread hung from her hand above the toaster.

"Tell Doc to get right over there. I'm on the way. Don't say anything to Jules. It's time for that talk." Blackhawk slammed down the receiver and turned to Maren. She set the bread down, completely losing her appetite.

"Maren, we have to go to the Redwing. Now. No Moonbaby this time. Give him a hug if you want but make it quick. Tell him you'll be right back."

Blackhawk grabbed his truck keys and walked way too quickly out the door.

Maren carefully put the slice of bread back in the loaf wrapper. She was trying to think. Her headache was worse now. *Was this to do with Moonbaby? Will he be OK? Did someone complain?*

She grabbed her purse and rushed out to the pen through the back door. Moonbaby was lying contently in the grass. He jumped up immediately, his hair standing up down his back. *God, he senses everything with me.*

"It's OK, baby," she said, as she ruffled his hair.

Moonbaby gave her a couple licks on the face, then stood back to look at her. It was obvious he wasn't convinced.

"I'll be right back, buddy. I promise." She kissed his head, laughing as she pulled hair out of her mouth. "You're losing your baby hair, little man."

She gave him one last reassuring pat and walked back the same way. She didn't want him to see her run to the truck waiting out front. Blackhawk had the engine running. He put the truck in gear as soon as he heard her door slam shut.

"What's going on, Grandpa?" Maren dug a piece of gum out of her purse. She hadn't even had time to brush her teeth.

"Jules brought in a wolf carcass. Jesse said its, *he's,* been dead some time. Didn't appear to be shot." Blackhawk's voice was shaking.

Maren couldn't understand why he was so upset. *It's not like there weren't a lot of wolves on the rez. And this one wasn't shot, at least.* She started to ask him when she noticed tears on his face. Maren's stomach pitched.

"Grandpa, what's *happened*?" She put her hand on his arm. She didn't know what to say, nor had she seen him that upset before.

"It's Big Silver." Blackhawk wiped his face quickly. "We are all going to talk. Now's the time."

Maren kept her hand sitting lightly on his arm until they pulled up in front of the Redwing Tavern. There was another older truck and a little black Jeep lined up at the curb. Blackhawk jumped out and stood, looking down the street. It was Dr. Don and he was running toward them. Maren got out and stood by her door.

"We'll wait for Doc." Blackhawk went over to Maren. He took her hand. "You are going to hear a lot today. All I ask is that you keep an open mind."

Maren felt him squeeze her hand and drop it. He didn't even look at her. He was already reaching out with both hands to grab Dr. Don's, who was still catching his breath. He had that same panic-stricken look on his face.

Maren grabbed her stomach and leaned over, her face twinging with pain. Her head pounded and her cramps were worse than before. "I don't feel so good, Grandpa. Really bad cramps."

Blackhawk and Dr. Don both looked at her. She couldn't tell what they were thinking but she was getting more annoyed by the minute. *Hello?? I need help … .*

"Come on in and sit down. Hopefully these will let up." Dr. Don took her arm and pulled her close to his side.

Well, thank god someone here sees I'm about to pass out. She leaned into Dr. Don's shoulder as they walked into the tavern, her heart pounding so hard she knew he could feel it.

44

There were three people sitting at the bar. One woman. She had shoulder-length blonde hair and was having a heated discussion with a younger Indian man, who was sitting on a stool next to her. Another older Indian was behind the bar and he pounded his fist on it. Everyone jumped.

"Hey, now. I want you all to meet my granddaughter, Maren." Blackhawk's voice got everyone's attention.

They all turned to face him and it was immediately quiet. Dr. Don pulled out a stool and sat Maren down, patting her arm.

The blonde lady came over to her first. She reached out her hand.

"Hi, Maren. I'm Dr. Shane. Just call me Cindy. I know these 'loud' fellows. They're harmless." She had a big, white smile that looked familiar.

"Oh my god! You're Kenny's mother. From the convenience store? He said his mother was studying up here. He looks just like you!" Maren took a deep breath. It was nice to see another woman. It made her think about how much she missed her mother.

"Oh, yes. That's right. He did mention some beautiful girl he talks to regularly. You do have to come to the resort one day. Kenny's going off to school at U of M—of course, you already know that." She gave Maren a big hug. "Really glad to meet you. My son has excellent taste."

Maren took a deep breath. A sense of relief floated over her. Her cramps had subsided. She started to thank Cindy when the young Indian man squeezed in between them.

"Hey. Nice to meet you, Maren. I'm Julian James, but call me Jules. Everyone else does." He shook her hand briefly and then sat back on his stool. He wasn't smiling. *Nice face. Kind of the cute, bad-boy type with that little goatee. Shiny, black ponytail to the middle of his back. He's younger than the rest of them. 30ish? Not bad.*

Jules glanced over at a large object that was wrapped in an old tarp, lying on the bar near him. Maren followed his gaze. *Whatever that is, it's huge!* She watched Jules smooth the edges of the tarp over, like he was trying to conceal its contents. That's when it first hit her—the smell. It was coming from under the tarp.

The older man behind the bar just leaned over and said," Hi, Maren. Name's Jesse. Jesse James, to be exact. No relation." He had a sincere smile for her. "That's my nephew, Jules."

Maren coughed. She nodded politely to Jesse. The smell coming from under the tarp was nauseating.

Jesse was older than her father was, she could tell that much. *And the only one without that ponytail or braid.* His hair was dark with a lot of gray, but cut off blunt-like just below his chin. He kept weaving his hand through it to keep it off his face. His humor was a relief in the midst of the awkward introductions and foul smelling heap on the bar.

Blackhawk interrupted. His voice was trembling. "Is that really Big Silver, Jess? I have to know."

Jesse walked out from behind the bar and up close to Blackhawk. He half-whispered, "Are you sure we should talk about this now?" He lifted his chin in Maren's direction.

"Yes, Jess. It's time. She's my blood. She has to know." Blackhawk gave Maren a reassuring nod. "Are you good with this, Maren?"

"For god's sake, yes. Spill the beans! I can't take this much longer." Maren's face flushed with anger. She bit her lip. The suspense was driving her crazy.

She was worried about Moonbaby, and even more worried about what was under the tarp.

Blackhawk walked straight past Jules and ripped back the canvas. He sucked in his breath, then stood there, motionless.

He's saying a prayer. Maren stood up. Everyone else, except Dr. Don, had looked away. It was obvious they had already seen the thing, and didn't need another look. Dr. Don brought both his hands to his face, and then dragged them down slowly. Blackhawk folded the tarp back down.

God, he looks really pissed. Jules just took a sip from the beer in front of him, and started picking at the label.

Maren walked slowly over, covering her mouth and nose with her hand. The stench was unbearable. She picked up the edge of the tarp with two fingers. Hairy. Silver-colored, matted hair. A bushy, black tail. It was huge, about four feet long. Bigger than any dog. She could see maggots wiggling in its stomach area and the rest of the body had a shrunken, petrified look. It must have been dead for a while. Its eyes were closed—or just gone. She recognized the creature. It was a wolf.

Maren shrunk back, trying not to gag in front of them. She turned her head so sharply, her ponytail whipped across her face. She pulled the hair out of her mouth.

"Why is this dead wolf here? Did someone kill it?" The words boiled out. Maren's nausea had changed to anger. She could imagine Moonbaby in its place.

Jules spoke up. "Because I found it. And no, no one killed it. It died natural. But I swear it's the same damn wolf that my sister used to call to in the woods—a long, damn time ago. Doesn't make sense, 'cause he'd be forty years old. But I recognize it. Same black tip on the tail. Same silver hair.

Found him by the hook, near where I got Moon. And I'd bet Moon's bounty money that this guy was the one that killed her—my sister Lara."

He drank the last of the beer and slammed the bottle down on the bar.

Maren watched the others. She backed up to her stool and sat down, thinking. *He's the one that killed Moonbaby's mother? What a jerk.* She looked over at Blackhawk, waiting for his reaction.

Blackhawk walked right up to Jules. He was as close as he could get without running him over. "Because, you ignorant fool, this is Marina's. This is Sylvester—Silver. Everyone knows it but you."

Blackhawk glared at Jules, then spit on the floor in front of him. He walked back over to the carcass and gently folded the tarp over. He petted the dead animal.

Jules jumped up, but didn't challenge Blackhawk. He headed for the door. "You can all go to hell," he said. He slammed the door so hard, it bounced twice before closing.

Cindy Shane stood up. "I'm sorry about this. Jules is mixed up. He's been a big help knowing this reservation so well. And all the wolf packs. I'll call him later."

She reached the door and paused. "Oh, Maren. Keep that Moonbaby of yours locked down for a while. Folks around here are getting pretty anti-wolf. Two more pet dogs disappeared in the last couple weeks. Jules talks about going out hunting, and I keep him busy with genealogies and some of my work. As long as he'll stand for it." She winked and left.

Jesse was the first to open his mouth.

"That girl's been good with Jules. She keeps him busy. Don't worry, Maren. We'll know if Jules goes off on some wolf-killing spree. Cindy will let me know."

Maren nodded at Jesse, but she wasn't thinking about Moonbaby at the moment. It was the big, dead wolf on the bar. *Cindy Shane saw and heard the whole thing. What does she know? My grandma, Marina, had a wolf? How could it be that old? Why was Grandpa acting this way? And now I have to worry about Moonbaby getting shot too?*

"Damn," Maren said under her breath. Her head throbbed. She took a deep breath and walked over to Blackhawk. He was fuming mad; she had never seen him so obviously angry.

"Grandpa, tell me what all this is about. Did he kill Grandma's wolf too? How can that be?" Maren grabbed Blackhawk's arm and didn't let go.

Dr. Don walked to the front door of the tavern and locked it. He walked back to Blackhawk and tapped him on the back. They both went to the dead wolf. Jesse handed them some heavy twine from behind the bar. They bundled up the wolf and tarp as best as they could.

Blackhawk made a final knot, his eyes glistening with tears.

"This is Sylvester Nightmoon. Nightmoon is Marina's name. Marina Nightmoon. My wife. This is her son."

Chapter Six

The Changelings

Maren stood still, her mouth half open. Dr. Don reached over and tapped her under her chin. He looked both amused and concerned.

"Maren, I know this all sounds weird—took me awhile to get a grasp of it too. But I've been here a long time. Blackhawk here, took me under his wing. He put his trust in me. They had a rough spell and needed a medical doctor. After that, I've been a full believer, and supporter. A miracle of nature like this can't be taken for granted. And I needed to understand the science of it, which I do now and, well, we're here to help you understand." Dr. Don eased Maren back onto the bar stool as he was talked.

Maren let Dr. Don move her. She felt as if she were watching a movie—that her body wasn't actually there. Her mind was running so fast, she was light-headed. She sprang back to reality when an awful thought popped into her head.

"Are you talking *werewolves*? Or just wolves fighting the Wendigo. Because how am I supposed to accept *that*?"

"Good god. No." Blackhawk answered immediately. "Not like werewolves … television style anyway." He sighed.

"Ahhh, the Wendigo … . Some believe the Wendigo exists in a physical body, that the 'smart ones' have kept it under wraps by killing anything its spirit inhabits. And then some believe Wendigo is just symbolic for greed and hate. And it is still the 'smart one's' job to fight that." He tapped his fingers on the bar and took another breath. "You will find many different ideas and versions on Wendigo. It's something we all figure out for ourselves."

"But the smart ones, as they've come to be called," Blackhawk paused again, "actually, we're—*they're*—called 'changelings.' Some tribes talk about 'shape-shifters,' things like that. But this is different. It's not an evil thing. The opposite, really. The ability—the gift—comes from an old gene that hung on with a few families. Its purpose was for preservation. And yes, against the Wendigo in any form. Not long ago it saved many Indians during the old Indian-white man wars. It's almost died out now, far as we can tell, but still there in only a couple families, here on the rez. I'm not sure about farther up north. It's been quiet—the way it should be. That's it. That's the legend. But it's genuinely real."

"Grandpa, you said 'we.' I heard it."

Maren wasn't going to drop that one. She sat quiet, dreading Blackhawk's answer. But it was Jesse James that spoke. Maren turned around. She had forgotten he was even there.

"The James' family has the blood, Maren. Not all of us. Just like not everyone inherits black hair or red hair. You get my drift. I am one. Jules, thank god, is *not*."

Maren couldn't tell by looking at him. That was for sure.

"What does it mean? What is its purpose? So you just turn into wolves and run around the woods? Killing things? Protecting things?"

Maren turned to her grandfather. She could tell by the expression on his face, he must be one, too. He looked way too guilty.

"Not exactly." Jesse laughed. "It's difficult to make the change. The old ones could do it much easier. It's painful, really. And some of us—well, don't want to *turn* back."

He nodded at Blackhawk and gave him a "your turn" look.

Blackhawk cleared his throat. "I am one. Haven't made the change in years. I think the family needs me in my human form. Right now, anyway. And Dr. Don here, he is not. But we desperately need his help. He's a blessing. And Maren, your father—Jonny, was one. I've waited for this time. You need to know. His problems, well, they weren't entirely his fault."

Maren searched her memory, trying to recall anything weird about her father, anything wolf-related weird. She remembered once when he was drunk, and crying, she thought he was feeling sorry for himself. He would go on and on about the Wendigo. But her mother always listened, and she was pleading with him to go back to the rez.

Maren remembered her mother crying. *What did she say? Yes. Go back and take care of yourself and the others—the others. Whatever that meant.* When she had asked her mother about it later, she just looked really sad. She had said, "You don't understand how complicated this is, Maren. When you're older, you will know."

Maren was furious with that response, thinking her mother was just making excuses for her loser dad. Now she wondered. She felt a sharp pang in her stomach. The cramps were back.

"Did he ever change, Grandpa," Maren said, clutching her side. "Because I never saw anything."

Blackhawk's eyes focused on hers. She got a sensation that he was trying to read her mind.

"Once. Jonny was nineteen. I helped him because he felt the urge so ferociously. It's different for each of us. He stayed away for several years, then showed up on my doorstep. I thought he'd never come back. But he changed back, and it was really hard on him. He decided to get some things done, then make the change back to wolf forever. He had seen something during his time as a wolf. He wouldn't talk about it. And then, your mother showed up here on the rez. You can figure out the rest."

"Did Mom know?" Maren could hardly believe what she was hearing.

"What do *you* think, really."

Maren was silent. She felt as if she had wheels in her head—clicking and spinning, backing up and stopping.

"He struggled terribly with it the rest of his life," Blackhawk said. "Couldn't change back because of her, and then you. Just couldn't do it. We all tried to tell him he was killing himself instead. But he was resolved. It's a sad story, Maren. I guess he always felt he was fighting Wendigo ... I don't know. But all of us are here to make sure nothing like that happens again."

Jesse had walked back behind the bar and was polishing glasses. He looked up now and then but didn't interrupt. Everyone was quiet. Even Dr. Don was quiet.

Maren thought of Moon, her beloved Moonbaby's mother. All the fuss that was made. All the fuss about Moonbaby. Maren's eyes widened.

"Oh my god. The 'smart ones.' That's what you mean. They were, are, whatever—changelings?" No one replied. Maren leaned over the bar. "Jesse. Your nephew—Jules. He killed a changeling wolf? He killed Moon?"

Another silence. Maren was getting used to how these Indians used silence as a part of communication. It was powerful on its own.

"Jules doesn't know or understand, Maren," Jesse said. "It's a long story, but he isn't ready to know. But you should know right now about Big Silver. Who he was. What it means."

Oh my god, he's right. I forgot all about the wolf laying right here on the bar. Maren walked back over to where Big Silver lay bundled in the tarp. She laid her hand on the body.

"Tell me about him, Grandpa. I want to know."

Blackhawk's face softened. "Marina had a small boy when I met her. I didn't ask her a lot about it. I figured she'd tell me if she wanted to. We were young, got to know each other. I found out she had changeling blood from a totally different family line. Canadian. The name was, translated, 'Nightmoon.' Marina had an Italian father, so, well, she was surprised, shocked actually, that young Sylvester—was a changeling."

Blackhawk nodded to Jesse who opened him another beer. Dr. Don waved his hand—no.

"He was a gorgeous boy. Wild as hell. Didn't talk much for a five year old. He had this silver-blonde hair with a chunk of black in it. Looked real odd. Anyway, Marina and I got married. Everything was pretty normal." Blackhawk took a swallow from his bottle.

"Then one full moon night, he changed. Fast. Without help. Marina cried for a while. Then I noticed she'd go out in the woods for hours. Think he came back to see her. It made her happy. Then of course, we had Jonny, your father. Silver quit showing up. Guess he thought his mother would be OK." Blackhawk paused.

"Then around that time, Old Malak James said he'd spotted a silver wolf with a black-tipped tail near his place. We were worried for a while, but nothing happened. We assumed he just went off to live his life. Maybe found a pack to hang with. Don't know. But this here is him. And he's forty-two years old, to be exact."

"Wow," Maren said, as she looked at everyone's face. No one looked the least bit surprised. "So Silver *did* die of old age then." She was hopeful for something positive amidst all the gloom.

"I believe so," Blackhawk said. "I hope so. Wendigo would have torn him to pieces. I also think he was probably Moon's mate. Jules found him near where he shot her. Makes sense. Two changeling wolves would seek each other out."

Maren tapped her fingers on the bar top. Moon, Big Silver, and her precious Moonbaby.

"So Big Silver was a little boy named Sylvester Nightmoon. OK, then who was Moon?"

Another one of those silences. Dr. Don and Blackhawk patted Jesse's arm over the bar.

Jesse finished folding a towel in his hands before he answered.

"Moon was my niece, Maren. Her name was Lara James. She was 16 years old when she disappeared. We had figured it out. Her father, old Malak, he knew too. Only one that couldn't accept her being gone was her little brother Julian, 'Jules.' He was eleven at the time. He figured the wolves had killed her—still does. He hates all wolves. Hell, just *hates*. His selfishness has weakened him. Made him susceptible to ahhh—bad medicine."

Maren's mouth was moving but no words were coming out. She jumped up so suddenly that the bar stool went crashing to the floor.

"Oh my god! Jules killed his own sister! Is he Wendigo?"

The Redwing Tavern was silent. Maren bent down and picked up her stool. She licked her dry lips. Blackhawk handed her his beer and nodded. She took a small sip and set it back down, hard. The briny liquid eased her parched throat. She lowered herself onto her stool. There were no words to change the horror of what she had just said out loud.

Chapter Seven

First Revelation

Several hours passed as the four of them made small talk. Maren realized it was how they handled the pain of losing Sylvester, Big Silver. It was some kind of tribute or respect thing. She had now returned from the small but clean unisex bathroom for the third time.

"Grandpa, I really don't feel that good. I need to stop at a grocery store before we go home, if that's all right. And I'm worried about Moonbaby. He seemed nervous when I left."

"You're right. We gotta go. It's been a long day."

"Blackhawk. Go home and spend some time with this great girl here. Jesse and I will give Silver a proper burial," Dr. Don said.

"That's right," Jesse added. "He's going right next to Marina in the old cemetery. We'll take care of it. You've done your best, my friend. Get some rest." He put one arm around Blackhawk and gave him a hearty pat on the back. Blackhawk nodded.

Maren took her grandfather's arm. "We'll go see him together sometime, Grandpa. I would like to see my grandmother's grave too. And," she paused, "I want to see my father's grave. His real grave here. On White Earth land."

Blackhawk squeezed her hand. She realized that the entire time she had been there in White Earth; she had never asked to go to her father's grave.

Outside the tavern, it was getting colder. It was late afternoon. Maren shivered.

"I'm not calling Mom tonight. We've been talking every couple days and each time she asks me what's going on, what has Blackhawk said, and so on. Now I know what she was waiting for."

Blackhawk opened the truck door for Maren.

"No doubt," he said. "Give it a day or two. We have a full moon tonight. On top of everything else. Let's keep Moonbaby in tonight. Just to be on the safe side."

Maren nodded. She was too tired to ask another question. What effect would the full moon have on Moonbaby? After all, he had two changeling parents. But then, he wasn't human. He was a different creature altogether. *Who knows.* Blackhawk would tell her anything important. One thing was certain. He was in danger if he got loose and she was going to make sure that didn't happen.

"You said you needed to stop at the store, Maren?" Blackhawk had pulled up in front of a little gas station/grocery store. "I think you'll find what you need here."

Maren's face flushed.

"Maren. We call it your 'Moon Time.' Remember? I was married most of my life? Did you ever stop and think about a female's cycle and the moon cycle—they are exactly the same. Twenty-eight days. Most of the time, anyway. Marina said that females are sacred. 'The moon spins the tides of the oceans—a woman—the tides of man's emotions.'"

"That's cool, Grandpa. I like that." Maren got out of the truck smiling. *Take it to Grandpa to make this not embarrassing. Twenty-eight days. That is weird.*

Maren returned to the truck with her package. She pulled a big piece of jerky out of the bag. "This is for Moonbaby. I hope he's OK."

Blackhawk smiled and nodded, but Maren could see that he was someplace else.

"What are you thinking about?" she asked. She hoped to keep the light humor they had just shared.

"Well, Maren. I was wondering if everything is OK. With your moon time. I know you didn't feel good today. Dr. Don was worried, too. I can read him."

"Yes, Grandpa, it really is. I had worse cramps this time and feel achy and sore. No big deal," Maren answered.

"It's full moon tonight. I wouldn't be surprised if you didn't feel well at all."

Maren's calm, happy dissipated. "Why's that?"

"Never mind. I'm probably making this into too big a deal. After today, that's all we need."

"You probably are," Maren replied. A satisfied, confident feeling floated through her. She didn't remember feeling so a part of something. Something important, even incomprehensible. *Wow, Mom was sooo right making me come up here.*

They pulled up in front of the little cabin and Maren ran straight to the backyard. Moonbaby was pacing in his pen, his hair standing up on his neck.

"Grandpa, something's wrong with Moonbaby!"

Maren ran over to the gate, reached to open it, when Blackhawk yelled, "Stop," way too loudly.

Maren stepped back from the pen, her eyes wide.

"Not without the leash. He looks about ready to bolt." Blackhawk made a "whew" sound. "Sorry for the scare, Maren. Look at him. Do you think it would be a good time to let him out without the leash?"

Maren grabbed the leash from the pen post and squeezed through the gate barely opening it. "Sorry, Grandpa. I wasn't thinking. Dumb move." She grimaced, then hooked Moonbaby on the leash and held it hard.

"You can put him in his old room with his dinner. I'll put some newspapers down for him. He's staying in tonight for sure."

Maren was glad to just follow orders. Her head was pounding and she felt "all thought out." She brought out the jerky she had bought and laughed when the wolf yanked it out of her hand so swiftly and precisely. *Those great big teeth and he never once touches me.*

Maren closed the door to Moonbaby's room. She was relieved that he was going to be safe in the house. She rolled her shoulders back and squeezed them together. *What a long day!*

"I'm going to take a bath, Grandpa. I'll heat something up for us when I get out."

"Sounds like a great idea, Maren. Take your time. This old man needs to sit in his recliner for a bit."

Maren smiled. She grabbed her bathrobe and flannel pajamas her mom made her bring. She was thankful for them; it was cold that evening. She shut the bathroom door and started the water, not too hot or it would make her cramps worse. She watched the water fill the tub almost to the top, her hand stirring it around. *I wonder if Mom knows all this stuff ... or more? Have to call her tomorrow.*

Maren stretched her body up straight and started undressing. She couldn't wait to take off her bra; it felt like it was crushing her chest. Maren got her shirt off and then reached under the bottom elastic on her bra; it was really pinching. She shrieked out loud as she reached around her back and ripped at the clasp.

"Oh my god, no, oh my god!"

Maren ran her hands frantically over her breasts and then leapt in two steps to the bathroom mirror. She swiped the steam off the glass with the back of her arm and peered into the glass. Her breasts were swollen, all right. But that wasn't the problem. Her two extra breasts had grown, not quite as large as the main ones, but full size breasts nonetheless.

Her eyes overflowed with tears. She turned from side to side, then full front view. She had seen enough. She tore off the rest of her clothes and climbed into the bathtub. The water comforted her. *I wish I could sink to the bottom and never come back.* Maren sunk down farther into the water, lowering her head, then her face. *All I have to do is suck in this water and I'll drown. Wonder if it would hurt.*

She held her breath for as long as she could, then sucked in a gulp of water. She jerked up to a sitting position, coughing and sputtering. *I don't want to die. Just want this to go away, please, please.* She wrapped her arms around her lower two breasts and cried. Then she was sobbing so hard her body shook.

"Open this door right now or I'm breaking it down!"

It was Blackhawk. Maren hadn't realized he was there, pounding on the door. She could barely catch her breath; her crying was out of control. Blackhawk threw his weight against the door, and Moonbaby started howling in the back room.

"Ok, Ok. Give me a sec." She stood up and found a towel, then her bathrobe. She couldn't stop the "after sobbing" spasms. She knew Blackhawk could hear them.

"Only a sec. I mean it." His voice was higher sounding, like someone was squeezing his chest. "Your wolf is having a fit. Say something to him."

Maren blew her nose, then yelled out weakly, "Moonbaby, it's OK. Quiet."

Her body shuddered with the aftermath of her crying jag. She took a washcloth and ran cold water on it. She pressed it against her swollen eyes and nose. Then she tied the belt on her robe and grasped the top tightly at the neck.

Maren took a deep breath and opened the door. Blackhawk sighed. His eyes searched her face, then stopped at her hand pinching her robe together at the neck.

"Damn, those hardwood doors are hard!" he said, rubbing his shoulder.

Maren couldn't help but half-smile. *Leave it to Grandpa to make a joke at the right time.* Her left hand choked her robe even tighter to her neck while her right hand brought the washcloth back up to pat her face.

Blackhawk reached down and pulled the drain to the tub. Then he put the toilet seat down and eased her over to sit. He half sat on the edge of the tub. "Do you have something to tell me, Maren?"

Maren looked down at the floor for a few seconds. She was mortified that she had behaved like such a baby, but anger was slowly replacing her embarrassment.

"I'm a freak," she burst out. "I have four breasts, and the weird ones just turned huge in a day. It's fucking ugly!" She threw the washcloth to the floor.

Blackhawk was silent. It seemed like an eternity to Maren. She rarely used the "f" word, but didn't care at the moment. She couldn't stand the silence.

"Just when everything seemed OK, even right! All that I heard today. Then this. This horrible, awful, ugly thing. It ruins everything!"

She looked around for the washcloth she had tossed, regretting having thrown it. Another flood of tears filled her eyes.

Blackhawk got up and went to her side. He lowered himself to the floor, making "Oooh, Owww" noises until he was sitting cross-legged on the wood floor next to the toilet. The absurdity of their seating arrangement forced Maren to blow air out her nose, stifling a laugh. She quickly unrolled some toilet paper and blew her nose again, making a snorting noise as she spit out a real laugh. *God, I'm going crazy!*

"Now that's more like it," Blackhawk said. He stretched across the floor to retrieve the washcloth and folded it neatly as if she wouldn't need it again. He patted it a couple times on his knee while he sat silent. Then he turned to her.

"Look at me. You're no freak, Maren. You're a changeling. Those four breasts … well, sometimes it's even six. They're what we call 'markers.' All female changelings have them. Males show with webbed toes and sometimes fingers. Always large canine teeth." Blackhawk paused to let it sink in.

"Do you remember your father, Maren?" he finally said.

Maren sat up straight. She squeezed the wad of toilet paper in her hands.

"Yes. He had an operation on his toes. And he was always going to the dentist."

"That's right, Maren. His canines, his front side teeth, would have grown. I'm sure he had to get them filed off. He had the webbing removed from his toes, that I know, and he didn't have the fingers' thing. That's a hard one to hide."

Maren sat quietly, rolling the wad of tissue into a ball and then picking it back apart. Blackhawk watched her a while, then unrolled several new sheets of toilet paper. He gave her the new wad as he pulled the sculpted tissue ball from her hand. Then he made a basketball dunk shot into a nearby waste basket. He cocked his head and gave her a 'Well?' look.

Maren couldn't help but smile once again. She was amazed at how her grandfather handled things, how he worked so hard to make her feel good about herself, how he told her things. He never preached at her. He always let her work it out. He just gave her the information with only truth as he knew it. Her mother had told her that was the Indian way. No controlling others, just guidance to help them choose their own path. She had said,

"When you don't coerce someone, they have to make their own decisions. They then have to take responsibility for them. No blaming someone else." Maren really understood it now.

"What do I do now? How do I hide *this*?" She jabbed at her chest area.

"I can only tell you what the women have done in the past. And not to hide who they are from themselves, but to keep the changeling legend under wraps. Pun not intended."

Maren looked at him, but this time couldn't smile.

Blackhawk continued. "People just aren't going to accept half of it, you know. Then there's the media, and you can only imagine what a circus that would be. I've got the ACE bandages Marina used. I saved them. You could buy your own, of course, but these are special. You can use them if you wish. You just wrap the bottom part. Marina had six—just so you know."

Maren looked down at her grandfather sitting there, Indian-like, while he told her what only a few days ago would have sounded like some utterly impossible, unbelievable fantasy story. Except, it was real. Exciting and yet, scary. She only wished she would have known more, earlier. All her life, feeling so different. She felt that old surge of anger run through her again.

"Why didn't anyone tell me *anything* all these years? Left me feeling like a total freak, only wishing I could be *normal* all these years. That really pisses me off right now." Maren was thinking about her mother, wishing she could scream at her.

"And what exactly could we have told you, Maren? Would you have believed even one part of this? We were waiting for you to come home. Up here, I mean. That's all. Don't hate your mother, Maren. She had no control over any of this. She was a blessing to Jonny. Always know that."

Maren nodded. She was crying again, but softly. Not about now, but for the girl that she'd never be, or never was. A totally different life was ahead of her. Secrecy. *Changelings?* She was exhausted.

Blackhawk got up, took her hand, and walked her to her room. "Try to sleep now. It's full moon. I suspected this might happen now. Moonbaby is an influence. Know that. Notice he's quiet. He knows."

Maren nodded, robotically. She suddenly remembered she hadn't put her pajamas on under the robe. Blackhawk must have noticed her hesitation to get into bed.

"I'll get them," he said.

He disappeared for a second and returned with her pajamas from the bathroom. He handed them to her and then, with a serious face, said," And remember. Tomorrow is another day."

Maren made a noise as a small laugh burst through her lips. "Oh god, Grandpa. 'Gone with the Wind'? You are something else."

Blackhawk laughed with her for a minute. Then he took her hand and patted it.

"And so are you."

Chapter Eight

Letting Go

Maren woke the next morning pulling herself out of the strangest dream she ever had. She was running in the woods. She could smell the fallen leaves. Their acrid smell burned her nose. Then another scent rushed in over the leaves. It was warm, no, it was hot. She was running toward it, closer and closer. The smell was sweet, not sweet like candy, but sweet to her. She almost had it ... then, something behind her distracted her. It had a bad smell. She turned her head to see—she jerked awake. Her eyes opened. *Weird. There was something delicious there ... and something evil.*

Maren laughed it off. *Who would blame me after all this wolf and changeling stuff!* She turned to get out of bed and froze. Her face went sober. She ran her hands under her pajama top. *Now why couldn't this have been a dream too?* Maren finally dragged herself out of bed and stood there for a minute trying to remember everything. She knew she was going to have to dress differently, that was for sure.

She picked up her ugly, old camisole bra and whipped it against the wall. It was strangely satisfying to see it hit and slide down to the floor like a squashed bug. *At least I'm done pretending with that stupid thing. Because I'm special. Something. A changeling?*

Maren made her bed quickly, then dug frantically through her clothes. *Layers, I need layers. Long t-shirts with baggy shirts over that. Oh, and the wraps! Need to buy some of those.* She found a couple shirts and hung them on the hook on her door. Something on the floor caught her eye. It was a leather type bag, laced. *Grandpa must have put this in my room last night.*

She picked up the bag and sat down on her bed. It was nice leather. *Probably deerskin.* She'd seen the things her father had, the Indian things he kept hidden away. Finely tanned deerskin jackets and other things. She had dug through his old chest. She hadn't a clue what some of them were, but the bag reminded her of his things. Even the smell was eerily familiar.

Maren scrutinized the bag. It was a natural color, kind of a pearly grey. An odd, beaded symbol was sewn near the bottom. *Very nice beadwork.* She pulled the laces open and reached inside. She grabbed a soft wad of something and pulled it out. It looked like some kind of cloth strips. Bandages. Not regular old ACE bandages but woven stretchy material and very soft. Yes, they were ACE bandages, Maren decided, but something had been done to them. She smelled them. A soft, woodsy smell. *Maybe some kind of herb?* She unwound one and sucked in her breath when she saw the end of the wrap. There was that same beaded symbol beautifully done and more elaborate than the one on the bag. *Meticulous.*

Maren had seen beading before. Her mother had made sure she knew about it … the heritage thing. Maren remembered scoffing at it, but now she was in awe of the craftsmanship.

She held the wrap out and rubbed it across her face. *Wow, how could anything feel this good.* She quickly whipped off her pajama top and started winding the wrap around her breasts. She decided she'd use both of them. The first she wound loosely so that it fit more like a sports bra around her normal breasts. Then she took the second one and wrapped it firmly around the other two breasts. She was careful to make sure the beaded end was on the outside end of both wraps. She secured them with four gold pins that were attached to the ends. Maren wrapped her arms around herself and closed her eyes. *How could they feel so good? What was on the material that made them so amazingly different?* She would certainly find out.

She walked to the mirror and turned side to side. Maren laughed. *Me standing in front of a mirror and smiling?* Now, it felt natural. It was way better than she'd ever felt before and that was good enough for her. Maren smiled and grabbed a long-sleeve, t-shirt hanging on the door. She dug around in her father's closet and found an old, faded flannel shirt. She put that on over the t-shirt and tied it at the waist. It looked just right. *Grandpa was so right about all this, so right.*

Maren finished getting dressed, bouncing around the room and then to the bathroom while she brushed her teeth and hair. Back in the bedroom, she took the leather bag, folding it neatly, and put it on her dresser. She would look at it more later, and ask her grandfather about it. Its familiarity haunted her.

An impatient Moonbaby finally got her attention. He had resorted to scratching on the door between them. *Poor Moonbaby!*

"Hold on, baby!" she yelled out. She burst again out of her bedroom door into the short hallway.

"Grandpa, where are you? I love these things!"

Blackhawk came out of the kitchen, crossing his arms in front of him when he saw her. Maren spun around for him, her shining, auburn hair flying around her like a whirlwind. Blackhawk held his breath while he watched her. Then he exhaled as if he were expelling all the stress of the last few days in one long breath.

"You've made this old man about as happy as he remembers being."

Maren ran to him, threw her arms around him, and whispered, "Thank you."

Blackhawk laughed at her, and shook his head. Maren was sure she saw his eyes tear up. He quickly turned and said, "Fresh fry bread in the kitchen. Gotta' haul in some wood. Can you take your little guy out? The pen should be OK today."

"Sure thing, Grandpa."

Maren grabbed two hunks of fry bread, stuffing them in her mouth as she dug through the coats hanging in the hallway. Winter was coming early to northern Minnesota. The air in the cabin had turned icy overnight.

She got Moonbaby's leash and collar and whipped open the door to his room, hoping to surprise him. No way. He was right there and leapt straight up in the air. His back feet had to be two feet off the floor.

"Wow," Maren said as she took in the powerful, graceful sight. "You are one fantastic creature." She wrestled around with him a little, slipped on his collar, and led him out to the pen. He immediately ran to the far end and relieved himself. He bounded back to her waiting for her approval.

"Good boy! Be right back with your breakfast, Big Man."

Maren ran back into the kitchen and fixed Moonbaby a special plate of dog food and breakfast scraps. *He's going to love this, the big monster.* She whistled to herself as she stirred everything up and headed back out to the pen.

As soon as Maren got within five feet of the pen's gate, Moonbaby turned and started running back again to the far end of the pen. *Weird.* She stopped and watched him. He made a swift turn then was bounding full speed back to her.

"Whoa! Stop!" Maren yelled. The plate fell out of her hands just as Moonbaby sailed cleanly over the six-foot high chain link fence. In only a matter of seconds, Moonbaby had disappeared into the woods.

Maren ran as fast as she could around the cabin toward the woodpile, where Blackhawk was splitting logs.

"Grandpa, Grandpa!" Maren stopped near him, bending over to catch her breath. "Moonbaby jumped the fence! He's out!"

Blackhawk completed his last swing into a log. Craaackkk. He left the hatchet buried in the ten inch diameter log and turned to Maren. His face was void of any concerned expression.

"Calm down, Maren. I knew this day would come. We can't prevent it. He's a wolf." He walked over to her and put his arm around her shoulder.

Maren pulled away. "But someone will shoot him! We have to do something!"

Blackhawk looked at her for a moment. Then he bent down and started yanking on the sunken hatchet. "We wait for him. You have to learn patience and trust. You cannot control any of the events that are bound to follow. There's nothing more I can say. I'm sorry, Maren."

Maren stood and stared at him. She couldn't believe what she was hearing. She didn't realize she was clenching her fists. "Then I'll find him myself."

Maren ran to her car that hadn't been driven since she had arrived at White Earth three months before. She remembered she had left the keys in it. Surprisingly, the car started without too much trouble. Maren sped out of the driveway spewing gravel. She had no idea where she was going but had to do something.

About two miles down the road she started to feel silly. *I just don't get his ideas sometimes. He is different. Native Americans are different, more than I ever imagined. And that's not even considering the whole changeling thing. Now what the hell should I do?*

Maren realized she was now on the main drag of White Earth. There was the Redwing Tavern. There was the clinic. She headed for the clinic and pulled up in front, turning the car off. Maren put her face in her hands and pushed on her forehead. *God, I've got a headache. What a fool I've made of myself. Now I have to drive back.*

She heard a soft tap on the side window. She looked up to see Dr. Don standing there. He looked concerned. She lowered the window.

"Is everything OK?" Dr. Don had that same non-hysteric tone.

"Oh, I don't know. Moonbaby jumped the fence and I just freaked out." Her face tingled as the familiar warmth spread down her neck. She shut her eyes knowing once again, her face was red as a beet. *Damn, I hate that!*

Dr. Don opened her door and said, "Come on in and have some coffee. We can talk."

Maren plopped down on a worn, corduroy chair in the waiting area. She watched Dr. Don as he delicately poured the coffee into the mug, then carried it over to her. The cup looked like it was floating in air. *He's so sure of himself. His hands move so smoothly, like a dance. Now I can definitely see the surgeon in him.*

"Grandpa didn't seem to care," Maren said as she took the hot mug into her hands. She took a small sip. It tasted like coffee, but kind of earthy. "What kind of coffee is this? Tastes good—but strange."

"My special blend. Has a little St. John's Wort and chamomile in it. Calming. Helps with the shakes."

"Oh." Maren blushed. She knew exactly what "the shakes" were. Her father had them plenty when he was alive. Alcohol withdrawal.

Dr. Don, thankfully, started talking. Maren's face was burning and she couldn't think of appropriate words.

"I'm a flawed man, Maren. I know you know an alcoholic when you see one. I know what you've probably seen and heard. I knew Jonny. Good man. But he was a drunk. I'm not making bones about this. No sense not to be upfront and honest about all this."

Maren eyes softened. *God, it would be nice to talk to someone who really knows. About everything. Nothing more to hide.*

"I haven't had a drink since that day you smelled it on me. Kind of shamed me back to reality. I think I am needed now and I don't want to screw this one up. Believe me, it's tough. Tough as hell. And your Pops is right about Moonbaby. He …"

"You're not the only freak show here, Dr. Don," Maren interrupted. "For starters, I have four boobs. And back at home, I'd occasionally vomit to try to stay thin. Now how sick is that!"

Dr. Don spewed a mouthful of coffee onto the floor. He coughed and wiped his mouth with a handkerchief from his pocket.

"Well, glad to see you can be forthwith."

Maren cringed at what and how she just said what she did. *I really am changing. Wow, that did feel good, though. And Dr. Don with his odd words*

… he's really cool. The thoughts made her frown change to a smile. Maren couldn't repress the giggle that came out.

"By the way, Maren, how is your mother doing?" Dr. Don was making the appreciated subject change, Maren noticed. "Only saw her for a few minutes at the burial. I know she needed some time with Blackhawk."

"You know my mom?" Maren hadn't thought about her mother living on the White Earth rez. It was so long ago.

"*Everyone* knew Laken O'Neill. We all were vying for her attention when she first moved her. The good-looking new teacher on the rez. That red hair. She was so Irish, and we loved her accent. Yes, I had a thing for her. You probably wouldn't know that but, anyway, Jonny won her. Your father. None of us stood a chance." Dr. Don's thoughts made him smile as he sipped his cup of concoction.

"Well, I'll tell her you said hi when I talk to her next."

Dr. Don spit out his coffee/brew a second time. His face turned scarlet. Maren laughed out loud, knowing exactly how that reddened face felt. It was always a dead giveaway.

"Whoa … you really *did* have a thing for her. Weird to see her in that way."

"Yes I did and not a bit ashamed to admit it. How is she getting along? Losing your father must have been devastating to her."

"It was. And more than it was to me. I'm sorry to admit. I was so angry with him. But I'm beginning to see some things now. I'm not the naïve little girl I was a couple months ago."

Dr. Don sat down after refilling his coffee cup. He smiled. "No. Probably not. But still a lot to learn, to know. You will tell Blackhawk if anything unusual happens?"

"Like more unusual than what has already happened?"

They both looked at each other and laughed. It felt good to Maren to have this new friend. Not that she didn't think the world of her grandfather, but Dr. Don was different. Her father's age. Someone else that knew her, her family, the changeling thing. Maren sat her mug down and leaned forward.

"Dr. Don. Will something be happening to me? How will I know? Will it hurt? Can I control it? What … ?"

"Whoa, whoa, young lady. Now those are questions your Pops needs to answer. I'm not one of you, remember? I can try to help, but I don't know the experience of it, the inner thing. You know what I mean."

"I'm sorry. I know. You're just easy to talk to. I'm a little frightened of Grandpa some times. He's so, uhmm, awesomely strange. I mean, I really love him, and no one has ever treated me better than he has. He has so much … uhmm …"

"Wisdom. Yes he does. He was the tribe's shaman for years. He knows and sees, beyond being a changeling. No one else really knows about the legend anymore. Except old Malak James, also a shaman of old. He's a recluse now. Losing his daughter, Lara—Moon—remember? And then his son being so damned impossible. I haven't seen the man in years."

"That's really sad, Dr. Don."

"Hey now. Just me rambling on. I have something for you. Just a second."

Dr. Don got up and went into a back room somewhere. Maren sat there in the chair. She felt as if she had melted into it. It was so relaxing and warm. She felt at peace. She closed her eyes and drifted off.

"Oh, oh. Think you had too much of my brew." Dr. Don had walked back into the room. He had something that looked like a leather necklace in his hand.

"Wow. Was I ever out. How long were you gone?"

Dr. Don laughed. "About five minutes at the most. See what I mean. Herbs are nature's own medicines. A lost art. I managed to pick some of it up. Blackhawk has a lot of knowledge but his wife Marina, your grandmother, knew it all. She was a true medicine woman, yet, a modern herbalist. A lot of knowledge, that woman."

Dr. Don knelt down next to Maren's chair. She could smell his woodsy smell. It was comforting to her. It took her a minute to focus on what he had in his hands.

"Oh my god! It's that symbol. It's on my wraps. My, ahhh, thingies that … ."

"I know what you're talking about. Yes, the same. It's the changeling symbol. That curly 'H' with the 'W' hanging below it. This was made by a silver worker—a long time ago, I presume. It was your father's. He never did tell me where he got it. But he did make me promise, when he took it off, the first time as far as I knew, last time he was here on the rez. He wanted me to make sure you got it, *when you came home.* That's exactly what he said. He knew, Maren. He knew what you were. He knew you were a lot stronger than him. From your mother's side, he said. He just plain never knew how to tell you. Couldn't deal with it himself, as you know. But he *did* know that you'd be here someday. And here it is."

Maren's eyes scrutinized the necklace with the tarnished silver symbol while Dr. Don talked. The leather looked like deerskin, of course. Everything made by the northern Indians seemed to be of deerskin. It still looked soft. The end was knotted. It was plain but beautiful in its simplicity. The silver was delicately tooled. *It must have been a real pain to make.*

Maren took it in her hands, feeling the coolness of the metal. She put it around her neck. She was immediately struck with a sense of strength. Her father. A vision? She couldn't quite grasp it but felt a sense of power. *Now he would always be near.*

"Thank you," she said as she squeezed the talisman in her hand, her eyes shut.

Dr. Don stood up abruptly, bringing them both back into the present. "One more thing, Maren. You have to learn to let some things go as they will. You can only control for so long. Eventually things will be as they are. Moonbaby, for example."

Maren launched out of her chair. "Moonbaby! I completely forgot why I was here. What *should* I do, Dr. Don? I'm so afraid for him. I don't know what I'd do if something happened to him."

"Your Pops is right, you know. Let him go for now. He's out exploring. He's different than other wolves or even a dog. He won't seek out humans, I know that. I think he will be seeking out other wolves. I'm sure he knows he's different. They all do. We just don't know what he is, exactly, being a wolf born of two changeling parents in their wolf phase. No record or story of that in any changeling legend. And we've checked, believe me. His father—probably *was* Silver but we don't know for certain. Not without DNA. And that would sure raise some eyebrows."

Dr. Don chuckled at his own words, then cleared his throat. "Go home. Take care of that old man. Figure out who you are. Moonbaby is doing the same."

Maren threw her arms around Dr. Don and squeezed him. "Thank you. I'm sure Moonbaby is off doing something gallant … like fighting the Wendigo," she said with a smile.

Dr. Don gave her a squeeze back then took her hands in his. "He just might be. He just might. Go live your life, Maren. Fight your Wendigo. I have all the faith in the world in you. So did your father."

Maren walked out of the clinic, the cold air hitting her in the face. His herbal concoction had relaxed her. Not in a woozy sense or even a "high." She just felt as if one layer of stress had been moved aside. She already missed Moonbaby. She couldn't help but worry. But she knew it was something that had to happen. Probably like a parent seeing a child grow up and leave the home. *God, Mom must miss me terribly. All alone, especially after just losing Dad. Oh, how selfish I've been. Just a self-centered teenager. God, I have a lot to learn. Moonbaby. He'll teach me. Moonbaby.*

Maren pulled into the gravel driveway of her grandfather's cabin. It was dusk. She couldn't believe she'd been gone that long. She ran out back first, just in case. Moonbaby wasn't there. Her heart sped up a bit, but she took a deep breath and walked into the kitchen from the back entrance. Blackhawk was cooking. It smelled wonderful. He looked up when the door opened. Maren could see the flood of relief on his face.

"Got some fantastic venison stew going here. Hope you're hungry."

"Starving."

Maren sat down at the kitchen table. She watched Blackhawk get out bowls, along with some fry bread. *Couldn't go without that.* She smiled. Then she saw his shaking hands.

"I'm sorry, Grandpa. I acted like a baby. I spent the day with Dr. Don. He was great. I should have called you. That wasn't right."

Blackhawk dished her up some stew and sat the meal down in front of her. Then he dished up his own and sat down, hard. Maren swallowed. *God, I really hurt him.*

"That's great. He's a good man. Good friend. Are you OK?

"Could only be better if Moonbaby was home, safe. But I'll wait, Grandpa. I will be here for him when he returns. No matter how long."

Blackhawk looked at her. His eyes had a worried look in them, as they searched her face. They stopped and fixated on her neck. *The necklace!* Maren reached up and grabbed the leather tie. She slowly pulled the silver talisman out from under her shirt.

She squeezed it in her hand, never taking her eyes off Blackhawk. A faint smile appeared on his lips. He shut his eyes for several seconds and nodded several times in slow motion. His eyes opened, but they were unfocused— looking straight ahead. He looked as if he were lost in a memory. Then he picked up his spoon and dug into the robust smelling stew in front of him. Maren did the same.

Chapter Nine

Unexpected Hero

Maren checked the backyard every morning. Meanwhile, she spent a lot more time on the phone with her mother. The subject of college came up several times, but it was way too late for the fall semester. Not that she had any plans of going *anywhere* until Moonbaby came back. Her mother didn't want her to go anywhere yet, either. She was even outright supportive of her staying with Blackhawk as long as she wanted.

That angered Maren. Her mother was just plain chicken. Even with their recent heavier conversations, Maren refused to bring up or even say out loud anything about her four breasts. The closest was to say "my differences," or "the thing going on with the legend." Her mother just didn't ask. Maren wanted her to; she owed Maren that much. Some little segue, anything. All those years without any talk, any support. Maren was damned if she would give her mother the satisfaction of making it comfortable for her. No way.

Maren helped her grandfather with all the house chores, particularly the cleaning. Blackhawk was terrible at it. Maren insisted they buy a new washing machine. Of course, Blackhawk did just that. It was obvious that he missed having a woman around the house.

Three weeks passed and no Moonbaby. Maren refused to let it get her down. She would often stop at the Redwing with Blackhawk. They always went early, when the bar opened, around 4:00PM. They always left by 6:00PM, and most of the time, earlier than that. Blackhawk refused to let her hang around after any of the regular and often rowdy patrons arrived. It was still fun. The best part was when the guys talked about the latest gossip on the rez. She was totally accepted and even enjoyed the mundane conversations—cutting enough wood for winter, the rice harvest, getting some meat in the freezer. The best, though, was the "not so nice" talk about Dr. Cindy Shane and Jules.

Apparently they were an item. Everyone was in an amused shock. How an educated, beautiful, blonde, non-Indian Ph.D. could fall for Jules was beyond them. Maren cracked up. She told them they were worse than a bunch of old ladies. Maren knew they loved teasing her, and told her things just to see how she'd react. She just loved being around them. It was all so different than the meaningless dribble she used to hear in high school, and these people weren't vindictive.

And Jules? She still didn't know what to think about him or what Cindy could possibly see in him. Was he truly evil? Maren knew that Jessie and Dr. Don would make a point of saying there had been no wolves shot or trapped. *Moonbaby.*

They made a point of calling Jules one evening from the Redwing to make sure he wasn't out hunting. "Hey, Maren. Cindy Shane wants to talk to you," Jesse said, as he held out the phone. There was a silence, then a lot of chuckling when Maren took the receiver. She rolled her eyes at them.

"Hello, Dr. Shane," she said. "How are you doing?" Maren was hoping she'd seen Kenny since he went off to college for the fall semester. Kenny and Maren still talked every week or so, and he did say he was coming home in a couple weeks to spend time with his mother at the resort. Maren wanted to ask him over for dinner. It would be nice to have company her own age. She needed a distraction from worrying about the missing Moonbaby.

"That's great, Dr. Shane—I mean Cindy. Thanks. Jesse is right here." After several minutes of "Great's" and "OK's" she handed the phone back to Jesse. "Jules wants to talk to you."

"Cindy was nice enough to ask about Moonbaby," she said, as she sat back down next to Blackhawk. "And she said Jules hasn't been hunting at all. Kenny will be at the resort visiting his mother next week so I'll ask him over for dinner. That's OK with you, Grandpa, right?"

"Sure thing. As long as you cook. Sounds like a good time."

As soon as Jesse hung up the phone, they started teasing her about Kenny. Whoo-hooing and just having a good time with it. Maren didn't care at all. She just smiled at them. She was thankful that she had this family of her father's that accepted her just as she was.

She realized they didn't care that she was "just a half-breed." A lot of the "Traditionals" did. The true spiritual Indians, as Maren saw it, actually *saw* the Indian in her. They didn't care that she had red hair or caramel-colored eyes. She just was—one of them. And they sure liked giving her a hard time .... .

Another week passed. Maren and Blackhawk were driving back from town. They had already stopped for groceries, said "Hi" to Dr. Don, who was busy taking care of an outburst of flu, and waved at Jessie through the window of the Redwing. Maren was unusually perky.

"Grandpa, just so you know, Kenny Shane is coming over this weekend. He just called. He's spending the weekend with his mom. Will that work?"

Blackhawk smiled. "It's *all* OK with me, my girl. You need to have some company your own age. I've been keeping you all to myself. We all have. Can't imagine this place without you, to tell the truth. I'm just a lucky old man. I'm thankful that this all happened. Of course, there are other things yet to discuss. They will let us know when it's time. Ahhh, yes. Bring that young man out and cook for him. Make him some fry bread. Yours is just as good as Marina's was."

Maren laughed. "I don't know if he'll eat it but I will."

Blackhawk pulled over onto the side of the road and stopped. He took a deep breath.

"What, Grandpa?" Maren clasped her hands tightly in her lap.

"I've been waiting for the right time. When I knew you were more, ahhh, stable." He cleared his throat. "I saw Moonbaby two days ago. You were taking the garbage out to the burn barrel. He was watching you from the tree line. He was checking up on you. He's coming back. Know that. He has something he needs to do. I'm not sure what it is, but it's important enough to keep him away this long, but still worry about you. I didn't know how to tell you or how you'd handle it. Just know he's there, and alive and well."

Maren put her hands over her face and cried. She hadn't cried as hard since the night in the bathtub, when she realized what she was. This time it was different. Pure relief.

"Thank you, Grandpa, Thank you. I'm so glad he's OK. I hope he comes home soon. I miss him so much, it's just weird. Can't help it."

Blackhawk pulled a hankie from his pocket and handed it to her.

"Not weird. Not weird at all. He's one of us. Don't know what will happen but we'll be here for him."

They returned to the cabin without another word. Blackhawk headed for the refrigerator. Maren followed him into the kitchen, rubbing her reddened eyes.

"Grandpa, I can't eat tonight. I really need to go to bed. I'm OK. In fact, I'm so relieved, I can't tell you enough. Thank you again. Love you."

Blackhawk gave her hand a quick squeeze, and began his evening meal search of the frig.

Maren headed for the bathroom to run a hot bath. She felt as if she had won the lottery. So exhilarated, yet so exhausted. Her stomach in a knot, she couldn't eat if she tried. She lay in the bathtub thanking God and anyone or anything that was listening. She barely made it into her bed before she passed out, sleeping straight through until 9:00AM the next morning.

Maren could see the sun was already up, trying to warm the frigid air in her room. She pulled the covers up over her head. She wanted to think pleasant thoughts of Moonbaby, running free in the woods, doing what he wanted to. Being a wolf.

"Holy shit! Maren, get out here. Now! No, call Dr. Don first. No, forget it. Get out here!"

Maren jerked up in bed. *What the hell?* Her Grandpa yelling at the top of his voice? A pang of panic hit her in the stomach. She jumped around the floor trying to get her legs into her jeans, threw on several shirts, then slid her bare feet into her boots. She grabbed her jacket that was hanging near the back door, and burst out into the back yard. She ran several feet, and then froze.

Was it real? She rubbed her eyes. It was Moonbaby. And he was huge. *He must have doubled in size. Black as coal, with that silver streak. Mind-blowing gorgeous.* Maren's knees gave way. She dropped to the ground. It was then that she saw Blackhawk standing about fifteen feet from Moonbaby. He was motioning to her—to stay put.

Moonbaby was standing over something on the ground. It looked like an animal, a big one with light-brown fur. Maren couldn't make it out.

"Is he OK? What is that laying there by him?"

Moonbaby's head jerked toward Maren's voice. His tail started to wag. Then in a fantastic leap he headed straight for her. She had no time to react as Moonbaby toppled her over onto the ground, covering her face with a thousand, slobbery licks.

"Whoa, get off, get off, you're too heavy!" Maren was laughing and crying at the same time. She rolled the gigantic wolf over onto his side, Moonbaby allowing it of course. He was making a wailing, howling noise. Maren was finally able to pull herself up, holding Moonbaby's huge head against her hip. He wasn't going to let her move anywhere just yet.

"I'm OK, Grandpa," Maren yelled out. "What *is* that thing out there?"

Blackhawk was kneeling down, his eyes fixed on the long, furry object at his feet. Maren saw him digging in his pocket, then pull out his cellphone. Maren watched impatiently, knowing that he always forgot he had the thing. He was obviously calling Dr. Don. He snapped the phone shut, then motioned for Maren to come over to him.

Maren gave Moonbaby another hug, and guided him toward his pen door. She didn't know why, since he could get out at his whim, but he walked in quietly. He looked tired and he immediately stretched out on the ground. Maren's hand went to her mouth as she inhaled. There were several long, bloodied scratch marks on his side and underbelly.

"Grandpa, I think Moonbaby's hurt. He's been bleeding."

"I wouldn't doubt it one bit. Come on over here. Dr. Don's on his way. He'll be OK."

Maren turned reluctantly from Moonbaby. She sprinted over to Blackhawk's side. "Holy shit, Grandpa! I mean, oh my god. What *is* it?"

"It's a cougar. Mountain lion, puma—whatever you want to call it. I know we have a couple around but they keep well out of sight. Obviously a male by the size of him. He's gotta' be seven feet long to the tip of that tail. Two hundred pounds, I'd bet."

"Oh, gross. He's all torn open. Did Moonbaby do this, you think?"

"Yes, I do think. Mighty tough job, too. It usually takes a whole pack to take down a cougar this size." Blackhawk grunted as he struggled to turn the big cat on its back.

"Let me help, Grandpa." Maren knelt down and gasped. "Looks like Moonbaby just pulled open his aww, stomach. What's that thing hanging out? Besides the guts, I mean." She laughed. "This stuff doesn't bother me anymore," she said, as she reached into the animal's open stomach.

"Apparently not." Blackhawk grabbed a section of the torn hide and held it out of the way.

Maren dug around trying to get ahold of the out-of-place object. It kept slipping back, getting lost in the bloodied mass of entrails. She finally grasped the object and held it up to Blackhawk. It was a two-inch piece of bluish, cloth tape with a metal d-ring and a round, metal object hanging off of that.

"Grandpa, it's a collar piece! A dog's collar! Look!"

Blackhawk snatched it out of Maren's hands, his own trembling. He rubbed the blood and mess from the round object. It was a name tag.

"Psycho. Not exactly what I'd name my dog. But I'd bet my ass it's from Jimmy Redbird's crazy pit bull. Now that would have been a fight."

"That jerk that's accusing wolves of killing his dog?" Maren swallowed hard as she looked over at Moonbaby, who was out like a light. "I feel bad for the dog, though."

"Yeah. I know. Redbird's only one of several 'jerks.'"

The sound of tires spinning to a stop in the driveway got their attention. A moment later, Dr. Don came running around the cabin to the backyard. He stopped next to the two and knelt over, his hands on his knees, catching his breath.

"Well this better be worth it. Left old Mrs. Tibbets sitting in the waiting room," he said, as he turned his head to the dead mountain lion on the ground. "I'll be damned ..."

"All of us," Blackhawk said, with a chuckle. "That's only part of it." He held the piece of collar and dog tag up to show Dr. Don. "It's Psycho's."

Dr. Don's eyes darted from the cougar to the name tag. He slapped his leg and laughed.

Maren nodded. "Moonbaby killed this cougar to prove that the wolves weren't doing this 'pet' thing around the rez. Then he dragged this huge animal all the way back here and he even did a partial autopsy for you, Dr. Don."

Her eyes watered. She wiped her face with her bloody hand. It didn't matter. Nothing mattered except Moonbaby was back. He was back and brought proof of his innocence—his and that of his wolf family.

"You all help me load this cat into the truck. I *am* going to do an official autopsy and let's just see what else I find. The size of this guy is enough. Must have been out looking for a new territory and decided to make easy prey like pets his choice of the hunt," Dr. Don said. "He just got lazy."

They all took a leg and dragged the huge cat all the way to Dr. Don's truck. It took all three of them to lift the dead weight onto the truck bed.

"Dr. Don? Can you look at Moonbaby's scratches before you go? He seems OK, but I'm worried." Maren took his hand before he had a chance to answer. Blackhawk slammed the tail gate closed.

"Hey, old man. Grab my bag out of the truck, will you? This girl is serious." Dr. Don smiled and made a look like he was being pulled against his will.

Blackhawk laughed. "No problem, you old drunk."

Maren smiled. That meant that Blackhawk knew Dr. Don wasn't drinking at all. He would never make such a comment otherwise. She squeezed her eyes closed briefly. *All these great friends and my baby is back … .*

Dr. Don and Maren kneeled over Moonbaby, who only opened his eyes for a second to glance at both of them, and then went back to snoring.

"This is almost impossible," Dr. Don said as his eyes took in the huge, black wolf. "He's doubled in size. Looks, well—mature."

"Thought the same, Doc." Blackhawk sat the medical bag down next to them.

Dr. Don took out his stethoscope and gently touched Moonbaby with it. He didn't budge. Dr. Don listened to the wolf's heart, stomach, and then looked in his ears. Moonbaby didn't move a muscle. He just went on breathing deeply and peacefully.

"From what I can see, you need to clean these wounds. Just some Betadine soap and water. They're just through the hide, no real internal damage from what I can see. Might sting a bit. I would love to do it for you, Maren, but Mrs. Tibbets is going to be a tornado when I get back to the office."

"Yeah, sure Doc," Blackhawk said. "By the size of him, I wouldn't want the job either. Guess it's up to our girl here." Both Dr. Don and Blackhawk were already shaking hands.

"Oh gee, thanks, guys." Maren had lain on her side next to her exhausted wolf. He was bigger than she was. She couldn't stop petting him.

"Now there's a Kodak moment," Dr. Don said. "Better get it done now, while he's aw, tired."

"Ha-ha." Maren said under her breath. *Nothing could be better, nothing.*

"Let me know on that autopsy, Doc. And, oh yeah …" Blackhawk dug into his pocket. "Here's the proof. Might be interesting to show around at the Redwing." He tossed the collar piece to Dr. Don, winking.

"Don't you know, old man. Don't you know. That carcass is going down there too. That will be sure to get a newspaper article, don't you think?"

They shook hands again. Then Blackhawk squeezed Dr. Don's arm. "You got it covered, Doc. Hey. Thanks."

Blackhawk's head was turned toward his smiling granddaughter, who was holding her wolf as he slept.

Chapter Ten

Kenny Shane

Maren couldn't help but notice the difference in Moonbaby. He'd been gone a long time. Dr. Don told her he was sexually mature. She knew that meant not to expect him to stay around long. They were just looking out for her feelings. She really believed he wouldn't leave again. But there was something peculiar ... . Every so often Moonbaby would walk around the property, his hair standing straight up while he sniffed the air. *What is he looking for?* Maren finally just brushed it off as boredom. What else could he do with his time but check out his old surroundings?

Moonbaby stayed in his pen during the day, when Maren went to town or stopped at the Redwing with Blackhawk. She believed that Moonbaby was doing it for her sake, that *she* was the one who needed reassurance, and he knew exactly what he was doing.

He had let her clean his wounds that day without a flinch. He just "knew." She was sure he understood more words than any average pet ever did. Just took it all in and watched everyone and everything. He "listened" to everything she and Blackhawk, or even Dr. Don said, ears twitching.

At night he slept on the floor in the room next to hers'—his old room—but now with the door kept open between them. He acted like a personal body guard.

Dr. Don did what he said he would. The whole rez was buzzing about the big mountain lion that Moonbaby killed. Even Redbird had to admit a wolf hadn't killed his dog.

Jules James, surprisingly, looked hard for supportive evidence when he went out hunting. He even came into the Redwing with some calf remains. He said they were partially buried under some leaves and debris; it was exactly what mountain lions do with their kills. Cover them and come back to eat at their leisure.

Jules was different. He called her and said, in his broken way, that he was glad her wolf was OK, and that some of the wolf-killing frenzy had died out. Maren had wondered how *he* felt about it, since he was the one with the wolf-hating reputation. She resisted the urge to ask him. That would have been too forward to an Indian.

Everything was wonderfully normal on the rez for Maren. She made some tentative plans to go to school in late January, now that Moonbaby was back, but only until summer break. It was a good time to start. She would only be gone a few months. That was one thing she was going to talk to Kenny about when he visited. He was going to hound her about it anyway, while adding that she was the prettiest girl he'd met. She smiled. It would be fun see him again.

Maren put Moonbaby in his pen. It was terribly cold but Moonbaby's thick coat prevented him from feeling any of it. And she was glad to have some time to sweep the massive amounts of wolf hair out of the cabin. *Remind me to get a non-shedding dog in the future*, she'd think to herself and laugh. There *was* no other dog, wolf—whatever—than Moonbaby, of course.

Maren made fresh fry bread and some stew from an elk that Jules had shot on a previous hunting trip. Cindy Shane had dropped it off, wanting to help Maren with the dinner plans. She was thrilled about the whole thing. Maren didn't have the heart to tell her they were just friends.

The last thing she needed was a boyfriend. A "good friend" was just fine with her. Moonbaby and everything else that was happening—she just couldn't deal with *that* added stress.

"He's hee—rre."

"Oh, Grandpa, Stop it. I'm nervous enough."

Blackhawk just chuckled and got back to reading the reservation newspaper. He spent more time in his recliner, Maren noticed. She knew the cold bothered him more than it used to.

Maren went to the door to meet Kenny. He was just getting out of his car. *Oh my god, he looks like a Viking god; the halls of Valhalla come to mind.*

"Hey, Kenny. You look great," Maren said, smiling, with the Viking image still in her mind. He had short, cropped white-blonde hair, nice fitting blue jeans, and a black leather jacket. *Wow, don't remember him being that good-looking.* She squeezed her hands together.

"Well, look at you. You're more beautiful than I remember. Really. What's happened to you?"

Maren raised her eyebrows and tilted her head. "What do you mean, what happened to me? Like there was something wrong before?" *God, I'm flirting again.*

"Awww, yea-ahh. You *have* changed. Grown up. Something. You were super before, but now you're awesome." Kenny reached out and swept her into a big hug before she had time to do anything about it. He released her just as quickly, with a big grin on his face.

"I see you haven't changed much, Mr. Arrogant. Come on in and meet Grandpa."

Maren guided Kenny into the house. She stood behind him as Blackhawk got out of his chair to shake his hand. She did a "fanning herself" motion so her grandfather could see. Blackhawk chuckled and shook his head.

"What?" Kenny looked back and forth between them. His outward confidence faltered a bit.

"Not a thing, young man. Nice to have you. Maren here, is just being a comedian, as she loves to do. Let's sit down at this table we rarely use. Hope you're hungry, cuz I am."

"Yes, I am. I'm looking forward to anything but my own microwaved stuff."

Everyone sat down and Maren relaxed. *It is nice to have company. Grandpa's right. I needed company my own age. Grandpa—he makes everyone feel so good.* Maren smiled warmly at Blackhawk.

It didn't take long for two refills of stew and all the fry bread to disappear. Kenny praised and praised Maren's cooking ability to the point that she thought her face would stay permanently red.

Maren jumped in her chair. She cleared her throat. Kenny had found her hand under the table and grasped it in his. She wasn't sure if she should pull it away or leave it. Her heart sped up. She was surprised at how exciting it was.

Blackhawk finally got up from the table. "OK. This old man is ready for his recliner." He walked around and kissed Maren on the forehead, and placed his hand on Kenny's shoulder.

"Nice meeting you, Mr. Shane. Drive careful home. Roads can get icy."

"Will do, Blackhawk, Sir. Thanks for having me."

"Let me show you my father's room," Maren said. "It's mine now, but has some cool things on the wall. Then we can go out and get Moonbaby before you leave. You absolutely need to meet my wolf."

"Cool."

Blackhawk had re-settled in his recliner. "Make that intro with Moonbaby nice and easy, Maren. Remember, he's only met Dr. Don so far."

"I will," Maren called out as she opened her bedroom door.

Kenny followed Maren into her bedroom, then reached around to close the door. Maren stopped his hand, then parked the door so it was half open, but blocking some of the view from the hall. It didn't take Kenny more than that to pull her close to him.

"God, your eyes are beautiful. They're almost yellow. They were more green. Copper. Brown. Whatever. Now they have this really intriguing golden glow. Weird."

Maren couldn't talk. She could feel his breath on her face, near her mouth. She could smell his cologne, and beneath that, his own warm smell. Kenny's eyes pierced her own. *They're so blue and wild, like an angry ocean.* She felt intoxicated; she'd never felt that before. Her high school kisses were clumsy. No passion. To put it bluntly, they sucked.

This was *way* different. She felt a warm sensation travel through her body. What would it be like to kiss Kenny Shane? Her mouth watered. She wrapped her arms around his neck as he put his mouth on hers. His hands caressed the small of her back, warm and strong. She was melting away, forgetting where she was—until.

Kenny's hands. On her back. They stopped suddenly, feeling the wide strips of cotton wrap ... HER WRAPS!

Maren jumped back so quickly, she fell down onto the bed. She pushed her hair back from her forehead. She couldn't bear to look at Kenny's face.

"What the hell? You just scared the hell out of me. Are you OK?" He sounded both hurt and pissed off.

"God, I'm so sorry, I just ... ." She couldn't finish her sentence.

"Holy shit—Maren, *Maren*?"

Maren looked up. Kenny was slowly backing up toward the rear wall of the bedroom. His light-colored Scandinavian face had lost all color and was distorted, like white paper was stretched back over his forehead. His eyes were solid dark holes in his head and his mouth was wide open with no sound coming out. Then she heard the sound. A low, rumbling, gurgling growl right behind her.

Her head snapped around. It was Moonbaby, and he looked like she had never seen him before. He was crouched down in the door between their rooms. The hair on his entire back was fluffed out and full. His silver neck ruff looked like a lion's mane, standing up straight, like it was electrically charged. But his face—his nose was curled down and wrinkled up so far that all his teeth showed, even those at the back of his jaw. Saliva dripped from his mouth. His eyes were glowing yellow-orange and bloodshot. And they were totally focused on Kenny Shane.

"Moonbaby! Stop! Now!" Maren screamed it out as loud as she could. Terror rolled through her as she saw that Moonbaby didn't even flinch. Another long, vicious, bloodcurdling growl rumbled deep in the back of his throat, making its way to his teeth where it vibrated for several seconds. It was a purely wild, wolf sound—one that was ready to take down his enemy—or tear out the throat of his prey.

The sound of a shot gun being racked cracked through the air. Blackhawk had a shot gun pointed directly at Moonbaby.

'No, Grandpa! No wait. Noooo!"

"Hell, yes. Kill that fucking wolf before he kills me! Look at him, Maren. Are you nuts?" Kenny shouted as he covered his face with his arms, his back against the wall.

Maren did look and that was all she needed to see. At exactly the same time Moonbaby launched from the doorway, Maren threw herself directly into his path. There was a loud smashing sound as Moonbaby's two hundred twenty pounds hit Maren full on. They both crashed to the floor. Blackhawk bolted into the room, grabbed Kenny by the arm, and dragged him out in less than a second. Then both doors slammed shut.

Maren lay dazed on the hardwood floor. She struggled for her breath, coughing. Moonbaby's weight had knocked the wind out of her. Moonbaby scrambled to his feet immediately. He threw himself against the hallway door, even though his prey was long gone. He shook himself, then stood there, still, as if nothing had happened.

Maren could hear some muffled voices and then Kenny's car start up outside. She could hear the gravel spin as he left, obviously in a big, angry hurry. She pulled herself to a sitting position, wincing as she held her middle. Maren closed her eyes and squeezed her forehead. She peered through

her fingers at Moonbaby. No trace of the monster she had seen only minutes earlier. She exhaled and threw her hands down.

"Look what you did. I ought to have let Grandpa shoot you. You just ruined
any chance of me having a boyfriend. How about even just a 'friend?' You
know, like a *normal* girl? No, you don't know. Because you can just go off
for weeks in the woods and be just what you want. I can't. I can't have normal. Get it? Thanks a lot, you big jerk."

Maren was already losing steam by the time she got through her well-
deserved tirade. Moonbaby had crouched down, his belly touching the
floor. He was looking at the floor. His ears were half-down. He whimpered.
Maren turned away, holding her middle. *The crazy shit broke my ribs*, she
thought. *Not feeling sorry for him.*

"Yes, you should be ashamed," she said, her anger melting by the minute.

Maren pulled herself up from the floor. She rubbed her aching side.
*What's going to happen now? What will Grandpa do? What will happen to
Moonbaby?*

Maren threw herself down on the bed and buried her head in her pillow.
She cried quietly. She thought she had already been through the worst life
could dish out. Now what? What if she really *did* lose Moonbaby? *It would
never have worked with Kenny anyway, not with this!* She yanked at her
wraps, breaking one of the delicate gold pins. She pulled and pulled until
they lay in a heap on the floor.

Maren heard Moonbaby sniffing around on the floor. *He's found the wraps.
Chew them up. See what I care.*

Before she could look down, her body was bounced up and back off the bed
so hard she grabbed the edges of the tucked in sheets to stay on. Moonbaby
had leapt gracefully from the floor, landing with a plunge and crash onto

the bed. She watched him as he maneuvered his body so that he was lying crosswise at her feet. He laid his nose in his paws and stared at her.

"My god, dog." Maren wrenched part of her bed quilt out from under the wolf and covered herself up. "Guess we're a couple of losers, aren't we, Moonbaby? Don't fit in anywhere."

Maren stuck her foot out from under the quilt to touch Moonbaby. She rubbed his nose with her foot and left it up against his head. She closed her eyes.

The bedroom door slowly opened. Maren turned to see Blackhawk standing there—minus the shotgun. He leaned in the doorway for a moment before he spoke.

"Guess we're going to have to handle a few things differently. Now that we know how Big Black there feels about you."

Maren sat up, holding her side.

"Really, Grandpa? Cause I couldn't live without him. He didn't mean it. He's like me. He's so different. He'll be better next time."

"Probably not, Maren. But we'll make it work. Get some sleep. Mr. Shane had quite a scare. Hell, so did I. But we're all OK. You might want to give him a couple days before you call him, though."

Maren smiled half-heartedly. "Doubt it, Grandpa. Nice try. He sure is cute; I'll have to admit that. But it's not what I want right now. Who knows? Maybe I never will. Do you think this jerk would ever let that happen?" Maren kicked her toe lightly at Moonbaby, who made a whining noise. "Kenny doesn't need someone like me, anyway. You know what I'm talking about."

Blackhawk sighed. Maren turned her back to the door, both feet now resting on Moonbaby's neck. It was a good five minutes before she heard Blackhawk close the door.

Chapter Eleven

Second Revelation

Several days passed after the Kenny-Moonbaby incident. Maren figured Kenny hadn't talked. There was no gossip at the Redwing and no one asked anything. She wondered how much wolf-hating Jules was doing lately, because if Kenny did talk, it would be really dangerous for Moonbaby. Jules did seem to have lost some of his anti-wolf fervor. Perhaps he was finding Kenny's mother, Cindy, more interesting.

Maren hoped to eventually run into Kenny again, after things cooled off. She missed their phone conversations. She was still embarrassed about "the other thing" that had happened, knowing she had hurt his feelings. She was relieved that she had gotten up later that night to retrieve her wraps. Fortunately, only one gold pin was twisted up. *Thank god for that, at least. What a mess ... .*

It was the first week of December. Frozen on the White Earth rez, and a couple feet of snow to boot. Maren went out with Blackhawk and Moonbaby to cut a Christmas tree.

Have I really been here this long? She tried to talk her mother, Laken, into coming up for Christmas or even Thanksgiving. She said she was too busy with all her school-teaching stuff. She was retiring. Maren was relieved to hear her mother making plans for the future.

"How 'bout this one?" Maren had spotted a luxurious, eight-foot blue spruce.

"Beautiful," Blackhawk replied. "This one it is."

Maren watched as he swung the axe repeatedly, hitting the same spot every time. *Wow, he sure is strong for an old guy. I remember Dad doing the same thing … .*

"You OK?" Blackhawk had felled the tree and was leaning on his axe handle, catching his breath.

Maren lifted her head. "Great. Just having one of my few very good memories."

"That's good to hear. Let's get Moonbaby and hook him up to this tree. He can drag it back."

Maren whistled twice. Moonbaby had been staying close to her. It would be odd if he had run too far. After about five minutes, he did appear. But he was walking, not running.

Maren started running through the snow toward her wolf. *Something not right, not right.* She got to him and knelt down, petting him, and talking to him. Blackhawk had also trekked over, taking a lot longer.

"Something's wrong with him, Grandpa. Look at his ears. They're half down. He looks sick. Hope he didn't eat something bad, or got poisoned or something."

"Now let's not get carried away here. Hook the tree on him with the harness. We'll help with these two ropes. It will be the fastest way to get us all back."

Maren did as she was told, watching Moonbaby the whole time. He was still strong, so she felt a little better. He just wasn't himself.

They left the tree outside and brought Moonbaby in. Maren rubbed him down with towels, getting snow and water off his coat. He went straight to his room and lay down on his old comforter on the floor. He wanted to be alone.

Maren came back out, rubbing her hair with the same towels. "What do think is wrong with him? See how he's acting?"

Blackhawk sat down in his chair. "It's full moon tonight, Maren. All of us changelings feel it. We all feel not so good during that time. I was wondering. You feel anything?"

Maren sat down on a nearby sofa. She folded the towel up in her lap. "Maybe a little. A headache, and of course—these things." She pointed at her breasts. "They swell up every full moon and my moon time, which now happens to be on the same schedule."

"That's normal. I've been wondering when you, ah, get the change urge. You'll know it when it happens. Just make sure to tell me if anything, I mean anything at all is different for you."

"You know, Grandpa. Genes or not. I don't think I'm one. I'm going to be nineteen next year. You'd have thought something would have happened already."

"Not necessarily. Your genes might be a little 'watered down' but I still suspect something to happen. Not sure what."

"What about Moonbaby? He's got two pure changeling parents, right? What will happen to him?"

Blackhawk got up and poured some coffee that had been in the pot all day.

"You know. Doc and I have discussed that. I think it affected his intelligence. His size. But he's wolf. And we aren't positive that Big Silver is his father. So, truthfully, I don't have a clue."

Maren and Blackhawk sat in the living room with a great fire going in the fireplace. They made plans for the Christmas tree. Where to put it, what to put on it. They ate leftovers which is what they did until everything was gone. Only then did Blackhawk dig something else out of the freezer, or go to town and get some venison or other meat from Jesse at the Redwing. It was always meat with fry bread, or stew and fry bread. Sometimes wild rice.

Maren enjoyed the simplicity and good taste of the meals. Blackhawk told her they added vegetables in the summer and potatoes in the fall. It was all fine with her. She was surprised that she didn't gain weight, but then she wasn't starving or throwing up. She just wasn't obsessed about it anymore. It all seemed so silly to her now—to worry about such things when there were much larger issues available to worry about. *Superficial nonsense.*

Maren was washing dishes in the sink when she heard a strange thumping sound coming from Moonbaby's room. She ran to the bedroom door and whipped it open. Moonbaby was in the corner. His comforter was torn to pieces. He was rolling back and forth on the floor, his body hitting the wall.

"Grandpa, something's really wrong."

Maren ran to Moonbaby's side. He was unaware of her presence. His eyes had rolled back in his head, showing only an eerie, grayish-white color. He was frothing at the mouth. Every few seconds his whole body shook and convulsed. Maren tried to hold him but the strength of his convulsions threw her to the floor. His leg bones quivered; their shape distorted. She watched in horror unable to talk. She heard Blackhawk's cell phone pop open.

"Doc, yeah. It's Moonbaby. He's acting like, well, like he's going through the change. No, I know. But his hide, it's hanging off of him, and god, his muscles are twisting all over the place. Be there in fifteen."

Blackhawk snapped his phone shut. "We gotta get him to Doc's. Now. Don't know how. Maybe let's try to get him on another blanket and drag him a ways. Gotta try something."

Maren ran to get her coat. She went to the closet and found an old moth-eaten wool blanket. Blackhawk jammed on his boots, leaving the laces hanging. He grabbed his heavy, down jacket. Together they pushed and pulled Moonbaby's bulk onto the blanket. He was all dead weight. The two of them could barely get him across the wood floor to the door.

"Now what?" Maren said, trying to catch her breath. "There's no way we can get him to the truck."

"I'm going to get the truck and back it up to the porch. Maren. Try to get him to get on his feet. Do what you can. Put his collar on. You never know."

Blackhawk dug his keys out of his pocket and charged outside.

Maren's heart pounded. *Gotta do something. He looks like he's going to die.* She bit her lip, fighting back tears. *I'll be damned if I'm going to cry. No more. He needs me. Gotta do something, anything.*

"Moonbaby, Get Up. Get Up!" Maren grabbed the wolf's head and screamed into his face. The wolf's eyes focused for a moment. Then his eyes rolled back again. Maren screamed his name over and over. She pounded on his body and shook his head back and forth. Finally, he yelped and tried to pull himself up.

Blackhawk opened the front door. He went to Moonbaby's side and they both pulled and lifted the wolf until he was standing, wobbly, on all fours. His whole back end looked misshapen.

"Come on, Big Black. Get in the truck. Gotta do it. Come on." Blackhawk's voice got Moonbaby's attention.

Maren nodded at Blackhawk and they both pulled and tugged. Moonbaby finally got his front legs onto the seat. Maren and Blackhawk, together, were just barely able to lift his distorted hindquarters into the truck. There was just enough room left for Blackhawk to squeeze in behind the wheel.

Maren zipped up her heavy coat, put up the hood, and grabbed the blanket.

"I'm getting in the back. I can make it to Dr. Don's. Just drive, Grandpa, drive. Please. Hurry."

Maren jumped over the tailgate and hunkered down in the bed of the truck. She pulled the blanket over her and held it, wrapping her hands in it.

Blackhawk didn't question her. It was the only option. There was no time to wait and see if Maren's car would start in the cold.

They arrived at Dr. Don's in ten minutes. Dr. Don, fully clothed in his Minnesota winter garb, was pacing back and forth outside. He propped open the door when Blackhawk pulled up to the sidewalk, almost hitting the steps. Maren jumped out of the back, shaking, her nose and eyes running from the cold wind. She whipped off the blanket and handed it to Blackhawk who was already at the passenger door.

"Shit. I couldn't tell if he was breathing, Doc. Kept pounding on him until he moved." Blackhawk's hands were shaking. "Damn. This has got to be OK. Just has to."

They laid the blanket out on the snow and pulled the big wolf out of the seat. He hit the ground with a thud. His eyes came open. They glowed yellow in the streetlight, but were unfocused. He didn't or couldn't move. *Oh, no.* Maren knew it had taken everything he had to make those couple steps to the truck. There was nothing left.

All three of them pulled and tugged the big wolf up the steps and into the office.

"In the side room there," Dr. Don said. "I have some blankets down."

They all looked at each other with a "one more time" look on their faces. They managed to get Moonbaby into the room. Maren and Blackhawk collapsed while Dr. Don had his stethoscope out and listened to Moonbaby's body—everywhere. He gave Blackhawk a serious frown and wrapped up his stethoscope. Then he removed Moonbaby's collar.

"His heart is strong as hell. That's for sure. But all this other movement's got me concerned. Especially internal organs."

Maren's body went rigid. "*What* other movement? He looks like he's dying. What do we do?" She did her best to keep the panic out of her voice.

Dr. Don pulled both of them up from the floor. "Coffee. In the waiting room."

Maren dropped into a familiar corduroy chair. Her face and hands were getting some feeling back. She shook them out in front of her. Blackhawk got two cups of hot coffee and carried one to Maren. He sat down and glanced at Dr. Don.

"Maren. He's in the throes of 'the change.' Metamorphosis. Hell if I know into what. But his muscle tissue is changing. That starts first. Bone transformation follows and looks like it's already begun. And that's painful. I've seen it." Dr. Don looked toward Blackhawk. "Thank god, he's unconscious."

"Into what, Dr. Don? What will happen to him? Can you give him something for the pain? Anything?" Maren doubted she could bear hearing Moonbaby scream in pain.

"No. Doesn't do anything but slow everything down and just makes the whole damn thing last longer. I know. I've tried it," Blackhawk said.

Dr. Don walked over to a steel table that had syringes and medical paraphernalia on it. He was drawing something out of a bottle. "Just in case … Blackhawk?"

"Yes. Definitely." Blackhawk said, and then turned to Maren. "We might have to—put him out of his misery, Maren. We don't have a clue what's to become of him. It's for all our safety. And his. It doesn't mean we will have to use it. I just want you to know. In case."

Maren put her head in her lap. She was so tired. *I suppose he could turn into some monster wolf thing. Oh, god, don't let that happen. Please.* She lifted her head up.

"I know. I trust you both. Totally. You'll do everything possible. I know that. I've watched you both with him. I know you care almost as much as I do."

"Lie down on the sofa, Maren. Get some rest while it's quiet. You too, Blackhawk. Put your feet up. It's going to be a long night."

He didn't need to tell Maren twice. She took the wool blanket they had carried Moonbaby in with and wrapped it around her. She stretched her aching legs out straight and fell asleep.

Maren jumped straight up, yanking the blanket off her. *What was that noise? Was I dreaming?* She rubbed her face with her hands and re-did her ponytail. *God, I was out.* Then she heard it. A whimpering. Then a howl. A sharp yelp. Then a chilling, animal scream.

She leapt off the couch. Blackhawk and Dr. Don were just shutting the door where Moonbaby was. Both their faces were white. They weren't talking.

"Let me see him! Let me in!" Maren tried to push past them but they held her back.

"No. Not yet." It was Blackhawk and he sounded scared, but firm. "Not yet, Maren. I mean it."

Dr. Don took her hand and Blackhawk released her. They walked over to a table and chairs. All three dropped into chairs at almost the same time.

Blackhawk spoke first. "He's making a change, Maren, but we're not quite sure yet to what. Doc's been monitoring his vitals. He's OK. But we may have to…you know. Depending on what comes out of this. You understand that, my girl, I know. And whatever happens, I, *we* want you to remember your Moonbaby as he was. Not some 'thing' that just wasn't meant to be. Trust us, Maren, as you never have before."

"Wow. Yes, of course. You really *aren't* sure what's happening."

Maren was so used to them having the answers to everything. All she had to do was look at their faces.

"OK. No matter what. I don't want him to be some freak of nature. I don't want us to have to hide him. Take away his life by putting him in some closet. No. He's got to fit in somewhere. I'll be OK."

Maren remembered her life in high school—avoiding everyone, every-thing—wanting to die. Until she came to the rez. "I'm OK, really. Just, shouldn't we be monitoring this or doing something?" Her eyes welled up with tears. But she wasn't going to cry. No way.

"I can't go in there, Maren. There's nothing else I can do—till it's over. The change. I can't bear watching when I can't help." Dr. Don looked like he was in pain himself.

"Oh. It's OK, Dr. Don." Maren stared down at her hands, opening and clos-ing her fingers.

Blackhawk reached across the table, took her hand, and held it. The next screaming sound came soon enough. Dr. Don grabbed Maren's other hand, then Blackhawk's. They huddled forward in a circle around the table. Dr. Don began chanting an Indian rhythm. Slow and soft. Blackhawk joined in. The wolf scream came again, and again. Maren squeezed her eyes shut, trying to concentrate on the soothing sounds and the hands clasping hers. She hummed along. Thirty minutes of the horrifying yowling. Then blessed silence from the bedroom.

Their singing stopped. Maren disengaged her numb hands from the two men at her sides. She kept her eyes closed. There was a new sound. Different. More whiny. Not painful. More like a scared animal sound. Then a whimper, like a baby wolf. Like Moonbaby sounded months ago, and then a scuffing, thumping sound. Something dragging itself across the floor.

They shot up out of their chairs. Blackhawk gently pushed Maren's shoul-ders downward. She sat down. Dr. Don was already at the door. He opened it a crack, then six inches. He held the lethal syringe in one hand. Then he stuck his head in. Dr. Don took two steps backward, his mouth open. It looked like he was trying to say something. No sound came out. He stood, silent. The syringe fell out of his hand. He didn't shut the door.

Blackhawk reached the door in seconds. He peered in. Then, just like Dr. Don, he backed up. He grabbed Dr. Don's shoulders and shook them. Tears ran down his face. They were holding each other, crying, laughing. Patting each other on the back. More crying and laughing.

"Grandpa!"

Blackhawk looked over at Maren. She saw the sheer relief on his face. "Come and see for yourself." He sounded exhausted.

Maren lunged for the door. She stuck her head in then threw the door wide open.

"Oh my god! Is this for *real*?"

No answer from the two still embracing each other, hands on each other's shoulders, their heads hanging between them. They were trying to catch their breath.

Maren stepped into the room. Hunched in the corner was a hairy, human figure. Thick, ebony hair hung shaggy-like over a perfectly sculpted human face. A hairy face, but perfect.

A gleaming chunk of silver ran through the hair from the forehead and disappeared over the top of the head. Long, sinewy limbs. It—it was a he—sat in a crouched position. His yellow eyes searched the room. He made small, whimpering sounds.

"Go to him, Maren. He knows and trusts you best," Dr. Don said.

Maren's eyes saw what she saw, but her brain just couldn't process it as fast. "*Moonbaby?*"

The creature turned his head to her position in the doorway. He tipped his face toward the ceiling and sniffed. He tried to move. His gangly, muscled limbs scrambled on the floor. The awkward movements made her feel sorry for him. She didn't know if she should watch or turn her head. Finally, he lumbered toward her in an all-fours movement, stopping about six feet in front of her. He crouched down.

Maren walked three steps into the room. Right in front of her was the human version of Moonbaby. Chunks of shed hair were lying around the room. Blood and what looked like tissue or hide—something like that, lay in clumps. Grotesque and bloody. His skin was light. Part of it mucous and blood-covered, like he had just been born.

His hands had wolf-like claws on them and were webbed, like a wolf's. Other than that, they were real hands. Maren couldn't see his feet, but she assumed they would be odd too.

"Oh, my baby. Moonbaby. You did it. On your own. How could you possibly …."

Maren didn't finish her sentence because the new Moonbaby scooted himself tight to her. He wrapped his arms around her legs, and tucked his head against her knee. Maren reached down and stroked his black-haired head. Then she looked over to Blackhawk and Dr. Don with a "what now" expression.

"OK. Good. Take it slow," Blackhawk said. "He knows you and trusts you. One step at a time."

All of a sudden the new Moonbaby reached his head up and stuck it directly into Maren's crotch.

"Whoa ..." Maren jumped back, pushing Moonbaby hard.

Moonbaby slunk down and cowered. Dr. Don and Blackhawk both covered their mouths, trying not to laugh out loud. It didn't help. In another moment, they were roaring with laughter. They looked emotionally drained, but obviously appreciated the humor of the scene. Blackhawk regained his composure first.

'OK, Maren? Didn't Moonbaby, *the wolf*, do that? Often, as I recall?

"Well, yeah. But this is a guy ... I think?"

"That's right." Dr. Don replied. "But he's still a wolf. Remember, he hasn't had human cultural manners' ... instruction ... yet." Dr. Don could barely finish the sentence.

Blackhawk and Dr. Don covered their mouths with their hands again choking back laughter.

"He's just making sure you are who you are," Blackhawk sputtered. "Wolves, dogs ... they have a deeply sophisticated sense of smell. Something we humans have long lost. Most of it, anyway."

Maren had to smile. They were acting ridiculous, but she knew how insane the whole ordeal had been. They deserved some major stress relief.

"We're scaring him," Blackhawk choked out. "Really, Maren. Sorry. This old drunk made me laugh like I can't remember. Not since Marina and I ... well, can't talk about that."

"Good god. You two are worse than a couple of horny teenage guys!"

Both Blackhawk and Dr. Don were laughed out. They just shook their heads back and forth, and wiped their faces with their hankies.

Maren smiled and shook her finger at them like they were naughty boys. She directed her attention to the new human Moonbaby. He was watching them all. His yellow eyes bounced back and forth, as they took in everything in the room.

She walked slowly toward him where he had backed up all the way to the wall. She stretched out her hand, palm down, just as she had when she first met him. Then she stroked his head, half-petting, half-patting. He lay down around her foot and fell asleep, oblivious to the commotion going on near the door. He was exhausted.

"Um, guys? What now?"

Dr. Don was still patting at his face with his hankie. "Hawk, you're all right."

"You too, Doc. By god. You had more faith than I did."

Blackhawk's eyes were still watering. Maren wasn't sure if they were tears left over from their joking or tears of joy—probably both.

"Sorry. My god. Can't remember being so happy. So relieved. Not since you showed up, anyway. Maren. This is a damn miracle. First of its kind anywhere ... as far as we know, anyway. We're good. By god, and we are blessed. Thanks to the Great Spirit and all who are looking over us."

Blackhawk clasped his hands in front of him and closed his eyes for a minute. Then he looked down at Moonbaby on the floor.

"He needs rest and food. I remember that much, at least."

Maren got another blanket and wrapped the strange, new, sleeping human in it. Then she took a bowl of water and another of meat and set it nearby.

She stood there a moment, just looking. She was bewildered, but joyous. She couldn't remember ever feeling that much of anything—all that she had felt since Moonbaby and the changelings' stories. Joy, sorrow, happiness, fear. Just feeling. Then seeing her grandfather really laugh, really feel that same joy. It was something she had learned from Moonbaby. As a wolf. He felt everything so strong, so *now*.

She crossed her arms and squeezed. New adventures and new responsibilities. Scary, but also thrilling. Regret, too. Regret of stupid things she'd done and said. Her life would never be normal—not how she had envisioned normal, anyway. It was as it was. Now she could embrace it. It would be *her* life.

Dr. Don put makeshift beds together for them. No one would be leaving until they tackled the next few steps. He threw a sleeping bag down for himself, falling asleep immediately. Blackhawk had the comfy, corduroy chair with an ottoman so he could stretch his legs out.

Maren leaned back on the sofa, thinking and watching everyone, savoring the quiet.

"Grandpa?"

"Yes, my dear girl."

"I think we're going to need a new name for him."

Chapter Twelve

Damien Jon

Maren woke with a start, trying to get time organized in her mind. *Moonbaby.* She jumped up from the couch, realizing she had slept in her clothes, had no toothbrush or hair brush, and was absolutely starving. Immediately, she smelled fried eggs and bacon. Coffee too. She could hear talking in the back room of the clinic. She re-did her ponytail and smoothed out her clothes the best she could. She went into the clinic bathroom and rinsed off her face and her mouth, trying to feel a little human again. *Human. Moonbaby.*

Maren walked toward the back room where the intoxicating food smells were coming from. It was all quiet in Moonbaby's room. She resisted the impulse to peek in. She tiptoed by. Blackhawk and Dr. Don were talking away, as if there were no cares in the world. They stopped when she entered the kitchenette room.

"Maren, he's fine. He must have woken up and ate the food. Back asleep right now. We were just trying to make a game plan. Any ideas?" Blackhawk took a big sip of his coffee, watching her face. Then he handed her a plate of food, obviously one he had prepared for himself.

"Thanks. Starving."

"That's my girl." Blackhawk began dishing up another plate while Dr. Don dropped a couple more eggs into the frying pan.

"We need a reason for why he's here, out of the blue," Dr. Don said as he dumped two more eggs onto Blackhawk's plate.

"Easy," Maren said between mouthfuls. "He's my friend from Wisconsin. From my rez down there, Lac Courte Oreille. Ojibwe, too, Dr. Don, but a lot more, ah, city like. In a very small way. More white people. It will go like this—this friend came to visit me, to see what this northern Minnesota rez was like. You know. More traditionals." She winked as she shoveled the buttery eggs into her mouth.

They looked at each other. "Sounds good to me," they said in unison.

"I've been thinking," Maren said, as she scraped her plate. "What should his name be? I can't remember if you answered me last night, Grandpa. I was pretty tired."

Blackhawk set his plate down.

"I have a favor to ask you. Just one—to consider, of course. He looks a lot like I remember Sylvester, when he was a little guy. Not exactly, but close and Marina loved him and missed him so much. I was thinking. Her father was Italian. Damien was his name. Would you think about that? Kind of a tribute to my wife, your grandmother. And her son, Sylvester. Moonbaby's father. She would have loved it. But OK if ... ."

Maren interrupted. "I love it." She looked down for a minute. "Could we add Jon, like Dad's name? Damien Jon?"

Blackhawk broke into a big smile. "Yes. That's perfect. Damien Jon it is."

"Damien Jon it is." Dr. Don said. He clapped his hands together. "But we should give you fair warning. He's been examining his feet, his hands. Even took a piece of jerky and ate it from his hands and fingers. That's astounding, as far as I'm concerned. But what I'm wondering, Maren, is if you've ever seen a man at full mast before."

Maren spit out what was left in her mouth, trying to stifle a laugh. Blackhawk raised his eyebrows at Dr. Don.

"I guess that would be my business now, wouldn't it?" She tried to keep a straight face.

"Yes it would," Blackhawk interjected. "Just so you know, he's been examining himself. Probably some stuff he can see that he wouldn't as a wolf. Just fair warning. Remember, he's like a child in that manner. Not in intelligence, but in knowing how humans do things. We don't know all what he'll remember having seen the world as Moonbaby. He's learning how his human body works. Remember. He was chastised by you last night. Not on purpose, but just how it turned out." Blackhawk sat his fork down and sighed. His food was no doubt getting cold.

"Animals, and wolves even more so, read body language like a language expert reads a hieroglyphic." Dr. Don butted in. "Complicated, and something humans have lost the art of—succinct body language. Do you know what I'm saying? He most certainly will do embarrassing things … in light of cultural norms."

"I get it, you two. I'm good with it. No problem. Just want to help him adjust."

"Now that's why Blackhawk here is going to teach him how to use the latrine. Take his Willie and aim somewhere in particular. He's already sprayed all four walls." Dr. Don looked amused.

Maren laughed. "Yes, I *do* get it." She shook her head, looked at them both, and smiled. "But I do think clothes would be the first order of the day."

Dr. Don reached behind his chair and handed her a bundle.

"You get the honors. Just motion to him as if you were putting them on yourself. If he's going to resist anything at first, I believe it will be the restraint of clothing," Blackhawk said. "An important necessity, of course. And he trusts you the most."

"Great. Can I go in now? Want to get this done," Maren said, patting the clothing bundle in her arms.

"We've been waiting. All yours." Dr. Don motioned toward the door. Blackhawk sat down and stared at his plate of cold food.

Chapter Thirteen

The Human Life

Maren stopped at Damien's door. She knelt down and took stock of the clothing bundle. A pair of old, worn jeans, size thirty-two waist, long inseam. *Must have been Dr. Don's a long time ago,* she thought, smiling. A really nice, purple plaid flannel shirt—obviously new. A slightly yellowed, long-sleeved underwear shirt, a pair of old boxer shorts, and a balled up pair of thick wool socks. *Now this outta' be fun.*

Maren slowly opened the door. The room smelled of urine. Maren did everything she could to keep from wrinkling her nose or flinching. She knew Damien's eyes would be fixed on her every nuance. She looked straight at him, tipped her chin slightly, and said softly, "Hello, Damien. That's your human name. I've brought you clothes."

She set the pile on the floor. Then she took the socks, sat on the floor, and pretended to put them on herself. She pointed to her own socks, and then placed Damien's in front of him. She smoothed them out so he could see the shape. Next she grabbed the boxer shorts. She stood up and went through the dressing motions. She unzipped her jeans slightly and pulled at her own underwear, hoping he understood they went on first. She continued the pantomime with all the clothes. Then she nodded and motioned with her hand "to go ahead." She closed the door behind her.

Maren leaned against the wall in the hallway. She wasn't sure how long or what the result would be when she opened the door, but felt she had all the patience in the world for this new person. She cared, yet the "butterflies in her chest" feeling was a little disturbing. It reminded her of the one kiss she had shared with Kenny Shane. And she hadn't even kissed *this* very good-looking young man. Her face flushed. A crash behind the closed door interrupted her thoughts.

Maren threw open the door. Damien was lying on the floor. He had a distorted "smile" on his face and was making strange giggling noises.

"Are you all right, Damien?" Maren bent down on one knee, trying not to scare him.

Damien scrambled to his feet, moving his socked feet back and forth on the smooth, linoleum floor. He had all the clothes on perfectly. Maren's mouth opened to talk. She didn't know what to say. *Good boy? That's not right anymore, though I doubt he would care. But, wow, look at him. That purple shirt with his gorgeous black hair. I think I'm really going to be jealous. Glad there's not many girls around right now.*

Damien had backed up to the side wall in the room. Arms out at his sides, he leapt into the air, landed, and skied across the room on his wool-socked feet. He hit the opposite wall with a thud, fell to the floor and started his weird, yelping wails.

He's laughing. Oh my god, he's playing. He's trying to have fun. Maren dropped the rest of the way down to the floor. She burst out laughing herself. Damien stopped and stared with his yellow eyes. Then he started again, this time trying to mimic her. *He's trying to make his laugh sound normal. He's amazing.*

Both Damien and Maren were laughing loudly when Blackhawk and Dr. Don pushed open the door.

"Looks like us yesterday, wouldn't you say, Doc?"

"Yeah," Dr. Don replied. "And your laugh sounded like wolf-boy's here."

"God, you two." Maren said. "Look at him. Moonbaby ... I mean Damien. He thinks this is all funny. Sliding across the floor in his socks. He's just making a good time out of this."

Blackhawk nodded. "Yes, that's what wolves tend to do. My turn. Bathroom lesson. And not too soon." He pinched his nose for a second, then walked toward Damien.

"Got to show you something, young man. Just me and you. In the bathroom. Trust me. New things to learn with this new body."

While Blackhawk talked, he was moving his hands. Smoothly. No jerking. Nothing startling. *It's almost as if he's using sign language, like a deaf person would learn.*

"Wow. That's cool. Is that something I could learn?" Maren stood up. She backed away so she could better watch them, how they interacted.

Damien had already gotten up and walked over to Blackhawk. He stood in front of Blackhawk, searching his face and hands.

"Not exactly, my girl. Maybe someday. It's the language of the changelings. Something we, ahh, just know after we change back human. Kind of a combining of wolf and human speak, I guess you'd say."

"I know what you mean, Maren. It's pretty amazing." Dr. Don moved out of the way of the door so Blackhawk and Damien had no obstacles.

Blackhawk slowly put his hand on Damien's back and eased him forward out of the room. Damien was shuffling his feet as he took each step.

"Doc. Find this young man some boots, will you? He doesn't like the feel of the floor and no traction."

"Right away, Hawk."

It was only the second time she heard Dr. Don call her grandpa, Hawk. *Must have some meaning to them. Something special.*

Maren stood in the hallway watching Damien and Blackhawk make their way to the bathroom. Just before they closed the door, Damien peeked his head around it, and smiled. Maren inhaled. *That was like a guy-flirt smile. Did he mean it like that? I wonder just exactly how much of this he already knows.*

Dr. Don had found some boots. He brought them to Maren.

"Those look like new, Dr. Don. They're probably really expensive. Don't you have some old ones? What if he chews them up or something?"

Dr. Don laughed. "Oh, I doubt it. I think you see it too, don't you, Maren? He knows."

"You're right. It's almost shocking. By any chance, do you have a shower or bathtub I can use? I feel really grubby."

"Back down farther. By the kitchen. My living area. It's nice. You'll like it. After living in Minneapolis I got kinda spoiled with some things. Towels and stuff there. And grab a shirt out of the closet, if you'd like. We all live in flannels here in the winter. Have tons of them."

"Thanks, Dr. Don, again, for everything. I just never imagined my life would be this ... amazing?" Maren kissed him on the cheek.

"Somehow, little girl, I don't think you've seen the half of it." He ruffled her ponytail and took the boots from her hands. "I think I'll take care of this. I'm the only one who hasn't had a chance to talk to the new guy." He winked.

Maren headed toward Dr. Don's main living area, imaging the feel of hot water and unwrinkled clothes. She walked by the small bathroom which she assumed was for the clinic's patients. She could hear Blackhawk and Damien having a conversation. She wanted to stop and listen but decided it would be rude. Instead she turned the corner into the main living area.

Wow, this is really nice. A small living room with wood floors. A medium sized flat screen TV, sofa, and chairs. Behind that was a small bedroom. There was an old brass bed and wood dresser. Everything was neat. Folded clothes sitting on the bed, the closet door still open. *He must have dug this all out for Damien.* The last door led to Dr. Don's bathroom. That was the biggest surprise yet. A modern, tiled bathtub with shower. The tiles were stone, probably travertine. The sink was set in the same tile.

All the fixtures were new. *No kidding I'll like.* She turned on the water in the tub full force. She found a bag of Epsom salts nearby and dumped some in. Huge, fluffy towels were stacked on stainless steel shelving. Maren stripped out of her clothes and climbed into the tub. *I hope no one expects me out there for a long time.*

Maren emerged from the back apartment an hour later. She had left her hair loose after finding a blow dryer, and brushing it all out. She was still smiling about Dr. Don having a blow dryer, trying to imagine him using it. She stopped suddenly when she saw the three of them in the clinic waiting room. Dr. Don was bending down in front of Damien, tying his new boot laces. Damien had been staring at the procedure but his face turned immediately toward her.

"Wow," Dr. Don said. "You sure do clean up nicely." He stood up next to Damien, whose yellow eyes were fixed on Maren.

"Yes she does," Blackhawk said. "Come on over and meet Damien Jon properly. He's had a few lessons since you last saw him."

Maren was fixated on Damien. His black hair was combed back into a small ponytail at his neck. He had a thick shock of silver hair that ran off center over his head. His yellow eyes were blanketed with black eyelashes. They had trimmed his eyebrows to look normal, not too bushy, and his face was shaved smooth. His nose was large but not huge—aquiline, with that northern "Indian" bump on the bridge. Perfectly sculpted cheekbones and full lips. He was just as tall as Dr. Don. He was just plain gorgeous.

"Wow. He's beautiful. Just like he was as a wolf. I mean Moonbaby. He's perfect." Maren said, half-whispering. She wasn't sure how she was supposed to interact with him. Her heart was pounding.

"Now don't get all drooly here." Dr. Don said. "He's just kept to his gene pattern. He was a specimen of a wolf. Now a man."

Damien smiled. It was a weird, crooked smile, but was definitely a smile. And there was an obvious twinkle in his eye.

"Oh, Yes. He knows exactly what we're saying. So I think it's time we talk *to* him and not *about* him, don't you?" Blackhawk's eyes gave him away. He was enjoying the whole thing.

"Of course." Maren blushed as she walked over to him. She felt strange looking up at him, her eyes meeting his. She reached out her hand. *Am I supposed to shake his hand or paw, or whatever it is now,* she thought. *This is all way too weird.*

Damien grabbed her hand between his two. They were hands, but had strangely shaped fingernails. Maren looked down at them, remembering they were webbed from the knuckles to the first joint. Someone had tried to cut the nails to look more human.

"Hi, Maren. I remember you well."

Maren jumped back with her mouth open. *He talked and it was even understandable! Almost perfect. A little spooky.*

Damien didn't let go and pulled her toward him. Maren's body stiffened.

"Easy, my friend. She's not going anywhere." Blackhawk walked toward them moving his hands in the same human-wolf language.

Damien slowly lowered Maren's hand and released it. Then the same crooked grin appeared on his face.

Maren took a step back to catch her breath. "Look at that. He smiles like a dirty old man. It's a leer … maybe it's the teeth. It's even a little scary."

Blackhawk covered his mouth and Dr. Don laughed out loud.

"Yes, we're filing the canines down later," Dr. Don said. "Just going over basics today. You're going to have to take him home tonight, so we've got a lot of work yet. I've got patients coming in. Can't stay closed another day."

"Oh, you're right Dr. Don. We've been so consumed with this, I didn't even think."

"We're all good. Nothing to worry about."

Damien had moved back to Maren so lithe-like, no one had noticed. He gently picked up her hand again. Maren stood still. She assumed he was just trying to do it correctly. He brought her hand up to his face, against his nose. He inhaled deeply.

"Girl," he said. He let her hand go.

Maren turned to Blackhawk and Dr. Don, who were watching. "Oh, oh," she said.

Blackhawk stood there, his chin in his hand. "Ignore it, for now. I think he's trying to push your buttons."

Damien shot Blackhawk an angry look.

"Yes, Damien," Blackhawk said. "I know all about what you came from. The difference between me and you is that I was human *first*. You will behave yourself. Treat everyone with respect. Kindness." He was moving his hands along with his words.

Damien's eyes travelled back and forth between Blackhawk's mouth and hands. He stomped his foot defiantly then looked down at the ground. His posture softened. He was submitting.

"Much better," Blackhawk said, this time without the hand language. "Let's get packed up. Time to get back to the cabin. The fire's out by now and it's going to be cold as hell in there. Gas furnace only keeps it up to fifty degrees. Damien is going to use up some of that energy—chopping wood."

Maren watched Damien as she put things in a duffel bag Dr. Don provided. Extra clothes for Damien and some medication. One bottle had Blackhawk's name on it. *Hmmm*. Yet, it didn't seem important after all that had happened in the last couple days. There was a syringe in a plastic bag. She knew that had to be for Damien. Just in case. *Who knows what he'll do next.* It left her uneasy. She wondered what Blackhawk and Dr. Don thought about it, what they worried about. Damien seemed oblivious to it all, his eyes just continually scanning everything around him. He was obviously over Blackhawk's scolding. He smiled as he touched things, smelled them, and explored the clinic.

"Keep your cell phone handy, Blackhawk," Dr. Don yelled out the door. It was freezing as they all piled into the front seat of the truck. Blackhawk nodded and held the phone up. Then they headed for home, Damien in the middle—smiling.

Maren jumped out of the truck first, glancing at the Christmas tree laying there in the snow. *That's a million years ago.* She ran to the door, digging in her pocket for the key. She put it into the lock and turned it remembering they hadn't locked it during all the past commotion. Maren put the key ring back in her pocket and went into the house. She went straight to the thermostat and turned it up to 68 degrees. Blackhawk never turned it up. He always had wood to burn. Now she was just glad he had back up heating.

Blackhawk and Damien came in the door together. *Was that Damien talking?* It was a young man's voice. Soft and quiet. Already smoother than before. Every word he chose was used correctly.

"How can he do that? This quickly?" Maren waited for an answer. Blackhawk seemed completely relaxed, not one bit surprised. Damien had taken off the old overcoat he was wearing, walked toward the kitchen, and hung it next to Maren's. Then he stood next to her, his hands crossed politely in front of him. He looked like a house servant that was waiting for his next task. Maren stifled a giggle.

"The talking or that?" Blackhawk gestured toward Damien and smiled. "I know. It's amazing. He's combined his wolf memories—actions and words he knew—with his human mind now. That's pretty much what he told me anyway. I don't understand him real well yet. But I do think he's learned right away to hide his emotions. And that's amazing to me—since a wolf never does." Blackhawk looked directly at Damien with his last sentence. Damien didn't flinch.

"Ok. Well, I am going to get some stuff ready for dinner," Maren said. "Do you want to go sit down in the living room with Grandpa, Damien? By the way, that's his recliner chair there. Don't try to sit there."

Damien glanced around, then politely nodded a "yes." He went to the sofa and sat, then picked up a magazine that was lying nearby. He was immediately engrossed in it. After a few minutes he threw it to the floor. He stood up, frustrated, then picked the magazine back up. He turned to Blackhawk, looking like he was trying hard to say something.

"What's he saying? He looks upset," Maren said as she walked closer.

Blackhawk sat up in his chair. "Not sure."

Damien jumped up and grabbed Maren's coat off the hook. He dug into her pocket and pulled out the keys, holding them up next to the magazine. He made a turning motion with them.

"Keys to … the magazine? Huh?" Maren said, walking closer to Damien. He held the keys next to the magazine again and locked eyes with her.

"Want help," Damien said.

"I know," Maren said. "He needs "keys to the magazine," "keys to understand" it. An alphabet? Something that shows him how to read? Something like that. I'm sure."

Damien dropped the magazine and clapped his hands together. "Yes. Yes."

Blackhawk got out of his recliner faster than usual. "There are boxes of books in that storage room. His old room, in the closet. Some of your mother's things that were left here. A lot of early readers. They were books she used that she didn't want thrown out. Let's get them."

Maren was first to the closet, Damien behind her. She pulled box after box out and Damien ripped them open as fast as she could grab another one. She was digging out the last box when she paused. The room had gone quiet. She backed out of the closet on hands and knees. Blackhawk was on the floor next to Damien. Both were moving their hands in the "hand speak." Damien was motioning so fast that Blackhawk just threw his hands up in the air.

"This is what he wanted. I can't understand him completely. He's faster than I am. I think he'll know how to read in a matter of days. Damn, he's smart. Damn … ." Blackhawk struggled back up to a standing position. "I need to sit down somewhere comfortable."

"Sure, Grandpa. This has taken a lot out of you. Go sit and rest. I'm fine and, well, look at him. He'll be here for a while." Maren helped Blackhawk into his recliner. She thought about asking him about the pills she saw in the duffel but decided to wait. He had done enough for everyone. "You sure you're OK? Can I get you anything?"

"I'm fine, my girl. Don't worry about this old man. Worn out. But maybe now that I think of it, I could use some of that stew in there and … ."

"Fry bread," Maren said, finishing his sentence. "Absolutely." She smiled and patted him on the arm.

Maren decided to clean the kitchen while everything was cooking and it was all quiet in the other rooms. *Well, this should be interesting … us all eating together at the table.* She took out dishes and set the kitchen table. Then she tiptoed past Blackhawk who was snoring in his recliner and peeked in at Damien. At least she *thought* she would peek in. He obviously heard her before she could even look around the door. He met her face with a smile.

"Good. Real good," Damien said, as he held up a grammar book. Then he reached around to one of the huge piles of books next to him, dug three or four down into the pile and held up *Little Red Riding Hood.* "Not good. Stupid," he said as he sent it flying across the room.

Maren covered her mouth but couldn't prevent the laughter that came out. Damien's face had changed from a happy expression to one of anger. Maren went to his side. "Yes. Stupid book. Silly story. It's OK."

"Not … correct. Stupid humans." Damien paused. His body tensed.

"I know, Damien. You're right. Correct. It's a funny story for some humans. I don't like it either. Come on. Come sit at the table. I'll wake Grandpa up." Maren looked at Damien's face as he stood up. *Wow, he's really sensitive. This communication is going to be tough. How do I explain half this stuff … oh my god.* She took his arm as they walked toward the kitchen.

Damien stopped. His head turned toward Blackhawk who was still asleep in his chair. He gently removed Maren's hand from his arm and walked to Blackhawk. He knelt down and stared hard at him. He sniffed his face and hair. Then he stood up. Maren watched him. He looked like he was deciding either how to say something, or *if* he should say something.

Damien walked back to her and took both her hands. He stared down, moving her hands up and down in his as if he were trying to put his thoughts together. He looked directly into her eyes and said, "Grandpa is not good.

Sick. They know. " Damien sniffed again, his nose to the air. "Something wants him."

"What do you mean?" Maren realized she had said it too loudly. Damien was already looking at Blackhawk, who was just waking up.

"Are we ready, Maren? I was out like a light. Where's Damien? Is everything OK?"

Damien squeezed Maren's hands before he let them drop.

"Yes, Grandpa. Come and sit down. Damien's already here at the table."

Damien raced to the table and sat down before Blackhawk could turn his head around.

"Oh, good. Smells great, Maren. Thanks." Blackhawk made his way slowly to the table. Maren and Damien exchanged looks while Damien passed the fry bread and pot of stew around. Damien smiled repeatedly but every so often his face froze, his body twitched, and he stared at Blackhawk. Blackhawk noticed. He just shook his head at Damien as if to say, "Not now."

Chapter Fourteen

Human Hypocrisies

Maren woke with a start. She pulled the covers tightly over her head. There was a thump at the door. And another. She threw the covers off and sat up.

"Damien. Damn it! Why do you have to make so much noise? Can't you ever let me sleep?"

She heard the giggle from the adjoining room. *Damien. You are a pain.* She got out of bed and dressed as quickly as she could. *That weird sense of humor of his is driving me crazy.*

"OK, you win again. When are you going to realize that this all isn't just one big game for your personal fun?"

Maren could hear him press his face against the door.

"Because it is, isn't it?" Damien's voice was mockingly calm.

"Oh my god. Enough's enough!" Maren whipped open the door hoping he would fall into the room. He was always too fast. Maren looked at his tousled black hair and yellow flashing eyes. *God, he's cute.*

"Damn it!" She slammed the door shut.

"Everything OK in there?" It was Blackhawk at her other door to the hallway.

"Yes, fine, Grandpa. But Damien needs a whipping. He's driving me nuts!"

"Damien's chopping wood today, Maren. And he should be ready by now... ."

Maren heard Damien say "shit" in the next room. She snickered.

"And what's with all the swearing lately with you two?" Blackhawk said, as he walked away down the hall.

"Sorry, Grandpa," Maren yelled out. Then she went over to Damien's door and whispered, "Better watch your mouth, Damien. Just because you learn everything doesn't mean you can do and say everything. "

"That sounds just idiotic to me. Why learn if you can't use. You humans ..."

"Hmpff," Maren said as she tapped the door. She couldn't think of a good answer fast enough for Damien. He was truly unbelievable. He could talk almost perfectly in two weeks and he was so strong. He could chop wood all day just barely sweating. But all the questions! Exasperating. And mostly because he was right.

Maren finished doing her makeup and grabbed her toothbrush. She stepped out into the hall and right into Damien. He'd been standing there quietly waiting.

"Oh, Maren. When are you going to drop that act. You know you like me." Damien's breath was on her face. It always smelled grassy, woodsy. He told her he chewed some kind of herbs; it worked better than toothpaste and kept your teeth white and shiny. Maren hadn't been sure if he was joking or telling the truth. The last thing she wanted was to be the brunt of his new found pastime: practical jokes.

Damien put his arm against the door to block her from moving. "Still using that junk?" He was looking at the toothpaste tube in her hand.

"Yup. That's what us mere humans use."

Damien laughed and let her walk by only by lifting his arm so she had to walk under it. He grabbed his coat and headed for the front door, whistling—another thing he had recently learned.

Maren went into the bathroom and closed the door. *God, he's mixing me up. Sometimes I want to slap him. Sometimes—hold him. Don't know about that. Could we be together? Who knows what I even am.*

One thing she was sure of. She was attracted to Damien. But there was more to it. More than just wanting to see what it would be like to kiss him. More than it was kissing Kenny Shane. There was something else. She missed Moonbaby, the wolf. It was so complicated. When she looked into his eyes, there was Moonbaby, just as if he were right there. Because he was! She spit out her mouthful of toothpaste and rinsed her mouth.

Blackhawk had brought more books into the living room after putting some away. He was always doing something for Damien. Always teaching him. Showing him pictures. Telling him stories. *It's so exhausting, but he never quits.*

She looked at the Christmas tree, all decorated, in the corner of the living room. *Now that was a pain. Trying to explain all that to him. Especially the part about religion when Grandpa was a traditional Indian. He didn't believe the real Christmas story but telling Damien that it was pretty much a cultural tradition through much of the country was a real good answer.*

Maren smiled. She felt the same way. Her mother wasn't a true Christian either. She always said that Jesus Christ was a wonderful man and prophet and left it at that. Maren didn't know what to believe anymore. How did changelings fit into the whole religion thing, anyway? She'd have to ask Blackhawk about that, how he worked it out.

"We're all going to the Redwing tonight for supper," Blackhawk said, interrupting her thoughts. "It's time we introduced your 'friend' from the Wisconsin rez. Should be interesting." Blackhawk winked at her.

"Do they know, Grandpa? I mean besides Dr. Don?"

"The family? Oh, yes. They're chomping at the bit to meet him. I guess we're going to have to say, for the rest of the ears around, that we brought Moonbaby to the wolf reserve. To spend a few weeks getting to know other wolves. We all need to get our stories straight. Get them down. We need to rehearse it all so we don't slip." Blackhawk took a deep breath and clutched at his chest.

Maren ran over to him and eased him onto the sofa. "What's the matter, Grandpa? Something's wrong. I saw your medication when we brought Damien home, and Damien says you're sick." She didn't care that she blurted it out. It had been on her mind too long.

"Well, he did, did he? Smart young man." Blackhawk sat up straight. It looked like whatever happened, had just passed. "It's my heart, my dear. Nothing to get too upset about. I plan on hanging around a bit longer. The pills help. Can you grab me one? Bottle by the frig."

Maren came back with a pill and glass of water. "Are you sure, Grandpa? I assume Dr. Don's been seeing you? Should I call him?"

Blackhawk swallowed the pill and drank the glass of water. "Nope. It's OK. Doc's got me under control. I promise we'll talk later. Now go call your mother and see if she's still coming over New Year's. We're all looking forward to her visit."

Maren patted him on the arm and went back into her room. She heard Damien come in and go to Blackhawk. She assumed they were still talking the hand language because the words she did hear out loud weren't ever complete sentences. They only talked like regular people when others were around. Maren used to wonder why Blackhawk still did it. She decided he just wanted to keep the knowledge. That's the way he was. He held onto everything "changeling."

Maren lay down on her bed after she hung up with her mom. It would be good to see her. After all, it had been six months since Maren had come to White Earth. So much had happened. And then there was school. She wanted to go in late January but had no idea how she could leave Blackhawk to handle Damien or vice versa? So much to figure out. At least her mom finally decided to get away from the teaching over Christmas vacation. She was even talking about selling the house, saying she didn't want to live there by herself anymore. She missed Jonny too much, she said, to keep staying there. She promised to discuss everything when she came up. Maren could hardly wait.

Maren picked up a bag of beads and string. She had one of her wraps and decided to repair a couple spots where the beads had fallen off. She had found a book on beading while straightening up Blackhawk's bookcase, and took to it immediately. She practiced on one of Damien's shirt—making the little changeling symbol on a cuff. Blackhawk had smiled so big she almost cried.

She held the wrap in her hand and sewed. *Wonder what is going to happen with me? Nothing in all this time. Grandpa never says a thing. Everything's been about Damien. Has to be. He's the one now. He's a pure wolf changeling and I'm pretty much just a "maybe" something. Oh, well. I've never been this happy.*

They all got into Blackhawk's truck around 4:30PM. That's when Blackhawk liked to go. There weren't so many people at the Redwing that early and hopefully no tourists. Blackhawk said that was a summer thing. Who would spend a winter in northern Minnesota if they didn't have to? He was right about that.

"You both look wonderful," Blackhawk said, as he pulled out of the recently shoveled driveway.

"Yes you do," Damien said, winking at Maren.

She knew he loved to ride in the truck—especially if she was along. He always pressed his thigh against hers. At first it annoyed her, but then, there wasn't really any room in the front seat for all three of them. She looked down at their legs touching. His so muscular in his jeans. And so warm. They had discovered his body temperature was higher—just like a wolf's.

She looked up at him to see if he was smirking, which he did way too often. But he wasn't. He was just looking at her. He had tied his black hair into a ponytail. The silver streak gleamed. He was very clean—always taking showers and washing his hair. He said he just loved the water. But his eyes—they were mesmerizing. So yellow with the long, thick black eyelashes. Maren decided he just was too perfect. *Looking* anyway ... .

"Do we have this all down now?" Blackhawk asked. "I mean, the guys know who you are Damien, but we have to learn to play this game to be safe. Just in case anyone hears something. It gets easy to slip up. Got to be on top of this."

"It's full moon tonight," Damien said as he gazed out the window, ignoring the subject. "And don't worry. I haven't felt much of anything to worry about. Think I can hold it back. Just know I can. You feel anything, Maren?"

"No. Never have. Just achy. That I could go without," Maren said. She waited, and then added, "I'm not you Damien. No changeling signs for me."

"Hmpff. We'll see." Damien turned back to the window.

That irritated Maren. He was always trying to push her buttons. "Well," she said, "I think what we *do* need to worry about are those yellow eyes of yours. They are completely weird."

"All right, you two. We're here. Best behavior," Blackhawk said. When Blackhawk made a plain statement, it sounded like a command. He just had that kind of authority.

They all walked into the Redwing. Dr. Don got up immediately and came to them.

"Blackhawk. Good to see you. Maren. Gorgeous as ever. And Damien. Damn. You look like you walked out of one of those Gentleman's Quarterly's magazines." Dr. Don hugged Maren, patted Blackhawk on the back, and then reached out to shake Damien's hand.

"Good to see you again, Dr. Don," Damien said, shaking the outstretched hand vigorously. "And under much better conditions." They both nodded at each other.

Jesse James walked out from behind the bar, greeting Blackhawk and Maren. He stopped in front of Damien. "By god, he does look like Sylvester—if the little guy had grown up. Don't remember him real good, but yeah. It's there." He shook Damien's hand. Jesse's face looked troubled.

"Are you OK, Mr. James, Sir?" Damien smiled and glanced at Maren. *Good god, he's showing off.*

"'Jesse' is fine with me, young man," Jesse replied. "It's just that you *do* look like someone else I knew, a long time ago. Weird. Never mind. Come and sit down. Beer, anyone?"

"I'll have one, Jess. You might let Mr. Jon here—Damien Jon, try one." Blackhawk sat down next to Dr. Don, who shook his head "no" to the beer. "Oh, and we're going to try a steak tonight, Jess. Can the two kids sit at a table over there? I have business with Doc."

"Sure. Over there is good. I'll take your order in a minute. Got some great rib eyes in."

Maren and Damien walked to a table across the room and sat down.

"Well, isn't this sweet," Maren said, sarcastically. She immediately regretted her tone when she saw Damien's face.

"Don't be that way for once, Maren. Besides, your body language always speaks differently than your mouth. Are most humans like that?"

Maren glanced restlessly around the room, reassuring herself that no one could hear their conversation. "Sorry. Just seems we're always pushed together, and well, I'm not always sure if you are comfortable with it. That's all." Maren grimaced—the familiar face flush again. *Why do I always act that way to him? I'm just so damn nervous around him.*

"And, yes, humans are known for being somewhat deceitful," she continued. "There are manners, customs—yes, sounds ridiculous. I don't know why we say one thing and do something else. Why we lie. Sometimes it's to keep from hurting someone's feelings."

"Interesting. Don't you think you hurt my feelings when you always want me to think that you *don't* like me? I know you do. Your body screams it out, Maren, so *that* is ridiculous to me."

Maren's face burned. She picked at her napkin. "Can we just order some food? I haven't had a real steak in a year, I think."

"Sure. I'm excited about trying it. A real steak. A big piece of meat. Not chopped up and cooked to death in a pot of other stuff. And *no* fry bread."

Maren looked up at him and started laughing. Damien joined in. *He's really trying. He's so incredibly good looking. Hard to handle that sometimes.* She looked over at the bar where Blackhawk, Dr. Don, and Jesse were talking away. *They're getting the story all down. Good.* Jesse glanced her way and nodded. He walked over to their table with two bottles of beer and waters.

"Maren, wasn't sure if you wanted a beer? Your Pops said Ok."

"Sure. I'll have some of it. With Damien. Thanks. And I think I can order for us both. Your medium rare rib eye is great for me. With that great wild rice. And Damien, I'm sure, wants it rare." Maren held back a smile when Damien licked his lips. "And probably the biggest cut you have. Just a little rice. Right, Damien?"

"Perfect." Damien nodded.

Maren tapped her foot while they waited for Jesse to make their food. She hated the uncomfortable silences with Damien. The worst part was he just sat there looking amused. Everything was so funny to him. She couldn't take it any longer.

"What's so damn funny, anyway?"

"Ha. You know Pops doesn't like you swearing, Maren."

"He can't hear me right now and there's no better choice of word with you," Maren said, feeling just a little guilty. She glanced over at Blackhawk again, just to be sure.

"Let me tell you what's so funny. You. People. Humans. Like I said. Saying one thing and meaning another. How do you actually tell when someone is truthful? When they really mean something? Is it always a guessing game? A little tiring."

Maren thought for a moment. "You know, you're right. We are a bunch of hypocrites most of the time. That means … ."

"I know what it means. I have spent enough time going over that diction-ary. So many words for the same thing. Wolves have it much easier. We read each other. There's no lying. We have the same emotions—love, hate, jealousy, joy, sadness. But don't see a reason to hide it. You humans are always trying to … ah, manipulate the situation. Hope that all works for you. Seems a waste of time to me. Stupid, actually." He looked down for a moment. "Especially when you aren't able to sense the 'other' things that are out there."

What the hell does that mean? She was relieved when Jesse showed up with the food. Damien was trying at times, to say the least.

"Ummm, this looks great," Maren said, "and nice and juicy the way I like it." She cut into her steak and put a large piece into her mouth. "Wow. Delicious," she said, the words barely understandable with her mouth full.

Damien cut his huge, bloody rare steak into four pieces. He shoved two into his mouth, and gulped them down.

"You're supposed to chew it, Damien. You're such an animal."

Damien took another piece and "chewed" away on it, looking right at Maren. Then he burst out laughing, trying at the same time to quickly swallow his mouthful. He finally managed to say, "*Me*, an animal? Look at yourself, you little hypocrite."

"What are you talking about? I have manners."

"No. I'm talking about the *juice* you like so well. It's blood, Maren. Nice and warm and salty. Blood. Calling it 'juice' doesn't change what it is. You like the taste of blood. Now, *that* is funny."

Maren swallowed. She stared down at her plate as a wave of nausea came over her.

There on her plate was a recently butchered piece of a cow, seared on a grill, and swimming in blood and melted fat. *Oh my god, he's right.* She took a big gulp of her beer. It didn't help. Her entire body ached. Her legs were shaking.

"I don't feel so good. And it's not just what you said. My head is pounding. I had a headache earlier—now it's bad. My body just hurts." Maren picked up a napkin and wiped sweat from her forehead. "Could be the flu—just don't feel right. I'll be back in a minute. Just enjoy your dinner. Sorry." She got up and walked straight to the bathroom at the back of the bar.

Maren stood in the little bathroom against the wall. Waves of nausea passed through her although she didn't throw up. She sank down to the floor, holding her head. The sick feeling was getting worse, and fast. She huddled down on the floor in a fetal position. It was getting darker and darker in the room, although the light was on. *Oh my god. I'm passing out. I can't talk. Damien, where are you? Help me. Damien.*

Chapter Fifteen

Starr

Maren felt herself being pushed. Everything was black. Faint voices in the background were saying her name. Her head pounded. It was excruciating. She didn't want to open her eyes feeling as if her head would crack open. But the voices got louder. She could hear Blackhawk and Dr. Don—talking loud and fast. She felt arms pull her up against a chest. The heart in it was beating so loud and hard, she wanted to yell out, "Quiet!" But she couldn't. The arms held her tighter. The smell was familiar and soothing. She felt fur against her face. Moonbaby! Her wolf was there with her. Moonbaby.

Maren struggled to open her eyes. It hurt but she wanted to see her beloved wolf. She could see a purple flannel shirt. Black hair. It was chest hair her face was touching. A man. *No, no, I want my wolf. Where is Moonbaby? Oh no, something's happened to him.* "Moonbaby, come back," she said aloud.

'I'm right here, Maren. Right here. I won't let anything happen to you."

Maren turned her head, slowly and painfully, to see the face that was talking.

"Damien, what's happening to me? I'm scared." She barely got the words out. She grabbed ahold of his shirt. "Don't leave. I think I'm dying."

"Never. I'll never leave you. And you're not dying."

Maren felt herself being lifted up. Damien was carrying her and they were out of the bathroom. Then Blackhawk's face was close to hers. He looked frightened. *Oh no. Something is really wrong. I am dying.*

"Where are the other customers?" Maren tried to lift her head to see around her. It was too difficult. "Don't let anyone see me like this."

"Maren. It's OK. Jesse had everyone leave. Try hard to keep your eyes open. It's the most important thing. Do it. I know it hurts. You're OK. You're going into the change. I need you to focus. What do you want? Doc and I need to know. We can help you either way. You have to tell me, my girl. You have to decide. We can help."

The change? Oh, no. Me? A wolf? I don't know anything about anything. No, can't happen. "No, Grandpa, no," Maren said as loudly as she was able. "I'm not ready. Please. Don't let it happen. I'm scared." She looked up at Damien's face. His eyes were fiery, yellow-orange. She had never seen them look like that. Then just as quickly, the glow dimmed and they were back to their sun-yellow color.

"She's not ready, Pops. It would be real hard on her. Can you do something? I don't think she's strong enough to stop it herself. Look at her hair already," Damien said. Maren could hear the panic in his voice and he never panicked.

"I need your talisman, Maren. Around your neck. The one from your father," Blackhawk said. He reached around her neck and pulled it over her head, trying to keep her long hair from tangling in it. "I need some hot water, Jess. Now. And we've got to get her to Doc's place. Closer than home. We have the herbs for this. You still do, don't you Doc?"

"Sure do, Hawk. I'll go start the jeep. Damien can hold her in the back seat. You follow with your truck, Hawk. I'll start that too. Hurry." Maren could hear the front door bang open and shut.

"You're right, Grandpa. It's not as bad when I keep my eyes open," Maren lied. It still hurt like hell. "What about my hair? Damien, what? Is it falling out? You're scaring me."

"It's *not* falling out, Maren," Blackhawk replied. "You need to drink this tea. The hot water releases the metals in the silver of your changeling symbol. It will help hold you back till we can get the good stuff at Doc's. I'll explain everything later. Just trust me now."

"I do, Grandpa. I trust you. I trust all of you." *God, I have to.* Maren leaned her head over so she could sip from the cup Jesse was holding to her mouth. She so wanted to close her eyes, to lean into Damien's chest and just disappear. But she knew that was not what would happen. She struggled to hold them open; her lids felt so unbearably heavy.

Damien was shaking her again. She forced her eyes open. He sighed with relief. They were at Dr. Don's and he had a bowl in his hands. She was on the sofa and still in Damien's arms, on his lap. He cradled her head in his elbow, propping her up into a half-sitting position. Dr. Don knelt down and spooned a green, mushy substance from the bowl.

"Let me do this. I have to be of help somehow here. I'm the only plain, boring human here," Dr. Don said, smiling.

Maren tried to move her arms to take the spoon, then realized she couldn't do it. She was totally helpless.

"Damn. I'm so weak," she mumbled. She let Dr. Don spoon feed her the herbal concoction. As soon as it hit her stomach, she felt a change. The tenseness left her muscles. Her head stopped pounding. She felt as if something strange and wild pulled away from her body. *How strange. It's like a dream when you're flying. Except I can feel the other me fly away. No, wait … don't go. Who's there? In the shadows … something is watching me. No, go. I'm not ready. Go. Please, go.*

"She's going out. We're good." It was Dr. Don talking. Blackhawk said something back but she couldn't hear it. She heard their footsteps walk away.

"I love you, Maren. I'll love you forever."

Was it Damien? No, it was Moonbaby. "I love you, Moonbaby," she said, as a warm, dark fog enveloped her.

Maren woke the following morning with a horrible neck cramp. Her head was on the arm of the sofa in a terrible position. Someone had covered her with a blanket. She sat up, squeezing and twisting her neck. Damien was right there, in a sleeping bag on the floor. *He never outsleeps me and he always hears me get up. I hope he's OK. What happened? Oh my god, yes. I was going to change!*

Maren patted herself frantically. Everything seemed normal human. No hairy body. No claws. She skimmed her tongue over her teeth. Normal! She felt her chest. The same. *At least I didn't grow another pair of these! Oh, yeah, my hair. What about my hair?*

Maren jumped up and ran to a mirror on the wall. *Well, it's a mess, but looks the same. No wait. It's silvery on the top. What's this? Oh, no.*

"It's OK, Maren. It's beautiful." Damien had gotten up and was standing behind her.

"What? My hair turning white overnight? Like some kind of bad joke?" Maren bent down and turned but couldn't see the top of her head. It was all gray at the roots, like it was growing out that way. It had some kind of pattern. Some kind of shape.

"Maren," Damien said, putting his hand on her arm. "This isn't odd for females—female changelings—to have this happen. Not the same as this, but usually a color change. This kinda' looks like a star. A silver star on the top of your head. It's beautiful."

Maren turned around, tears in her eyes. "What else? What else can make me a freak? I already have … ."

"I know what you have," Damien interrupted. "I know what you are. And it's time to quit acting like a baby and take pride in it. What you are. You just might be one of the very few of our kind left. Look at me? Do you think this has at all been *easy*? Quit being so damned selfish." He yanked the sleeping bag from the floor and disappeared down the hall.

Maren dropped onto the sofa. *God, he's right. I'm glad Grandpa didn't see that. He'd be so disappointed. Or Dr. Don. After all they've done for everyone. God, I'm a selfish brat. But it was scary. Something out there. Watching me.*

She struggled to gain her composure. *Just dreams. I was in the middle of changing.* Then she stood up, ran her fingers through her hair, took a deep breath, and headed to the back kitchen where she knew they'd all be.

"Something smells good," Maren said, as she poked her head around the door. "Can I join you?"

Damien was sitting next to Dr. Don, eating bacon and eggs. Blackhawk was cooking. He turned around. He looked better than normal. *He looks like a great big load was just lifted off his back. No doubt. Waiting and knowing all along this was going to happen to me.*

"Good morning ... Starr," Blackhawk said, smiling.

"Huh? What does that mean?" Maren looked around at everyone. They were all sharing some private joke.

"Your hair," Damien said. "We all think it's cool. And you need a wolf name. I guess no one told you that. Pops here, your Grandpa—his is Hawk. That's why Dr. Don calls him that once in a while. Lets it slip. And you know mine. You named me. So no complaining on what it is. I certainly didn't have a choice." Damien had that twinkle in his eye. He was getting a kick out of the whole thing.

"Just a moment, Damien. She can change it if she wants. You can, Maren. But it's ... ah ... bad luck." Blackhawk smiled. He also was enjoying the whole thing.

"I guess I'm good with it then. Starr? Could be worse." She gave Damien "a look." "Because of my now gray hair? A constellation of sorts?" Maren knew she was being a little sarcastic. *God, just so much to deal with...*

"It will most likely keep growing its normal color since you're back in this phase. You'll have to cut it a little, though, if you don't want anyone to notice. It must have grown four or five inches yesterday. A lot has happened. I want to make a toast." Blackhawk had ignored her tone. He picked up his coffee cup.

"To my beautiful granddaughter, Starr. Maren to the rest of the world. She will make a difference for all the changelings of the future."

Everyone lifted their cups and nodded. That was all. Maren felt hot. She looked at everyone, confused and embarrassed. All the fuss, and she hadn't done anything. Plus, she was being a rude brat. She cleared her throat.

"Well ... thank you, Grandpa, and everyone else. I wasn't ready. Sorry."

Maren walked toward the coffee pot to wipe her eyes quickly and poured a cup. The warmth felt good. She cradled the cup in her hands, unable to say anything else.

"And, Maren. It's Starr spelled S..t..a..r..r. We started out with 'starry' something, then just decided you were a special *star*, so we kept the extra 'r,'" Damien said. "And that, you are." He nodded at her and smiled. No sarcasm this time. His face looked peaceful.

Maren smiled back and tipped her cup at him. A jolt of recognition went through her mind. *Oh my god, didn't he tell me he loved me? Did I dream that? I told him I loved him? No, Moonbaby. But he is Moonbaby! Oh, did we really say that to each other?* Her face flushed. She snuck a quick peek at Damien. He was just watching her, no expression. *He knows what I'm thinking—what I'm remembering. I know it!*

"Come on and eat something, Maren. That change stuff takes a lot out of a person. Either way you go. Come sit down, my dear. And here's your necklace. Always wear it. The symbol means something specific. A lot to talk about," Blackhawk said. "Also don't think myself or Doc would have been able to carry you. Literally. Damien did." He reached over and patted Damien on the shoulder.

"Glad to help, Pops. I remember *everything*," Damien said, pausing, while he looked at Maren. "… about my wolf days." He winked.

"Thank you, Damien. For taking such good care of me," she replied, forcing a distracted smile. She set her fork down. "But something's been bothering me. I wanted to ask you both … this sounds a little silly, but when you changed … Damien, Grandpa … did you ever sense a presence? Something a little scary? Maren's eyes flicked back and forth from Damien to Blackhawk. *I sure hope that didn't sound silly.*

Dr. Don dropped his fork on the floor. Everyone froze. Damien looked at Blackhawk and waited for him to speak.

"Maren. You're learning a lot very soon," Blackhawk said. "Yes, there is always something dark 'out there' whether you are a human or a wolf. But now you've felt it in its purest form. Quite amazing because usually you wouldn't understand or really see it until you've actually made the change. Anyway, my advice is to be strong. Be who you are. Don't let it put fear or hate into your heart. That's when you become its prey."

"Well said." Dr. Don had picked up his fork and was wiping and re-wiping it on his napkin.

Damien walked over to her and whispered in her ear, "You are amazing. It can never harm you." Then he kissed the top of her head and went back to his plate.

Maren watched him sit down. Everyone went back to what they were doing—eating, as if nothing had happened. *They're right. They are absolutely right. Nothing that worrying can ever change. Not a bit.* Maren smiled as she put a piece of bacon into her mouth. *Wolves … .*

Chapter Sixteen

Wolves in the Closet

Maren didn't say anything to Damien about what was said between them that night—the love word. But she did have a zillion questions about what it was like to go through a change. To really just let it happen. But what then? And the really scary side of it. Were they telling her everything?

She wanted to go to college. Be somewhat normal. Have a life other than all the "changeling" stuff. But then there was Damien. Thinking about leaving him was actually painful. What would he do? Find a nice Indian girl on the rez while she was gone? After all, he was a full-blooded Ojibwe Indian— changeling. How could she blame him? She always made a point to make sure he thought she didn't care. Except that night. That night when she was the most vulnerable she ever was.

Damien sat on the sofa pouring through more books. He couldn't seem to get enough of them. Then it was her computer. Blackhawk had asked her if they could fool around on it for a while. How could she say no? Then she'd check and Damien had erased his search history.

How can he figure out all this so fast? Grandpa doesn't know that much about computers. It's so irritating.

"Frustrated about something, Maren?" Damien sat his book down.

Maren slammed her laptop shut. "Nope. I'm just fine." She'd be damned if she was going to let him know how she felt about his *super* this, and *super* that.

"OK. Just saw that same old 'pissed off' look on your face. Do I ever do anything you like?"

Maren shut her eyes. *What the hell is the matter with me? He's not doing anything wrong and I want to strangle him!*

"Yes, you do actually. It's me. I'm just worrying about going to school. I'm supposed to go in a couple weeks, you know. I was just wondering how you and Grandpa will be. OK, I hope?"

"Don't want you to go, Maren. But can't make you stay. That's your decision. Pops says so, anyway."

"I don't know what I want. I'm waiting for Mom to come; I need to talk to her. Of course, she can't wait to meet the changeling prodigy."

"You or me?"

"Don't make fun of me, Damien. I couldn't do it. I'm just chicken. It's actually embarrassing. I think I let Grandpa down." Maren twisted her hands together.

"You could never let him down. He loves you so much. I remember that feeling—back when I was a wolf little guy—the way you loved me. Sometimes I wish I could have stayed that way. Moonbaby. But now I'm a human. As much as I despise that idea sometimes, I want to be with you. That keeps me here. Human. Right now, anyway."

Maren's head jerked up. "What do you mean, right now anyway?"

Maren heard the house phone ring in the background. She hoped Blackhawk would get it. *Does he really miss being a wolf that much? I haven't thought of that ... if he wants to go back to that. Then what?*

Damien didn't get a chance to respond. Blackhawk came into the living room, upset.

"It's Jules. That was Jess on the phone. Cindy Shane just called him. Jules is threatening to kill himself. Locked himself in the bathroom with his gun. Jess thinks we should come. And for some reason, especially you, Damien. Not questioning him, nor do I know the reason. Get your coats. I'll warm up the truck."

Maren and Damien looked at each other and jumped up at the same time.

It was a long drive out to Julian James' cabin. Maren was worried. Not so much about Jules, although she didn't wish anything as bad as suicide on anyone. But it did bring back memories of her father. She had been too young to understand anything about why or how a person could get to that point. And why would Jesse want Damien out there?

Maren looked at Damien's face. His jaw was clenched. Every so often she heard a click or snapping sound. She realized it was his teeth hitting together. *Is he "biting" in his mind?* Right then they pulled up in front of the cabin.

"Damien. Are you able to handle this? Because if you have any doubts about your self-control, I would suggest you wait in the truck until I find out why Jesse wanted you out here," Blackhawk said, in his naturally authoritative voice. Sometimes it could even be downright intimidating.

"I'm not *good* about it. But I am curious. I picked up a scent just as we drove in. It was so familiar—but I just don't know how to place it. No. I'm not going to attack him or anything. But I do want to see the human that killed my mother. And how that could have even happened. My wolf mother was way too smart. Yes. I want to see this man."

Blackhawk looked hard at Damien. "Remember. That's not why we are here."

Damien nodded and took a deep breath. He opened the passenger door as soon as Blackhawk opened his. Maren followed and had to run to catch up to the two men. She took both their arms as they walked to the front door. The front porch light came on and a frantic Cindy Shane whipped open the door. Her eyes and nose were red and swollen.

"Blackhawk, thank god you came. Jesse is here and he called Old Malak. I doubt if he'll come. Jules still hates that man. I don't know what's going on but Jules started drinking hard a couple days ago and now he's saying he killed his sister? What does that mean? Jesse won't say anything. Said I had to talk to you—and this Damien guy? Who are you? God, please, can you help Jules? I don't know what to do and … ."

"Hold on, Dr. Shane. Hold on. We're here to help but Jules has always done just what he's wanted. I think he's just realized a lot of things he should have years ago. It's a hard thing to handle. We'll do what we can. Where's Jess?" Blackhawk sounded remarkably calm.

"He's sitting by the bathroom door trying to pound sense into his crazy nephew. He's pretty upset too." Cindy wiped her eyes with a towel she had been clutching to her. "Maren, honey. I'm sorry you have to see Jules like this?" She looked at Blackhawk and held her towel up.

"Maren is part of this. She's my granddaughter and my blood. She's here because she can help."

Maren looked at Damien and shrugged. Damien squeezed her forearm. They entered the old cabin. Damien took two steps in and froze. He tilted his head up and inhaled deeply. Then he turned to Blackhawk and started the "hand language" so fast that Blackhawk said, "Whoa. Regular talk here."

Maren tapped her foot anxiously on the floor. Damien was scowling and clicking his jaw. *Damn, quit gnashing your teeth together. It's more than a little scary. God, we shouldn't have come, shouldn't have come.*

"Are you going to be OK, Damien? Otherwise, we can both go back out to the truck right now."

"That's not it, Maren. Really. I smell my blood. My family. I'm trying to figure out what this is. It's real strong."

Damien walked away and sniffed his way to the bathroom door where Jesse was sitting on the floor. "Excuse me, Mr. Jesse, Sir. Who is in this room? I know him—can't tell you why. I just do."

Jesse got up from the floor with difficulty. His legs looked cramped and sore from sitting, obviously for a long time, while he talked to his nephew Jules through the door. He looked drained.

"Damien. I knew it. I knew it when I saw you. You're not only a James' but you're a Malone/James. You're the son of Moon and Silver. Moon was Lara James—Jules' sister, my niece. Silver was Sylvester Nightmoon—Son of Marina Nightmoon Malone and … ." Jesse paused and cleared his throat. He stood taller and faced Blackhawk. "I have something to tell you dear friend. Well. Guess someone else is here to do it."

Everyone turned to the front door at the same time. There stood an old Indian man. He had solid gray hair pulled back into a long braid. His weathered, darkened face looked sad. He wore old, deer skin garments. Maren thought he looked like a picture in a magazine about Native Americans.

Jesse ran to the door and took the old man's hands in his. "My brother. I thank you for coming, Malak. I've missed you, brother."

The old man nodded and clasped Jesse's hands in his. "Where is my son?" He said it more like a statement than a question. Jesse pointed to the bathroom door.

Malak walked slowly, but deliberately, toward the door. He stopped directly in front of Damien. Old Malak tipped his head up to look Damien in the eyes.

Damien moved his hands in only a couple smooth movements, the changeling hand speak. Old Malak just nodded, but his eyes were watering. Maren watched, looking at Malak, Damien and Blackhawk.

This was the first time she had seen Blackhawk in the background, disengaged. There was something wrong here—between these elder men. She had never seen this old Indian man before and she felt he had more power than Blackhawk did. Maren grabbed Damien's hand.

"It's all right, my young queen," Malak said, facing Maren. "It's a good time for all to have truth. Even us elders here." He turned his attention to the door. "Come on out, son. Don't waste your life over something that was meant to be."

The silence was deafening. No one moved. The sound of the bathroom door knob turning broke the silence.

Jules James stepped out of the bathroom. He stood there facing his father, Malak. His mouth was open, as if he wanted to say something to him. Jules dropped his revolver to the floor, while his eyes remained fixed on his father. Jesse quietly ducked in, grabbed the gun and disappeared.

"Father. I didn't ask you to be here. This has nothing to do with you. It's me. My blindness all these years. But you could have told me." Jules glared at old Malak until his face crumpled. Jules dropped to the floor, both hands squeezing the top of his head.

No one moved. Malak stood silently, with his eyes closed. Maren wished someone would say something—anything, to help Jules. He looked so tormented. But it wasn't her place. After all, she didn't really know him. And he had shot Moonbaby's mother for bounty money.

Damien pulled away from Maren, now sniffing vigorously in the air. He stopped when he reached Jules, his eyes widening. Then he knelt down next to Jules and closed his eyes.

Everyone was watching. But no one said a word. She wanted to ask someone, anyone, "What's going on?" Instead, she remained quiet.

Damien took ahold of Jules' arm, hard. He cleared his throat. Maren could tell he was trying to use his best speaking voice. "Jules. Julian James. You are my uncle. You are my mother's brother and I am trying to understand you. But I feel an old evil … I hope it has gone. It is weak now. I really hope it is gone."

Jules lifted his head. He sucked in his breath. "I murdered my sister. *Your mother.* I drove her away. Away from being *human*. Then I shot her. Bam! Just like that … poor Lara. Moon. Beautiful Moon. Evil is an understatement. I can't deal with this." He pulled his arm from Damien's and fell back into a sitting position.

"Son. You had the pull of the Wendigo on you. For many years." Malak's voice boomed across the room.

"Lara—Moon—she *needed* to die. She knew you would find her children. The pull of Wendigo would be broken. She knew you would *never* take the life of any orphan animal. You never did that. Even as a small boy hunting. Never."

"She knew that? She remembered?" Jules wiped his arm across his face. "This great James' family of changelings—and I was not one of them! I couldn't admit that Lara was special and I was … nothing! I hated her. And I loved her. The wolves … God. So damn blind."

"No, Jules. You had Wendigo all through you. It needed to be broken. Driven away. She gave her life so her children could live. Wendigo has always sought to destroy the changeling. From the beginning of time. It is gone … for now."

Malak paused for a moment. "I have a much larger betrayal. After Marina died … Hawk, I should have said something." Malak turned to Blackhawk, who took a step backwards.

"Sylvester Nightmoon was my son, Blackhawk. It was years before you came into Marina's life. I left and came back to find she had found you. Things will be as they will."

Malak folded his hands in front of him. "You raised my son—*my* Sylvester. A changeling like no other. Up till now anyway." Malak nodded his head toward Damien. "I want to thank you for that, my old friend. For doing all you have done."

Oh my god. Maren watched Malak and Blackhawk. For the first time she saw anger on Blackhawks's face. His eyes turned from their normal copper color to dark orange. *Just like Damien's … that night … when I almost changed.* Blackhawk gripped his hands in front of himself, squeezing and releasing them.

"Grandpa?" Maren could barely squeak out his name.

Blackhawk shook his head at her. "Let him finish what he has to say."

Malak dropped his hands to his sides. "My punishment has been difficult. My daughter Lara—Moon—gave her life so that Wendigo would be defeated. The life of a changeling is not a small thing. Wendigo wanted Moon's son—Damien here. He wanted his power. It is over for now. But only for now."

Jules stared at his father, Malak. His face looked softer, less anguished. Maren walked over to Malak. She took his weathered, wrinkled hand in hers. *This is Damien's grandfather. Damien is a James. On both sides— mother and father.* She felt the power he had—through his hand. She felt it on her "inexperienced" changeling side.

"I'm very pleased to meet you, Malak James. Damien's grandfather." Maren said. Malak was no taller than her so they were eye to eye.

"Do you know how special you are, Maren? I've wanted to meet you for so long. To know if it was really true. That you could possibly have changeling blood. Now I know. It's all over you." He eased his hand from hers and laid it on her shoulder.

"Your father Jonny and Sylvester were half-brothers. They'll never know each other. Now all I want—as an old man that will pass from this world soon—is to see my family again. My son, Jules, now free of the evil that held him hostage. My grandson—Lara's special son, Damien. And you. A future queen. You don't realize it yet, but it will come to you."

Maren didn't know what to say. *A queen? Queen of what? I've never even made the change. What about Wendigo?*

Blackhawk's eyes had returned to their normal color. He cleared his throat.

"That's right, Maren. Malak knows. He always knew more than I did. Malak here was head shaman. Not only of the traditionals here in the tribe, but of the changelings. I've missed his advice. I've missed his friendship."

Malak turned to meet Blackhawk. He took two steps forward with his hand stretched out. Blackhawk stood quietly for what seemed an eternity. Then he clasped Malak's hand in his.

"Silver Moon," Blackhawk said.

"Hawk," Malak replied back. Both men squeezed their hands together and nodded—their eyes closed.

"You look just like her. My sister." It was Jules talking to Damien. Maren swallowed hard. *Was Damien really as calm and cool as he was acting?*

"I do feel your sorrow—your regret, Uncle. I also know that no human would be able to take my mother's life—unless it was to be so." Damien was crouched on the floor. He reached out his hand and they both stood up, face to face.

"Damien. I knew who you were when I saw you," Jesse said. He was standing in the background, holding Cindy Shane's hand. "To me, you look just like my brother, Malak, when he was young. From old pictures. Just like him—but a lot taller." Everyone smiled at that, appreciating the relief of tension.

"And Blackhawk. I knew it when you brought Damien into the Redwing that night," Jesse continued. "It was like I saw my brother walk out of the past and into the front door." He patted Cindy's arm and walked over to Damien and Jules. "Welcome, nephew. I'm proud to claim you as a James."

"Now, all of you. Don't forget there's a little bit Malone in there too. On Marina's side, anyway," Blackhawk said. "Only she could give birth to two changelings of such power."

Malak nodded.

"My father, Jonny Malone," Maren said. "He and Sylvester. Half-brothers. Wow." She turned to Damien. "Looks like we're a little related, Mr. Damien Jon James," she said.

"Enough to keep the bloodlines strong, Maren," Damien replied. He winked at her.

"OK. What am I missing here?" Jesse said, smiling.

"I'm not missing it," Malak said. "What about you, Hawk?" His tone was considerably lighter.

Blackhawk shook his head and smiled. "OK, everyone. Let's let them figure that out."

"Why, thank you, Grandpa," Maren said, with a pretend, contemptuous tone. Everyone started talking, and then, was interrupted abruptly.

"Umm, hello? Everyone? You all just dropped the biggest bomb on me. Changelings? Human wolves? The evil Wendigo? And this was all supposed to be just an old legend," Cindy Shane said. She walked over to Jules and put her arm around him. "You know I love you, Jules. Doesn't matter. Any of this. You're a good, kind man. We do have a lot to talk about, though."

Jules kissed her lightly on the cheek and squeezed her. He turned to face everyone. "Cindy's good with all this. She understands the necessity of keeping the changeling legend—just a legend. She had a lot of this figured out before I did. Part of how I got thinking about it—the questions she'd ask. Anyway, our secret is safe with her."

"Could hardly put this in my fellowship study," Cindy said, throwing her arms up. "I'm going to have to give them something, though. I'll be thinking on that one. The need for the wolf in the wilderness? The outrageous ruthless slaughter? Don't get me started on my soapbox." Cindy laughed.

"Thank you, ma'am. We're much appreciative," Damien said. He looked over at Maren. She nodded, distracted. Her mind had been drawn back to her childhood. *Dreamcatchers. Dad always had one in my bedroom … said I did see a real monster … Wendigo.*

Cindy Shane said something to Jules and walked over to Maren's side. "Can we sit down and talk? Girl to girl?"

"That would be great," Maren said, deliberately lying. She was still unsettled with her thoughts. *Would she ask me about being a changeling? What do I say? About Kenny? Who even cares? Have to remember the monster … .* Her hands were shaking so she clasped them in her lap, dreading the coming conversation.

Cindy noticed. She took one of Maren's hands and squeezed it. "It's OK, sweetie. I'm not going to nose in. I'm terribly interested in this, though. And someday—if you ever need to talk—I'm here." Maren took a big breath and exhaled, hoping Cindy didn't notice.

"What I wanted to talk to you about is my son, Kenny. He says you two are talking. That you are friends. I'm glad about that. You will actually know someone when you go off to school. A couple weeks, I hear?"

"Yes. I think so. Still depends on some things here. I'm glad Kenny didn't stay angry with me—after what happened." Maren lied. *I really don't care. It's so small in everything else.*

"Well, *he* is not so fond of wolves." Cindy laughed and Maren forced a chuckle.

"I wouldn't think so," Maren said. "After what happened to him with Moonbaby. So sorry about that." Maren's thoughts shifted to the kiss and Kenny's hands on her back discovering her wraps.

Maren continued. "I'm just relieved nothing terrible happened. He's such a good guy. He said he's dating someone now?"

"Yes. A real sweet girl from Wisconsin. I'm sure you'll meet her over the holidays? I'd like to invite you all over here one night for dinner. Just to smooth everything over."

"That would be great, Cindy. I think Damien would like that too. Kenny bringing a girlfriend. It wouldn't be so threatening to that wolf ego of his," Maren said, rolling her eyes in fun, hoping the conversation wouldn't last much longer. *Where was Damien?*

"Yes," Cindy said, smiling. "Kenny did say you were too 'wolfy' for him. He didn't know *how* wolfy you really are," She chuckled. "You know, you two—Damien and you—make such a couple. I really hope the best for you, Maren. I've always liked you."

"Thanks, Cindy. Yes, Damien and I are close. Not sure what will happen with us, but I can't imagine him not being here. That probably says a lot." Maren's eyes searched the room for Damien.

"It all works out, Maren. Take it from an old lady. Look at me. Never thought in a million years I'd meet someone or feel anything again after

Kenny's father left. Time sometimes just fixes things." She hugged Maren. "Thank you for coming. I think Jules will be all right now. For the first time in years."

"Of course. Grandpa would never turn away from anyone. He's the best. And I'm really glad I was here."

"Oops. Jules is summoning me," Cindy said. "I think he wants to offer some drinks. You take care."

"You too."

Maren sighed with relief. She scanned the room. Blackhawk and Malak were still talking. Jesse was in the kitchen with Jules. And Damien was standing in the corner—looking at her. Maren patted the sofa and motioned Damien over.

Damien bounded over and plopped down hard on the couch. He slid close to her.

"Jeez, Damien. Do you always have to be the comedian? Look what all happened today? I'm emotionally exhausted." Maren rolled her eyes. *He was impossible.*

"Yes. A lot happened. But that is already in the past. That's how a wolf thinks. We're always 'in the now.' I was angry when I first saw Jules. Then I felt a connection—when I fully got his scent and knew he was part of my family. Now I'm happy because you wanted me by you. Do you understand that, Maren? It's a much simpler way to live."

Maren looked straight into Damien's yellow eyes. They glowed. Almost like a yellow light bulb. It was eerie and almost funny. She smiled. It was a girl's smile—a self-conscious smile. She couldn't help it.

"And now I want to kiss you," Damien said. "But I won't here. You'd be 'embarrassed' or whatever that odd human feeling is. Besides, maybe I'd be embarrassed. Haven't felt that emotion yet. And really, I'm not quite sure I know how to kiss correctly."

"Ha! After all those movies you've been watching? All those sex movies? Don't think I haven't heard the TV on after I've gone to bed. It's not difficult to figure it out—you have it so loud."

Damien laughed and slapped his legs. "That was for your benefit. I wanted you to know."

"Figures."

"Well? Any tips for me? Would you let me kiss you?"

Maren stared down at her lap. *How should I answer that? Should I tell him the truth? Will he tease me and make me regret it? Damn! Here goes nothing!* Maren cleared her throat. She turned to face him.

"Yes. I would let you kiss me. And I don't care how correctly you do it. But not here. Not now. I want to be alone with you. Maybe later."

Damien smiled softly. He took her hand and held it, hiding it between their touching legs. He didn't let go.

Maren looked around uncomfortably. "And Damien? What do you know about Wendigo?"

Damien squeezed her hand hard and cleared his throat. "I know that I sensed it when I was off as a wolf. I know that it is completely evil. And I know that I will keep it from you with my life."

Maren squeezed his hand back. A lot of commotion and talking was still going on around them. Her eyes traveled around the room, stopping at Blackhawk and Malak.

They were no longer talking. They both had serious expressions on their faces—and they were both looking at her and Damien.

Chapter Seventeen

Free As a Wolf

It was a long quiet ride back to Blackhawks's cabin. Damien pressed his thigh against Maren's in the front seat. This time she didn't squirm uncomfortably on the truck's small bench seat. This time it wasn't as if he were taking liberties—liberties that he knew she couldn't do anything about without making a scene. After he had held her hand on the sofa at Jules' place, she felt different. And she knew he did too. It was no longer a big game. She could tell by the look in his eyes. He *was* serious about her. She was able to push the Wendigo stories from her mind.

"Grandpa. Are you OK? You haven't said a word since we left," Maren said, patting Blackhawk's arm lightly.

"I'm fine. I *would* like to talk to you two when we get home. When we're done eating supper. That Ok with you? Nothing to worry about," Blackhawk said.

"Sure, Grandpa."

"Sure, Pops."

Maren glanced at Damien and he shrugged his shoulders, just enough so she could see. They pulled up in front of the cabin.

"Damien, could you bring in some wood for tonight? I'm just so darned tired. Need to eat and sit down awhile."

"No problem, Pops. You and Maren go on in. Be in in a bit." Damien nodded at Maren, like it was OK—not to worry. She was relieved. Damien knew a lot more about Blackhawk than she did. He could read so much more. Every subtle nuance had a significant meaning. That was one quality she envied. *Maybe someday when I have the guts to do the change.*

Maren made fried elk steaks that Jules had insisted they take with them. She made wild rice—the rice that was harvested right there on the rez. There was just nothing that could compare to it. And large glasses of milk. Damien liked milk as much as Maren did. Blackhawk insisted they drink it. Their suppers were a big deal to him—all three of them sitting down together to share a meal.

Blackhawk pushed his almost empty plate to the side.

"You two should know this. I'm not a healthy man anymore, as you already know. There's a couple things I've gone ahead and done. This place. The cabin and the land. It's willed to both of you. You two are all I have left— of my kind. I did talk to your mother, Maren, and she seemed pleased. And Damien—Doc's been working on getting you a birth certificate. So far it was Damien Jon Nightmoon—Marina's maiden name. Didn't think using Malone would be good. Too many questions. We're changing that to 'James.' Damien Jon James." Blackhawk paused, glancing at both their expressions.

"I know you two can make arrangements to live here part time or however or whatever you need. I was thinking Damien would make this his home while you're in school, Maren. He's quite self-sufficient. And I have some savings. It should last quite a while if you're sensible."

"Wait a minute, Grandpa. You're talking like you won't even be here in a couple weeks. When I go to school. I don't get it." Maren felt a knot tighten in her stomach.

"I won't be," Blackhawk said. "That's what we're going to talk about now."

Maren and Damien looked back and forth at each other and Blackhawk. *Even Damien didn't see this coming.*

"Old Malak and I got talking tonight. It was good. A good talk for both of us. Anyway, what I'm saying is I don't want to die in my human form. Neither does he. We've done everything we can do here—as humans. There's a new generation now—you two—and what becomes of the changelings is up to you. We want to make the change—this last time. We want to live out our lives in the woods—smelling the smells, seeing what we see, just going back to nature as we remember it. Already talked to Doc about this. He's apprehensive, of course, good man that he is. Now Malak wants it too. It shouldn't have surprised me. But it did. Anyway, would be good to have an old friend along."

"Grandpa? Are you sure? What if you can't change? What if something goes wrong? I wouldn't know what to do. I … ." Maren stopped talking. She realized she was whining, something Blackhawk didn't put up with. He had made up his mind. He just had a little half-smile, like he was going to sit and listen to whatever she said, but it wouldn't make any difference. He was that way.

"There are no guarantees, Maren. About anything. Old Malak and I discussed the whole thing. It is easier changing to wolf than it is wolf to human. Damien, you already accomplished that task and without help. So, what I'm saying is. I'd like both of you nearby. It will be at Malak's place way out there. If something goes wrong, well, Doc will know what to do. If all goes well, I'd like to take one last look at my beautiful granddaughter and you, Damien. Then you won't see me again."

Everything was quiet at the table. Maren stared at her plate. Damien spoke first.

"I'll do whatever you want, Pops. Whatever you need. And of course you know I'm here for Maren—to help her—as long as she lets me."

"Thanks, Damien. You turned out to be quite special. To all of us."

Maren finally spoke. Her eyes were watering.

"When are you going to do this, Grandpa?"

"After New Year's. I want to see your mother again, Maren. I want to see all the family and the James' family too. It will be a wonderful last gathering. Something we haven't done in years." Blackhawk stood up. "Thank you. I appreciate your support. Maren, don't you worry about your old grandpa here. It's the one thing I want now. The one thing I have left. If you don't understand now, you will later." He leaned down and kissed her on top of the head.

"Now why don't you two go enjoy that Christmas tree. It looks beautiful in the dark, with just those lights on. I'm going to bed. See you in the morning." Blackhawk reached over and gave Damien a pat on the shoulder. Then he walked down the hall to his bedroom.

Maren got up and started clearing the table and washing dishes. Damien helped. Neither said a word until Damien dried the last plate and put it away.

"Guess Grandpa won't be needing the winter gloves I got him," Maren said, nodding toward the tree. They had each agreed to get one another one thing for Christmas. Maren knew Blackhawk had his own form of religion—traditional Indian with a couple Christian traditions mixed in. The tree, for instance. He sure loved that tree. He said it was one way he could enjoy the smell of the sap and needles without "having to sit his ass outside and freeze."

Maren felt a rush of understanding pass through her. *Of course. I'm so blind. He so misses being a wolf. To enjoy simple things again. Nature. Being free. The smell of a pine tree.* She turned to Damien.

"It's OK. It doesn't matter, really. Come sit down by me. Let's look at the tree. Like Grandpa said." She took his hand and pulled him to the sofa. They both crashed down on it and laughed, making "shush" gestures to each other.

Damien took her hand. His face was serious. Maren stopped laughing. "So, Maren. Are you OK with this? Your grandpa? Being alone here with me?"

"If you mean Grandpa changing back to a wolf, and us handling his house and things together, I have to be. It's what he wants."

She paused a minute, then continued … her head tilted to the side, "If you mean being alone with you now, here, and Grandpa in his bedroom sleeping—well, I guess I'd say yes to that too. I'm OK with it."

Damien reached for her. He pulled her tight to him, their faces almost touching. Maren watched his thick, black eyelashes go up and down over his yellow eyes—eyes that were turning almost orange as her body was pressed against his.

"Your eyes are changing color," Maren said, breathing the words out.

"So are yours." Damien's voice was low and gravelly.

"Oh, just give that kiss a try, Damien. I'm not that experienced. I … ." Maren didn't finish her sentence. His mouth was on hers. Gently at first, then more urgently as he seemed to gain confidence. He pulled her tighter. They were half-sitting, half-laying on the sofa. Damien pulled her down so she was on her side, his body wrapped around hers as if she were in a cocoon. His hands ran up and down her back, over the thickness of her two wraps.

He didn't flinch and neither did she. It felt so completely normal, that she had the four breasts and he knew it. It was just the way it was. Maren finally pushed him back, softly, catching her breath.

"You passed the kissing test. By a long shot," Maren said, kissing him lightly on the nose. She laid her head on his chest. His heart was pounding. *His smell. It's Moonbaby. He's him but he's my wolf … so weird. Wow.*

"Maren. When you're ready. I want you to be my mate. Alpha female. And I want you to change. Just once. Be with me. Until then, I'll stay human as long as I can. That's all I can promise you." Damien stroked Maren's hair, twisting it around his hand, and letting it fall.

"I know, Damien. I know. I think more about it every day. It just scared me that first time. Besides, I couldn't bear to think of you out in the woods, chasing all the female wolves, and well … you know."

"Maren, Maren," Damien sighed. Then he laughed. "You are so wrong. There is only one breeding pair in a wolf pack. The two alphas. They are like the king and queen. Everything revolves around keeping them and the pack, well-fed and safe. That's the truth."

"Wow. But what if one of the young males in the pack has other ideas? What happens then?"

"Well, he either gets killed by the alpha male, leaves on his own, or, in the case of an old male alpha—could take over the pack. That rarely happens, though. And in our case, we'd both leave before I let any young wolf get you from me." He gave her a squeeze.

"What are we going to do, Damien? So much is happening. So much." Maren said, holding on to his arm. She was afraid to change, afraid of losing Damien, afraid of losing her Grandpa ... too much to deal with.

Damien pulled her up into a sitting position. He ruffled her hair. "You're a mess. We better go to our rooms." He nodded toward Blackhawk's room. "Wouldn't be right, wouldn't be ... ."

"Respectful." Maren finished his sentence, smoothing her hair back. "You are really something special, Damien. Goodnight, Moonbaby." She threw him a kiss at her bedroom door.

"Goodnight, Starr."

Maren stood behind her closed door, thinking. She heard Damien in the bathroom brushing his teeth, then his bedroom door close. Maren went to the bathroom with her toothbrush and face cleanser. She scrubbed off her eye makeup, looking into the mirror. The silver part of her hair had grown down the sides of her face in points. She was still trying to figure out if she should color it or leave it. Would they find it unusual at school? Probably not a whole lot different than some of the purple streaks she was seeing on TV.

She looked closer into the mirror. *My eyes. They've changed. They are more yellow now. I'm changing ... I can feel it. Wonder when the real change urge will come on again. I have my herbs, but if I don't go to school, if I'm here ... with Damien ... what should I do?* Maren exhaled.

She finished in the bathroom, tip-toed down the hall and into her room. She undressed and folded her wraps. It was time to wash them again in that herbal, woodsy stuff. It did help keep the swelling down. *Thank you Grandma Marina ... wherever you are.*

Chapter Eighteen

Herbs and Silver

Maren and Damien kept busy helping Blackhawk run the household. They planned on having a little Christmas celebration, probably more like a Yuletide. Damien had found another new talent of twisting old copper wire into art forms. It kept them laughing, which was a good thing. Maren worried about Blackhawk—if he would be able to make the change after all this time. Yet she could see every day that he was getting weaker. She saw that Damien noticed it too. He was being so attentive to Blackhawk.

Maren put another log on the fire. It was one of those Minnesota cold, winter weeks. Twenty five below zero for several days. And that wasn't even the wind chill.

"Damien, how much wood do we have left? Do you need to cut more? It's so cold out too," Maren yelled from the living room. She was hoping there was plenty. She hated to see Damien go out and spend hours in that weather. But he did. He dressed well but Maren was still amazed that he barely shivered. *Wolves* ... .

"Would you quit worrying? There's enough to last till *next* winter. I'm going to have to go to the Redwing and get some meat though. And flour. You know how Pops likes his meals—always the same."

"I heard that, Damien. You're welcome to conjure up something different any time." Blackhawk had just hung up the phone in the kitchen.

"Naw." Damien retired to his room, calendars and markers in his hand. Maren knew he was trying to figure out full moons, dates, and anything else that could help Blackhawk pick a good time. She also knew he was looking at how many moons she would be gone at school. She knew he was worried—worried that she would not be able to stop the change while being so far away.

"Maren. Good news," Blackhawk said. "Laken—your mother, I mean—is coming up around the 30th. I told her to make it a two day trip and go slow. Highways should be good unless we get a bad storm. I'll be calling Jules and Jesse. They can firm up the party date now. They insisted we go over there, you know."

"I know, Grandpa. There is more room there. It's not that far. It will be fun," Maren said, then paused a moment. "Umm, I was just wondering. Is Dr. Don invited?"

"Ha-ha! You aren't too subtle, Miss Malone." Blackhawk winked at her. "Of course he's invited. What you really want to know is if he is coming."

"Yes. I do. I think it will be good for Mom to see someone she knows that's her age. Someone that she cared about a long time ago. And Dr. Don isn't seeing anyone. He's been sober all this time, all by himself. I don't know how he does it."

"Well. The way I see it. After all these years knowing him and a lot of that time he was drinking heavy—I believe it is you, my girl. He really cares. He wants to make sure you'll be OK. And he knows the ropes. The changeling ropes, Maren. Remember. You can go to him anytime if you need help. He is going to give you his cell number too. For when you're at school."

Damien slammed his door shut behind him. He stood in the hallway, some papers in his hand. "I think it's a good time to talk about that and you, Pops. Can we sit down in the living room?"

Blackhawk nodded and Maren followed him into the room. He sat in his recliner leaving the sofa to Maren and Damien.

"Pops. January 5th. It's the Wolf Moon. I think it would be a good moon with a lot of energy—for you and Malak. I'm thinking the sooner the better?"

Blackhawk nodded and then looked over at Maren. He smiled softly. "The sooner the better. Actually been feeling something coming on. Something strong. I have to take advantage of that. I'll get a hold of old Malak. Sure he's been waiting on that call."

"Good. Now Maren? You're going to have to go through three or maybe four moons before that semester break. The Flower Moon on May 4th is scary for me. It's a fertility moon or awakening. It's usually used for the first change of a new changeling. If they'd had trouble. So its energy is all about transformation—just what you don't need off in the middle of Minneapolis by yourself." Damien flicked the papers in his hands against his knee.

Maren swallowed. "I think I'll take your advice on this. The full moon May 4th scares me. I would have to be here—with you. I'll work it out. Go back for finals—whatever I have to do. So I'd leave right after Grandpa and Malak, The Wolf Moon January 5th. And would have three moons to get through on my own? Oh, boy." She scowled. Repeating it out loud made it real. She turned to face Blackhawk.

"I have to know absolutely everything you both know now. Right now. I need to get some confidence with this." Maren tapped her foot for what seemed an eternity. "I'm waiting … ."

"It's about time I see that 'Starr' show herself," Blackhawk said. "Well, where do we start? The herbs … ."

Maren grabbed up her notebook, an old binder with her Grandmother Marina's writings in it, and three plastic bags of herbs Blackhawk had been storing in the cellar. She had never even realized the cellar was there, but wow. What a day it had been! Her fingers were sore from all the writing—all the note taking. Going down into the freezing cellar. All the hidden stuff! *And all Grandpa was waiting for was me to ask? To demand, actually. To show him I was really ready.*

Maren pushed her bedroom door closed with her hip. She tossed her armful of treasures onto the bed. She carefully separated out the flat paper bag Blackhawk said was irreplaceable. He had asked her to research on her computer how to properly care for the contents. Maren could barely wait to examine the bag. She delicately tipped the bag and let the brittle contents fall onto her quilt. It looked like very old parchment. Some kind of handmade paper. It was still intact but obviously fragile. Real fountain pen ink and elaborate letters. Wow. And there was that symbol! The one on her necklace—her wraps. That weird curly 'H' and 'W.'

Maren put on the old white gloves Blackhawk had given her with the package. He told her that was the only way he and Marina were preserving the precious antiquity. They just didn't know enough about how to do it. Now Blackhawk was leaving it all to her. The first thing she'd do would be a simple online search. Right now, she just wanted to read it. She propped her pillow and lay back on the bed with the first piece of parchment.

Maren woke in the middle of the night startled and reached for her bedside light. *Oh my god, I fell asleep. And no one even woke me for supper.* She carefully gathered the old papers and put them back into the bag. She still had the white gloves on. Maren packed everything up and stored the bag in a sturdy box under the bed. The herbs she put next to her closet door. She was planning on "cooking them up" in the next few days. They needed time in jars to reach their full potential. And she was going to need that potion for those full moons in Minneapolis.

She quickly slipped into a long t-shirt and ran to the bathroom. As she did her evening routine she thought about Damien. *Was he awake? Probably heard me at least. Funny, he never knocked or woke me. He and Grandpa probably had a lot to talk about. They need their time too. I'm almost always around. Good. It's all good.*

Maren slid into bed, propped her head up on her arm, and thought about all the amazing reading she had done. The symbol. H/W ... yes, there were actually two symbols and she hadn't known about the other until she read about it in the old manuscript. The one on her wraps and her necklace stood for 'human over wolf.' *That's why my father had it—why he gave it to me. I wonder when he quit wearing it ... if he ever changed ... why he did jump off that construction beam. Maybe he couldn't change back ... maybe. No one will know but him.*

Maren turned the talisman on her neck in her fingers, over and over. *The special silver in this ... mined from some weird place ... will have to ask Grandpa where that was ... a French name, maybe Canada?*

The papers talked a lot about the silver symbol, that anyone that does not want to be overtaken by the change, should never take it off her neck. Its power increased the longer it was against your skin. And the herbal potions. The same ones that Dr. Don had given her that night, the same herbs that Blackhawk gave her to make her own potion. That part had been difficult to read. It was the measurements. In liters and milliliters. Metric. Explained why her grandmother had re-written them in that binder.

Maren tapped her fingers on her notes. *I'll rewrite all this. Put it in a beautiful book for ...? Who knows? My changeling children? Who knows what the future will bring.* She smiled at how ridiculous it was. *Ridiculous but true! Anyway, no more paper bags or dirty cellar.*

Her hand stilled. *The other symbol...the W/H. Wolf over human. Grandpa will need that. The brand. I wonder if there's a branding iron somewhere. And the potions that go with that. Which I'll make for him. I can do that much. I can do all of it. Yes, I can. Moonbaby ... .*

Chapter Nineteen

Yuletide-Christmas

Maren, Damien, and Blackhawk sat quietly in the living room. Damien had stoked up a huge blazing fire. He always could find the right wood for the right time. Super dry and medium sized for a big display. A little newer log, not as dry, but huge—would burn all night. Maren was sure he learned everything Blackhawk had shown him in only a few months. Not only was he a beauty as a wolf, but he was truly a marvel as a human being.

It was December 23. Maren called it their Yuletide-Christmas because they combined both traditions into one and just picked the day. It was fine with her and Blackhawk. Damien didn't see the whole human holiday religious thing the same. He was a true example of a unique nature religion. Maren could see he was spiritual, but not in the "going to church" way. The world outside was his church. She understood that seeing the woods, the sky, the stars—everything from the eyes of a wolf would be unexplainable. It was something she started to yearn for, much to her own surprise.

"Well, should we open our gifts from each other?" Maren said. It was such a wonderful evening. She was looking forward to probably the last time they would all be together—alone. They still had the New Year's Eve party at the James.' Her mom would be here. Damien would meet her. Everything would be great. But then the Wolf Moon was coming quickly. She didn't want to think about that now. *Grandpa ... .*

Damien got up and brought a long box over to Blackhawk. He sat back down by Maren.

"Well now. What could this be?" Blackhawk tore open the box and pulled out a long, metal object. It had a weird end on it; Maren couldn't see what it was.

"Damien. That's just great. Yes. I want this. Old Malak will too. That's really thoughtful." Blackhawk stared at it for a long time, turning it around in his hands. He finally held it out to Maren. His eyes were watering. She jumped up to get it and took it back to the sofa next to Damien.

Part of it was copper wire—the stuff Damien had been playing with. The end was a different metal. She examined it. It was the other symbol. It was the W/H symbol. Wolf over human. It was a branding iron.

Damien took her hand. "It will help them. It will keep back any change urges they might not be able to overcome. It will make sure they don't start the change back to human in the middle of the woods. In the middle of winter." He paused. "As very old men."

Maren nodded. *Yes. He's right. Damien thinks of everything.* She got up and handed her package to Blackhawk. "Sorry. Didn't know all this when I got these."

Blackhawk opened his package which was the leather gloves Maren had bought him.

"They're beautiful, Maren. I'll be sure to wear them to the James' party. Thank you."

Maren got up and got her present for Damien. He motioned for her to grab the one from him too. Damien unwrapped his first. It was a black flannel shirt of top quality. On the cuffs and collar, embroidered with beads, was the H/W symbol.

"Did you do this work, Maren? It's fantastic. Beautiful."

"Thought it would give you some incentive when I'm gone."

Damien smiled. Then he leaned over and kissed her lightly on the lips. "Thank you."

Maren looked at her package from Damien sitting on her lap. *What could this possibly be? I'm almost afraid to open it.*

It was a small box. She shook it. It felt substantial. She carefully opened the box. She sucked in her breath, then lifted it out to view it. Beautiful copper woven with what looked like silver. It was a bracelet. And there it was. The H/W symbol, discreetly entwined with the intricate wire. The symbol was silver—highly polished. No one would even see what it was unless they knew the story.

"Damien. It's breathtaking. And I know you made this. Wow. This looks like it came from some high end boutique!" Maren slid it on her wrist. It was just tight enough to not come off without some effort. "Is this silver different? It looks heavier, thicker. I can't explain it."

"Actually this gift is from both me and Pops. He gave me the last of the wolfs' bane silver—that's what it's nick-named—from Marina's belongings. She brought it from Canada. I'm sure it, ahh, can't be replaced."

"Grandpa. Oh, wow." Maren ran over to Blackhawk and threw her arms around him in his recliner so hard it started to tip over. Damien was there, as usual, to save the day. He grabbed the back of the chair and pushed them back up. Maren and Blackhawk were laughing. Maren's eyes were watering. She didn't want to let go of him.

"All right now, my girl. It's all good. I can see Marina smiling at us right now. I can feel it. This was all meant to be."

Maren released her hold and slid to the floor. She ran her hand back and forth over her bracelet. "I'll never take it off, Grandpa. Never. I love you."

"And I love you too, my most precious girl. Life has so much in store for you. I'll be watching, you know. And Maren. Never say never. This is for you. For now. There'll be a day when you will take it off. For a while, at least. And then there'll be a day when you will give it to someone else. One day when you are an old woman. An old changeling like your Pops here. Right now, it's to be worn all the time. For your safe keeping. It has all our love in it, Maren. Mine and Damien's."

Maren couldn't think. She had no words. How she wished she knew the changeling language so she could say something extraordinary in a unique way to her grandfather. Something succinct and powerful—like she knew the language to be. She smiled at Damien. She was so filled with joy, she was sure it was a wolf's joy. She just sensed it.

"Sweetheart. Would you be so kind to this old man and bring him some of that hot eggnog? Just a shot of rum in that would be beneficial right now."

Maren jumped up—sprung up. It caught Damien's attention and he glanced at Blackhawk. Blackhawk nodded knowingly. *They all saw that! What did I just do? I am changing … not fully … but like Marina's notes said. You become wolf before you actually become wolf. Now she knew what it meant.*

"I'd be glad to. And maybe a shot and a half. It'll help you sleep well tonight, Grandpa." Maren knew her grandfather rarely drank but a few beers now and then. But she also knew that some liquor helped slow the change. She knew they had put vodka or something in the herbal thing she drank. It made sense. Alcohol was a depressant.

"Yes it will. And hopefully keep the dreams off. I know this Wolf Moon is my time. January 5th. Still got a couple things to do. But tonight, I think I'll just have a drink with the two most important people in my life. Have a little one yourself, kids. This is our celebration."

Damien jumped up to help Maren in the kitchen. "Don't mind if we do," he said, then started whistling way too well.

"God, Damien you sound just like a cardinal. How can you be so good at absolutely everything? It's maddening." Maren laughed as she said it.

They all sat quietly in the dark, sipping their eggnog and rum drinks. The fire was crackling and toasty warm. The tree still smelled of fresh pine sap. Maren looked over at Blackhawk. *He's happy. He's truly happy.*

Blackhawk started to snore. It woke him. "That's it for me, kids. Come give old Pops a pull out of the chair. I'm looking forward to that big feather bed and double quilts."

Both Maren and Damien took an arm and lifted Blackhawk onto his feet. Maren could sense that he had lost weight. And she knew Damien was giving him extra meat at breakfast and supper. Some of it didn't look very cooked, either. She trusted Damien fully. He cared about Blackhawk as much as she did and they both were just focused on him getting through the change alive. That was all.

Blackhawk kissed Maren on the forehead, as he did almost every night. This time he embraced Damien, put his hands on either side of Damien's face and then did some quick changeling sign. Damien patted Blackhawk on the arm. Blackhawk went into his room, shutting the door tightly behind him. He didn't usually do that so he could still get heat from the fire. They could hear him rustle around in the room then into the bed. It was immediately all quiet.

"Should we put some music on quiet-like? Something soft and moody?"

Maren looked at Damien. "What are you up to, Moonbaby?"

"Just want to cuddle by the fire with Starr."

"OK. But let me pick it. You're still experimenting with music and get the moods wrong way too often."

"All yours." Damien sat on the sofa. He took off his boots and stretched his legs out on the floor watching Maren. She walked over to the sofa and noticed right away that his eyes were turning orangey. She decided not to say anything. She sat down next to him and took off her short boots. She hooked her leg around his and leaned back, putting her head on his shoulder.

"This night couldn't be any better than this," Maren said. She turned her face to his and kissed him. Softly. Then she kissed his cheeks and eyes. She climbed up so that she was sitting on his lap. She could feel Damien's heart pounding. His breathing made a deep growling sound in the back of his throat.

"What's that weird noise you're making, Damien? It's a little scary sounding."

Damien pulled his upper body back and looked down at Maren's chest area. "Ahhh, I can feel all of your breasts against me and well, they have all swollen up. What are you expecting?

Maren giggled. "I'm sorry. That's funny to me that you would find that erotic. It's always been an embarrassment for me ... you have no idea." She looked at his eyes. Now they were blazing orange-yellow. "I guess you do.

It's normal with us … changelings. Forget sometimes." She suddenly felt shy and started to sit up.

"No, you don't. And take those wraps off. Hate those. Want the real you against me. All of you."

Maren stood up. Damien's black and silver hair had come out of his usual low ponytail. The silver chunk fell forward and hung across his face, like a silver waterfall over orange glowing eyes. His wolfy smelling body was erotic. Even his sweat smelled good to her. It was so full of different smells each saying something. *You become wolf before you become wolf … .* She picked up her boots. "In my room."

She turned and walked to her door. She could hear Damien scrambling, picking up his boots, tripping, and then fixing the couch back up. Then his breath was at the back of her neck.

She opened the door and shut it behind him. It was totally dark. Maren made her way to her bedside light and turned it on. It was light enough to see but not glaring like the ceiling light.

Damien sat down on the edge of the bed. Maren stood, thinking. *This will be the first time anyone ever has seen these … ahhh … four full size breasts. I trust him. I have to.*

Maren pulled her big sweater off over her head. Then she reached over to the pins that held her wraps. She undid them, feeling the release of pressure. It felt great. It was a strange freedom she would never be able to explain to anyone. Except maybe another changeling female? Not many of those around. Then she froze, holding the released wraps against her body as best as she could.

Damien stood up and moved tight to her. He lifted her hair and kissed her neck—it seemed like a thousand times. Then he took hold of the end of one wrap and pulled gently, letting it loosen and slacken, then pull again until it was off her body. He did the same with the second one. Maren looked down, unable to meet his eyes. She put her hands around his neck. His mouth found hers and he kissed her as he laid her down on the bed. Then he stood back up.

"You're astonishingly beautiful." Damien removed his shirt and jeans. He lay down next to her. He kissed and caressed her body until Maren interrupted the kiss.

"Wait," she said, breathless. She took her jeans and stockings off and pulled the quilt up around her. "Is this going to be strange? I mean I've seen dogs and animals ... umm, just wondering what ... ."

"Maren," Damien said, his orange eyes blazing in the dim lighting, "if there is one thing I actually prefer about being a human—it would be that I want to look into your eyes when I make love to you."

Chapter Twenty

New Year's Eve

"Hey! It's Mom!" Maren yelled out. She had been checking the driveway a hundred times in the last two hours. She threw her coat on and went out on the porch. Laken pulled up to a parking spot that Damien had plowed out earlier. At least the temperature was hovering around zero—much better than that 25 below. A regular heat wave.

"Mom!" Maren ran out to the old station wagon her mother still drove. She said she liked it and it had lots of rooms to carry books and all her teaching stuff. This time it looked like it was piled with clothes and personal things.

Laken Malone got out of the car and stretched. Her hair was still long and red, but shoulder length and curly. She had big furry boots on and a long down coat. She looked shorter than Maren remembered. She was 5'6, Maren knew. It had to be because of all the tall men Maren was around.

"Oh, honey, it's so good to see you!" They embraced for several minutes.

"You've changed, Miss Maren. You're so … mature! And what did you do to your hair? What is that silver stuff?"

"Never mind, Mom. I'll tell you all about it. Come on in and have some coffee. Grandpa's not doing the best, so don't say anything. And Damien. Mom, I have so much to tell you!"

"I'm sure you do."

Blackhawk reached her first and gave her a big hug. "Oh, Laken. So good to see you. You're still as beautiful as I remember. Come and meet Damien Jon James. Our new addition."

Damien walked up slowly. He was dressed in the black shirt Maren gave him. His hair was combed straight back and tied at the neck with a leather strap. He reached out his hand.

"Nice to meet you, ma'am. Maren's been driving us crazy ever since you called about two hours ago."

Laken took Damien's hand and held it. "My god, you're profoundly good-looking. It's almost shocking. Maren, how do you keep the women away?"

"Not a lot around in the middle of winter, Mom. Yeah. I know. It's a little disturbing sometimes."

"She's got nothing to worry about, ma'am. I'm all hers."

"Please call me Laken. I'm so pleased to meet you. And Pops … it's been awhile. The funeral. I wasn't too good around that time. Things are much better. I do have news. I retired. All done teaching for a while. It's a well-deserved relief."

"I'm so glad, Mom. Come in and sit down on something comfortable. That drive's a killer. We'll get your things. You have a lot with you. What do you want inside?"

"I know. More news. Anyway, my red suitcase is all I need for now. Thank you."

"I got it," Damien said.

Laken sat down and sighed. "Good coffee. Great. Some bad stuff on the road. Well, Maren. Tell me everything. Catch me up. Heard a few things from Pops but would like to hear from you. Your plans. How you are … ."

"Mom. I'm just great. Starting school after … on January 7th. Just for three and half months right off. I need to get back here. I can always take summer classes too. I'm just doing one thing at a time.

"You look so different. Your hair. It's unusual. I like it though. Your idea?"

"Not exactly."

Damien came in with the suitcase. He gave Maren a "where?" look.

"Put that in my room. She can sleep there. I'll take the sofa. I don't really care," Maren said. "I have a lot of stuff to do on the computer and like sitting in Grandpa's chair when he goes to bed."

Laken smiled. Her eyes traveled down her daughter's body, stopping at her breasts.

Maren noticed. "It's the way it is, Mom. I'm a changeling like Dad was. Haven't done it yet, but almost. They're all helping me control it until I'm ready. I've seen a lot, Mom. And yes, I now have four full breasts. Guess everyone was wrong when they said it wouldn't happen."

Maren couldn't help use a little sarcasm. She still resented her mother from keeping everything from her. "Besides. Damien thinks they're beautiful."

"Maren. That talk isn't proper right now and you know it."

"Really, Mom? The way I see it, it wasn't ever proper with you." Maren got up and went into the bedroom. She was surprised at how happy she was to see her mother, but how quickly she got angry. *Damn it. Couldn't resist. Damn.*

There was a knock on her bedroom door. "Maren. Let me in, please." It was Blackhawk.

Maren opened the door sheepishly. "I'm sorry. I just couldn't help it."

"I understand, Maren. But do you really want to hurt her now? It won't change a thing. She asked to stay here for a while. While you're in school. I think she needs to get away from everything back there. And Damien… well, I'm not sure if he won't want to change while you're gone. It will be too hard on him with both of us gone. He knows wolf better than any change-ling. Remember, he was born wolf. It will always be his first calling. No matter how much he loves you. Come on out and be friendly. Your mother misses you terribly."

"OK. Just give me a couple minutes, Grandpa. Thanks." Maren waited for the door to close then threw herself on the bed. *Oh, no. Damien. Don't leave. I'd do anything. I'll forget about school. Have to talk to him. Now.*

Maren took her compact out of her purse and powdered her reddened face, put on lipstick, and brushed her hair. She walked out into the hall to hear everyone laughing and talking. Damien's voice was the loudest. He was having fun. *How dare he. How dare he not tell me this.*

"Hey. Sorry. A little history with Mom. It's OK. Sorry, Mom. I really am glad you're here."

"Oh, honey. Me too. You've grown up so much. I'm afraid I've missed a lot. But I knew that when I sent you up here. You know that now, Maren, don't you? I'm not one of you. I couldn't help your father. I wanted you to be with your own kind. So that nothing bad would happen to you … when you completely realized everything. Can you understand that?"

"Most of me does, Mom. The little girl didn't. It's tough growing up." Maren cast Damien a "look."

"Yes it is, honey. Even as a regular girl. It's always tough making the right decisions. All the consequences."

"It's OK, Mom. Damien, can I talk to you a minute? In the bedroom, please?"

"Sure." Damien gave Blackhawk an "oh, oh" look.

Maren shut the door behind Damien.

"Why didn't you tell me? Why weren't you honest with me? So you're going to run around being a wolf while I'm in school?"

"And you're going to run around a college full of men being a beautiful young woman? Do you think I'm not worried? Don't you have a clue? What if you meet someone? Get tired of this whole wolf thing? Then what? What if you don't want me anymore?" Damien's face was grief-stricken. He sat down hard on the bed and stared at the floor.

Maren sat down next to him.

"God, I'm sorry. I never in a million years thought you would worry about that. Never. After what we did? Just last week? I love you. I don't want anyone else, ever. How could I anyway?" Maren tore open her shirt. She had quit wearing the wraps—at least until she went to school. She fell down on the bed, feeling ridiculously childish.

"Oh, Maren. Starr. I'd bet any guy, well not any, but some wouldn't give a damn about that. Maybe find it … Ahh, the word … oh, kinky."

Maren kicked at him with her foot. Damien grabbed her leg and pulled himself on top of her. He put his hands on her breasts and kissed her hard. Maren wrapped her legs around him, kissing him back. She could not resist Damien. It was just that way.

Damien disengaged himself from Maren and pulled her shirt together.

"Now put on a new shirt and come back out and be a lady. I'm not saying this wouldn't be fun, but you know better." He smiled and kissed her. "I want to be with you one more time before you leave. Let me explain everything then. And I promise you have nothing to worry about with me. You are my queen. You are my alpha female. Don't forget that." Damien stood up, smoothed his hair and clothes and walked out of the bedroom.

Maren got up and found a nice sweater. She put a t-shirt on under it. She re-did her lipstick again. *He's right. He's always right. But when I come back, I'm going to change with him. I will do it.*

Maren walked out, put a big smile on her face, and said, "So is everyone ready for the big party tomorrow night?"

The next morning was chaos. Maren's neck hurt from sleeping in the recliner and it was agony waiting for everyone to use the bathroom. Then there was the typical fry bread and scrambled eggs. At least her Mom thought it was a marvelous treat.

Blackhawk was on the phone the rest of the day trying to figure out who was riding with whom and how they were going to fit everyone in the truck. It was finally decided that Damien would drive her Mom's station wagon.

Maren and her Mom spent the afternoon trying to decide what to wear. A balance of style and sensibility since it was still around zero. Maren showed her mother the wraps and told her the story. Her mother actually cried. Then she hugged Maren and told her how sorry she was that she didn't help her more, that she just didn't know how. And that her father wasn't any help at all staying drunk to avoid any painful decision. It was the best and most intimate conversation she could remember having with her mother. But then came the dreaded one…

"So, honey, are you and Damien sexually active?"

Maren froze. She couldn't talk about what she and Damien had. She finally whispered, "Just once."

"OK, honey. You are certainly a woman now. I could see that when I pulled in. Your whole presence is different. You've grown emotionally. You're eighteen and can legally make your own decisions. This is important. You are both changelings. Damien is unlike any before. You have to have protection from pregnancy. You know that, don't you?

"Yes. I was going to talk to Dr. Don about it. Although it would be really embarrassing."

"Donnie Minnetonka. How is he doing, anyway?

"Quit drinking. It's been quite a while, actually." *Donnie? Yeah, they did know each other pretty well. Won't she be surprised to see him tonight.*

Laken dug in her suitcase. "Here. Brought this for you. Birth control. One pill a day, every day. You can refill them at any pharmacy. The prescription is from your doctor back home. Everything's OK."

Maren took the pill bottle. Then she hugged her Mom hard. "Thanks so much, Mom. I've had so many things to figure out on my own. This helps so much."

Laken reached down and took Maren's hand—the one that held the pill bottle.

"You're welcome, honey. At least I can be a mother in that way," Laken said as she moved Maren's wrist up. "Now this is one fabulous bracelet. Stunning. I've never seen work like this."

"Damien made it, Mom. It's copper and silver. It helps keep the change at bay. Same as this." Maren took her hand from her mother's and pulled the necklace out from her sweater. "Same as this does. All to help me when … ." She didn't finish her sentence.

Laken had put her hand over her mouth and collapsed onto the bed. She dug a tissue out of her pocket and dabbed at her eyes. "I'm sorry, honey. That was Jonny's. Your father's. I remember it well. He always wore it. Until the last year or so. I never knew what happened to it."

Maren sat down next to her. "I'm sorry, Mom. I never even thought. Dr. Don gave it to me. He said Dad wanted me to have it. He must have been up here? Before he died?"

Laken put her arm around Maren. "I suppose he was. He never said much at the end. You know, I tried to get him to change back. He never fully fit in as a human. But he wouldn't do it. I think that's why we both tried so hard to keep everything from you … like that would make a hill of beans' difference. Oh, we were so ridiculous thinking we could keep you from being who you are!"

"I understand, Mom. I've done the same with Damien. It's OK," Maren said as she hugged her mother.

Laken hugged Maren back and then stood up and took a breath of relief. "OK. Now put on those leather boots I brought. You'll look great in them. High heels, but warm. And as tall as Damien is, you two will look fabulous together. And this scarf. Tie it like this. With the sweater. Super."

"Thanks again, Mom. I missed this. All the 'girl' stuff. Not much of that around."

Laken smiled and half-laughed. Maren gave her a quick kiss on the cheek. *Wow, she really is pretty when she's happy. She really needs this … she needs to be here too.*

Maren ran out and got into the passenger's side of the old station wagon. It was warm since Damien, being the thoughtful guy he was, had gone out early to start it. *Or maybe he's trying to impress Mom. Doesn't matter.* She was excited about the big James' party. Blackhawk and Laken got into the backseat, jabbering away. Damien came out last and what a vision he was. Maren watched him walk to the car. Black, leather jacket and boots. It was the black shirt that she had given him. His jeans were just right. *Wow, how can I leave him alone? I must be crazy. He's actually getting into this—being the hot guy."*

"Everyone ready?" Damien climbed in behind the wheel and Maren scooted possessively close to him. She put her hand on his thigh. "You look fantastic."

"You too, Maren. As always." He patted her hand reassuringly. She exhaled, relieved.

The drive was fairly long. Maren couldn't believe all the cars at the James' place. A couple she didn't recognize. Then, there it was. Kenny Shane's. He was there … hopefully with his new girlfriend. *This should be fun.* She looked at her mother smiling away in the back seat. She couldn't wait for her to see Dr. Don there.

Jules was at the door greeting everyone. He looked like a different man than she had seen a couple weeks ago. Cindy Shane came out. She was stunning with that blonde hair and her big, white smile. Blackhawk got out and escorted her mother. She and Damien were last. He helped her out of the car, then stood quietly, sniffing the air.

"If that bastard Kenny is here, I'm going to kill him for real this time."

"Oh my god, Damien, you remember that? As a wolf? You're kidding."

"I remember his scent. His scent around you. And yours by the way … when you were with him." Damien actually glared at her.

"Just a minute, Mr. Damien James. Things were different then. I don't care about him that way. I love you. And I'm sure he brought his girlfriend."

"Hmmm."

"You want trust, Damien. You just better be able to trust me. This works both ways."

The place was fixed up nice. No doubt Cindy Shane had a lot to do with that. Maren grabbed Damien's hand and walked straight up to Kenny Shane and a beautiful dark haired girl. She looked uncomfortable.

"Kenny. I'm so glad to see you. This is Damien James. These are his relatives. He came up from Wisconsin to visit and, well, decided to stay awhile," Maren said, eyeing Damien carefully.

"Maren, you look great. Hi, Damien. Nice to meet you. This is Mariah. She's also from Wisconsin. Appleton, actually."

Everyone shook hands. Mariah immediately started asking Damien about Wisconsin, which he knew little about.

"Oh, lived on the rez there with my aunt. Just decided to come back and get to know my family better. I like it here. If you can hack the cold, it's beautiful in the summer."

Kenny leaned in closer to Maren. "Hey, was just wondering what happened to that crazy ass wolf you had. Is he still alive?"

"Alive and well, thank you." Damien spoke in the coldest tone Maren had ever heard from him.

Kenny looked back and forth between Maren and Damien. "Well, good then. Going to hang out with Mom. Help her out. Nice seeing you all." Kenny grabbed his girl's arm and practically dragged her off.

"You big jerk," Maren whispered to Damien, stifling her laughter.

"No problem. Anytime."

"Well, I'm going to call him and fix it anyway. He didn't deserve that, Damien. They will be the only ones I will know at school, you seem to forget."

"Yeah. Thanks for reminding me," Damien said, trying to sound lighthearted.

They both walked over and got hors d'oeuvres and drinks and sat on a sofa to watch everyone. Maren quickly spotted her mother who had found Dr. Don.

"Look at them, Damien. I know they have feelings for each other. It's so nice to see both of them smiling, isn't it?" They both laughed. Just then, her mother looked over her way.

"Shit," Maren mumbled under her breath. Laken pointed a finger at her and swished it back and forth. Then she smiled and turned back to Dr. Don.

"Whoops. Guess I'm busted," Maren said. "She knows I knew he was going to be here and didn't tell her."

"Looks like they're just fine," Damien took her hand and kissed it. "Which reminds me. Are we fine, Maren? Can we make this work?"

"Absolutely. Can't be any other way." Maren leaned her head on Damien's shoulder and they smiled and laughed the rest of the evening.

Everyone was leaving. Blackhawk, Malak, and Dr. Don had been talking seriously for the past hour. Maren's mother made her way around, rein-troducing herself. Jesse and Jules said they remembered "the red-haired Laken" from her years teaching before she had met Jonny Malone. They all looked like they were discussing good times. Her mother finally came over to her.

"Now don't get smart about this. Donnie, I mean Dr. Don, is taking me to his clinic for the night. He said I could stay in his living quarters and he'd sleep in the clinic front. He said you'd been there and know all about it, that I'd like it. Blackhawk's place is fine, but I sure would like to try out that big, tile bathtub he has. Is that all right with everyone?"

"Mom. That's great. And it's completely true about his bathroom. It's awe-some. All four of us have spent a few nights there ourselves." Maren looked at Damien and he nodded emphatically. "Yes, do that. Dr. Don is wonder-ful. Go ahead. Just call if you need a ride back or anything, Mom. That's a good idea."

Laken stood there for a minute. "OK. But don't get your little match-making head going. I know that look of yours, my dear. Donnie and I go way back. I trust him. And thanks for bringing me here tonight. It was wonderful seeing all these people I used to know." She bent down and kissed Maren. She took Damien's hand. "Take good care of my special girl."

"You can count on that, ma'am—I mean Laken."

Laken motioned for Dr. Don's attention. He was shaking hands and embracing both Malak and Blackhawk. Maren knew what that was all about. Final plans. Wolf Moon, January 5th. Just a couple days away. She shivered.

"Damien. Could you sleep with me tonight? Just sleep. Come in after Grandpa goes to bed. I feel so lonely thinking about all that's going to happen in the next week. Everything. It's too much."

"You know it. I'll be there. I feel it too. A little human for me worrying about something that hasn't happened yet. You're rubbing off on me, my Starr."

They walked to the door holding hands. Blackhawk nodded at them. He was coming. It was going to be a long ride home.

Chapter Twenty One

Wolf Moon

Maren packed up the quart jar of mixture she finished making, wrapped it in several t-shirts, and put it into her duffel bag. *Hope this is potent enough.* She took a deep breath. Damien and Blackhawk had stood by her side while she cooked the herbal mixture—straight from her Grandmother Marina's ancient recipe. *Well, it worked fantastically before and I followed directions exactly.* She had even taken a mouthful before sealing the jar. Blackhawk had insisted. She certainly didn't need to start the change herself when all this was going on.

Maren took one more deep breath, squeezed the amulet around her neck, patted her bracelet, then started putting her neatly folded clothes in the bag, arranging everything so it wouldn't get wrinkled.

Dr. Don had shown her the "military roll," how she could fit even more things into a small space and keep them from wrinkling, by rolling each clothing item into a tube-shaped parcel. He had looked pleased that he could be helpful.

Maren knew he needed to feel useful and thanked him profusely. Now she wondered if she would see him before she left. *Maybe I'll stop at the clinic on the way out.* She left only a couple items out of the duffel bag—enough to get her through the next two days. She zipped the bag shut.

Sitting on her dresser was one small jar—the *other* mixture. Maren picked it up and held it to her chest. Blackhawk had not even let her touch the jar until it was sealed. He was afraid any contact with the potion could affect her. The W/H elixir. They would use it tonight. Blackhawk and Malak. They were leaving the human world sometime very early in the a.m.—one way or another.

Maren could *feel* the mixture through the jar. *So warm. Swirling around inside the jar...by itself?* She quickly pulled the jar from her chest and slammed it onto the dresser. She took one step back. Then she slowly leaned forward, her eyes fixed on the jar's contents. It *was* moving. Like someone was gently stirring it. *Wow. Grandpa's right about this stuff. This is the last thing I want to happen to me right now.*

It was January 4th. Blackhawk and Damien had divvied out assignments to everyone—even her mother, Laken. Right now the moon was waxing; very early morning the full moon called Wolf Moon would show itself. Maren was both excited and petrified. Damien had sat down with her and told her that Blackhawk might not survive the change. To top it off, he said he was more worried about Malak, that he could smell a sickness on his grandfather. Damien had mentioned cancer or something like that. He couldn't quite tell but knew it was worse than Blackhawk's problem. He was all quiet after that. Maren had to remind herself that Malak was Damien's family— his grandfather—Moon's father. The whole thing was unsettling.

Maren had finished dressing and brushing out her hair. Her mother had trimmed it for her but even she refused to color it. The silvery star of hair would have to stay for now. She found a small towel and picked the "WH" concoction off the table. Then she put it into a shoebox that was lying in the closet. *That's better. Don't want Damien getting near this stuff.*

She put the box back on her dresser and covered it with a sweatshirt. Then she grabbed her makeup and toothbrush and headed for the bathroom. She paused, then tossed the toothpaste into the garbage. She grabbed the little jar of herbs that Damien used instead.

Maren walked out into the living room where everyone was sitting. Her mother hung up the phone. Everyone was looking at her.

"Well. Donnie said everything is as set as it's going to be. He's bringing everything he can think of—medically—and I told him we have everything here under control. He said again, 'Don't forget the herbs and the branding iron.' I feel for him. He's both nervous and well ... sad. It's going to be hard on him, Blackhawk. Losing you." Laken turned her face. Maren knew she was fighting back tears.

Damien gave Maren a little nod and then went over to Laken. He put his arm around her. "You're so right, ma'am. It's going to be hard on all of us."

"I told you to call me Laken, you big handsome devil," Laken said, smiling as she wiped her eyes. She grabbed Damien's shoulder and squeezed it. "Thank you, sweetie."

"All right now, all of you. The circle of life. From an end always comes a beginning. From where you came, you will return. I know that means something different to everyone here. But to me—I'm either returning to the rest of my time here on earth as a wolf, or I'll be returning to the very earth from which we all originated. Maren. Damien. You know where I want my bones to lie. Next to Marina and Big Silver's. You know there won't be any funeral service here ... I don't believe in any expensive coffin that's just going to go back to the earth with me. Doc knows what to do. If I'm in my wolf form—and I don't make it—he and Damien are taking care of getting me into the ground. Quietly. Same goes for Malak. If all goes as planned, you will see us in our old wolf forms," Blackhawk said. He looked over at Damien, who nodded.

"Ok. Time to head to Malak's place. It's out there a ways. Will take half an hour with bad roads." Blackhawk looked at his watch. "Damien. The branding iron."

"Got the herbs, Grandpa," Maren blurted out before he could ask. She ran into her bedroom and patted her eyes dry without messing her eye makeup. *Ok. I can do this. For Grandpa. He wants to see me strong. He's depending on me … the future of the changelings? God. Ok. I'm good.*

Maren came out of her bedroom with the shoebox. The sweatshirt fell to the floor. Damien was there in the hallway, waiting for her. He had her coat and scarf. He took the box carefully out of her hands and put the coat and scarf over her shoulder. Maren watched him as he stared at the jar. His eyes started glowing. They were turning orange.

"Damien! Cover it up! It's really strong."

Maren's words snapped him out of the trance-like state he was entering. Blackhawk came around the corner with a towel and threw it over the box.

"Forgot to warn you about the herbs. Either of the two mixtures. Around any full moon, you want to stay away from the one that you don't want to happen. I should be carrying this box." Blackhawk took it out of Damien's arms. Damien bent down in slow motion and picked up the sweatshirt.

"Wow. Really felt that. Really felt that." He turned quickly away from Maren.

Oh, no. Oh, no. He wants to go. Maren put on her scarf and coat. She stood there, wringing her hands while she watched the rest dig out their coats, scarves, and gloves.

Maren finally headed out to the old station wagon. Everyone was taking so long and she was starting to sweat in the house. She froze by the car's passenger door. *This is too weird. Deja' vu. Everything the same as when we went to James' party. But not right.* She turned around and saw her mother, Damien, and Blackhawk huddled by the front door of the house. Laken didn't have her coat on. She was still in the doorway. *Something's wrong.* Maren walked slowly back to the house trying to rid herself of the ominous feeling that was overwhelming her.

"What's wrong?" Maren said, searching everyone's eyes, absolutely dreading the answer. Blackhawk went over to Laken and embraced her. He whispered something in her ear. Laken nodded while burying her head in Blackhawk's shoulder. Then he released her and headed for the car.

"Mom?" Maren moved close to her mother. "What's happening? Where's your coat?"

"I'm not going, honey. This is your thing. This is Jonny's side of the family. It's a special ceremony and I really don't fit in it. Maren. I've been through enough with your father. Some good. Some bad. This is your thing now." She kissed Maren on the cheek and then bent down and picked up a box covered with a towel. She handed it to Damien. "Everything's here, Damien. I wish you all the best and my love."

Damien smiled and tipped his head to her. "I'll be out at the car, Maren." He turned and left them standing alone on the porch.

"Mom. It's OK. I understand how you feel. And don't you worry about me. Not about this. Not anymore." She hugged her mother. "I'll be fine. No matter what happens. I'm pretty much ready for anything at this point." She smiled and waited until her mother could smile back. Then she turned and headed for the station wagon.

Damien had the car running and was drumming his fingers on the steering wheel. Blackhawk was in the back seat, his head tipped down, most likely meditating. Maren slid in next to Damien.

"OK?" he said, as he put the car in gear.

"Yup. I'm good. This is right, you know. It's better for her. I'm not sure how she got pulled into this anyway." Maren was quiet a moment and then added, "It must have been me. I didn't even realize it." Damien took her hand and squeezed it.

The drive out to Malak's was long and silent. Maren thought about Dr. Don. He was probably out there already getting things ready. *I hope he'll be OK with Mom not there. Maybe he'll even be relieved. He's got enough to worry about.*

Maren looked again at Damien's face. He was distant. Every once in a while, he patted her leg. But Maren knew something was really eating at him. *He wants to change. Please don't let me lose him.* She turned to look at Blackhawk in the backseat. He was smiling, his eyes shut.

Maren looked past Blackhawk to the snow covered road behind them. *How different things can be in just a very short time. Last time we were all riding in this very car to a party. Damien laughing, me laughing. I'm losing Grandpa. Am I losing Damien?* Maren felt herself go cold inside. Her heart felt like steel. She doubted that she could squeeze one tear out. *Hmmpf. So this is what bitterness is … .*

Malak James' place was lit up with a large lantern by the entrance. It was another log cabin but not anywhere near as nice as Blackhawk's. There were two cars there. One was Dr. Don's. The other looked familiar. *Of course. It's Jules. Would Jesse be there too?* Maren's heart pounded. She squeezed her hands together. Blackhawk got out and hurried toward the house.

"Can you wait a sec? I need to talk to you," Maren said, just as Damien threw open his door.

"Sure." He pulled the door shut and turned sheepishly to Maren.

"Oh my god, Damien. Your eyes are orange. You're going to do it. Aren't you. You're going to go off with them and leave me." Maren's voice was icy.

Damien looked down. He took both her hands and kissed them. "I'm so sorry. I just can't *not*. I have to." He got out of the car and headed to the cabin.

Maren sat silently in the car. She stared straight ahead. She gritted her teeth. Then she got out slowly and walked up to the door, which was left partially open.

"Maren. Come in. Doc's been looking for you." Malak said. He was sitting at a table with his son, Jules and brother, Jesse. They were holding hands around the table. It looked like some kind of ceremony.

Dr. Don walked over to Maren. "Let's go into the kitchen. I have to talk about something important." He took Maren's hand. She looked over her shoulder to see Damien staring after her, a sad, hopeless look on his face. He turned back to Blackhawk. It looked like they were arguing.

"I suspect by that look that you know. It's my fault. Look at me. It's my fault. I can't let those two old men go back out into the wilderness at this time of year and fend for themselves. Your Pops is stubborn. And a little irritated with me right now. I talked Damien into going with them. He didn't want to leave you. But you'll be at school. Think about it. He knows when you'll be back. He'll be here. I'd promise you that on my life." Dr. Don paused a moment. "Sometimes the right decisions are the hardest."

Maren tensed up. She wanted to slap Dr. Don. "Well then there's nothing left to say." She turned and walked back out into the living room. She sat in a chair and stared at her hands. *Sometimes the right decisions are the hardest ... who said that? Dad. My father always said that. Oh my god, Jonny Malone said that all the time!*

Jesse and Jules got up from the table. They disappeared outside and came back with the herbs and branding iron. Malak added more wood to the fireplace. He had replaced his deerskin clothes with an old terrycloth bath-robe. Blackhawk had done the same. They stood in front of the fireplace with a bound chunk of some kind of pine needles. Malak lit it then blew out the flames. They waved the wand of smoking needles around them while they chanted something in another language.

Maren felt a hand on her arm. It was Jules. He pulled her gently down into a kitchen chair. "I'm sorry Maren. I know what you're going through. I'm losing my father. You're losing your grandfather. But believe me when I say this, your man there—Damien—my brother—he's a leader. If he said he'll be here for you when you come home, he will be."

"Thank you, Jules. I have to believe. It's all I have."

"Good girl." He kissed her on the top of the head. "Starr."

Dr. Don had his medical bag out in the living room. He gave each man some kind of shot. Then Blackhawk and Malak went into the one bedroom in the little cabin and shut the door. Dr. Don knelt on the floor with his eyes closed. He was praying—in the same language she had heard by the fireplace.

"That's old, original Ojibwe," Jules whispered in her ear. "Not many of us know it anymore. I don't. Jesse remembers some of it. Kinda sad. One of the things I plan on doing. Learning more about my people. Who I came from. Oops. Looks like you've got company." Jules squeezed her hand and walked away. Damien stood right in front of her.

"Maren. Starr. I love you. Don't ever forget that. I will see you soon. Three moons after this one, Maren. Three moons." Then he turned and walked through the living room past Dr. Don. He tapped him on the shoulder and then went into the bedroom and closed the door behind him.

Maren stood up. She was motionless. Everything she had felt in the last month seemed like it never happened. She felt empty inside. Not sad, not happy. Nothing.

"Ok. Maren, Jesse, Jules." It was Dr. Don's voice. "We are all here to wish our loved ones a safe journey to their other side. I will be in the room with them. I am here to ... take action if something goes wrong. I have both Blackhawk's and Malak's full permission and trust in this. Damien will be traveling with them. For a short while. When I come back out, I want everyone to stay seated. Remember. They will be changeling wolves. Not truly a wild wolf, but it will be startling to them. It's been many, many years for the old ones."

Everyone was quiet. Dr. Don opened the door, paused, then turned toward Maren. He shut his eyes and nodded. Then he picked up his medical bag and started to close the door behind him.

Maren jumped from her spot and in three leaps landed by the bedroom door. She just managed to grab the edge of the door and Dr. Don's hand on the doorknob.

"Now that was fast, Maren," Dr. Don said.

"I want to be in there. I *have* to be in there," Maren said, holding Dr. Don's hand so he couldn't pull the door closed.

Dr. Don looked at her for several moments. Then he turned to the three men in the room. "Any objections?"

"I'm glad." Damien spoke first. He was sitting cross-legged on the floor next to his grandfather Malak. There were some old blankets and quilts spread around on the wood floor. Blackhawk was lying back on the one small bed in the room. He didn't look like he felt very well.

"Can't see why not," Blackhawk said, holding a wet cloth next to his face. "And don't get alarmed, my girl. Had a reaction to the antibiotic shot Doc there insisted on giving us old guys." He gave Dr. Don a stern, disapproving glance.

Dr. Don glanced back and replied in the same stern tone. "They *needed* it."

"Whatever she wants," Malak said. Damien was helping him get comfortable and had rolled up his sleeve. "Guess we're going to get the branding out of the way first. Don't think Doc wants to mess with some cranky, old wolves later." He looked over at Blackhawk and chuckled.

"Ok then," Dr. Don said as Maren pushed by him and went to Damien's side.

"I'm so glad you're here, Maren. You need to see. And know." Damien put his arms around her and whispered in her ear. "Remember Wendigo? It's out there. It's OK. I love you."

Maren pulled back, ready to ask him what he meant. Instead she whispered back, "I love you too. No matter what."

"I can definitely use your help, Maren," Dr. Don interrupted. "Say your goodbyes because I need you over here. I will feel more comfortable with you by me. Don't know how the old guys will react. If they'll be able to tell you're one of them. I don't have that much experience with this."

Dr. Don turned to the door. "Jesse. Jules. Maren's going to be in here. Jules, can you put the iron in the fire and hand me those herbs? Don't get them close to your Uncle Jesse. He should be in the kitchen drinking the same stuff I gave Maren earlier. Don't need more than three wolves showing up here today."

Maren could just make out a "No problem" coming from the other room. Dr. Don's hand reached out and grasped the jar of swirling herbs from Jules' hands. He shut the door.

Maren released herself from Damien's arms and backed up. She felt the hair on her neck and arms stand up. She looked over at Damien. His eyes were dark orange and she could see some saliva at the corner of his mouth. He looked down at the floor. *Wendigo? What did he mean? It's just a scary story that everyone seems to use for anything that goes wrong. Just an old nightmare to me … .*

"Better do that branding now," Damien said, taking deep breaths. "I don't want to be near it. Having a hard enough time." He focused his eyes on something on the floor.

"Yeah," Malak said. "Damien's not going to even need the herbs."

Maren went to Dr. Don's side. He nodded. Maren opened the door just a couple inches. "We need the iron. Now," she said through the crack.

A couple seconds later she pulled the glowing iron through the door and closed and it. Dr. Don took it from her and went straight to the bed. He pulled back Blackhawk's robe and plunged the end of the iron against his thigh. Blackhawk held back a shriek by biting on the pillow. Dr. Don then went directly to Malak and pushed the slowly cooling end against his upper arm. Malak barely flinched. The smell of burning flesh permeated the room. Damien bolted to the other side of the room, trying to get as far away as possible. Maren grabbed the iron, opened the bedroom door, and slid it out. Then she picked up the jar of herbs sitting on the floor.

"Whoa. Better let me handle that." Dr. Don jerked the jar from her hands. He poured two small glasses full and gave them to Malak and Blackhawk. They downed them like they were shots of liquor. "OK. It's done," Dr. Don said. He turned the cover on the jar tightly and held it out the door. Someone—probably Jules—grabbed it. The door shut and Dr. Don locked it.

Maren leaned against the bedroom door. She slid down into a sitting position and slapped at her face with both hands.

"Are you OK?" Dr. Don grabbed his medical bag. "I do have the other herb here. You might want to take a shot."

"I think I'll do that," Maren said. She dug into the bag and found the jar. She slugged down two swallows of the bitter tasting concoction, and closed her eyes. *Whew. Better. Now I know. I felt it. I felt the feeling of wanting to change. The first time, ever. Now I know, Damien. Now I know … .*

"I'm good, Dr. Don." She stood erect and smoothed her hair. She even redid her ponytail to prove it.

Dr. Don took a deep breath. "It's not going to take long now. I thought Damien would be first, but he's holding back. I think he's worried about the elders. He's not going to be able to stop it soon. He'll go into a coma-type state that as I recall, he'll have no control over. This part now, when the change just starts coming on—you can still hold back a little."

Boy, do I know that. Don't I ever.

"OK. What should we be doing now? Anything?" Maren asked. Damien was crouched on the floor by the wall, his face turned away from hers. *He doesn't want me to see his eyes. I can tell. He's going to go out any minute.*

"Well, Blackhawk and Malak are out." Dr. Don walked over to each of them and listened with his stethoscope. He paused at Malak's side. "Skipping a bit." He fiddled with the scope, obviously worried.

Maren had other concerns. Damien had crawled onto a blanket not far from Malak and was curled up in a fetal position. Every so often he would stretch out in a spasm.

"Can he feel that?" Maren flinched every time Damien's body twitched and jerked.

"I don't think so. At least they don't remember a bit of it. Try to relax, Maren. This part takes several hours. You don't want to watch every move."

No I do not … .

"OK, Dr. Don. I'm just leaning against the door here and think I'll shut my eyes. I just got really tired all of a sudden."

Maren opened her eyes. She was sitting on the floor. *What was that? I just drifted off.* She sat up straight, squeezing her stiff neck.

"Shhh," Dr. Don said as he sat down next to her. "Don't want to startle you. You were out for about twenty minutes. I knew the herbs might make you drowsy. Everything's OK but, well. You might want to see this."

Maren rubbed her eyes. Her first thought was Damien. He was still on the floor near his grandfather, Malak. Except now he was nude. Dr. Don must have removed his clothes. Both Malak and Blackhawk had their old robes lying on top of them. They weren't wearing them.

Maren turned to Dr. Don. "Was that for my benefit? Because it doesn't matter. I'm OK with seeing a naked old man and well—Damien, of course."

"I know. I couldn't help it. Just part of my manners, I guess." Dr. Don blushed. "And mainly out of respect for the elders here."

Maren took his hand. "You know, you're a really nice man, Dr. Don. I'm glad Mom has a friend like you here. She was worried about not coming. Mainly about you. All the responsibility you take on. I know she was torn about coming."

Dr. Don patted Maren's hand. "I think it's about time you just call me Don. I told your mother not to come. I knew it would be real hard on her because of Jonny. Just thought it best."

"You were absolutely right, Dr..... , Don, I mean. I thought ... ." Maren jumped. She heard two popping sounds. "What was *that*?"

"You're going to hear a lot of that. And worse. That noise was bones shifting in joints. Some shortening, some lengthening. It's amazing, actually. Look at Damien's hip. See how it's shrinking back making a much narrower pelvis? Their bone is unbelievable. The cells can compress or expand. That's the science part. Blackhawk actually let me look at some of his cells under a microscope. They—and you—are a miracle of nature. Don't ever forget that."

Maren watched Damien, who was nearest to her in the room. The hair on his body was growing and thickening. She couldn't see his face; it was buried in the blanket, but furry silver hair was pushing out down his neck and across his narrowing shoulders. The rest was black. She could still see some of his human head hair. Some seemed to be connected to what was growing out; the rest lay in chunks on the floor.

Pop! Craaack … . Maren shifted her attention to Blackhawk lying on the bed. He was twisting around, his robe now lying on the floor. Maren covered her mouth with her hand. *Oh my god. He looks freaky, scary actually.* Blackhawk no longer looked like the grandfather she loved so dearly. He was a being in transition—another life form.

His thighs had shortened immensely and were now a mass of different tendons pulling and stretching. His human knees had disappeared and his calves were half the size. The ankle of the foot was huge and the main portion of the foot itself had grown long into the ankle. It was now an animal's hock. The ball of the foot had become the paw of a wolf, the bottom calluses becoming the pads he would walk on. The toes were narrowing and the nails were now huge claws. *Wow. I get it. We aren't really that different at all. Not at all.*

"Don. It's beautiful. It's actually beautiful." Maren stood up to see better.

"You're right, my girl. Look at the face and the, ahhh, genitalia. That's amazing."

Maren cocked her head and raised her eyebrows. "OK, Dr. Don. If you insist." Her sarcastic smile disappeared as she saw Blackhawk's penis being pulled into his belly area, the skin around it stretching over it to form the pocket-sheath that all canines had. "Wow," was all she could manage to say.

Maren turned her attention to Blackhawk's face. The nose portion was elongating and pulling back into a grotesque grin that exposed all his teeth. His forehead had flattened back and his ears seemed to move higher. Maren focused closer and saw that the jaw was stretching out and the back of his head was moving up, bringing the ears with it. Hair was growing out everywhere. Some was grayish-white, an undercoat, and another layer was silkier, dark hair. He was dark brown mixed with gray. Blackhawk's entire wolf body was much smaller than Moonbaby ever was. "Hawk" was smaller built, but even as a wolf, had long legs and a sinewy musculature.

Maren studied the transformation barely taking time for a breath. Damien was now almost completely "Moonbaby." She no longer worried about him. He was young and strong. After all, he was a wolf first. And what a wolf he was. He was bigger than the two older ones combined. But then Malak—Damien's grandfather, Maren reminded herself, didn't seem that good. His whole process seemed erratic, just not smooth. His breathing was slower and uneven.

Dr. Don noticed too. He grabbed his medical bag and knelt on the floor next to Malak. He moved his stethoscope to several spots on Malak's chest. He yanked it out of his ears and threw it down into the bag.

"What's wrong, Dr. Don? You're frightening me." Maren squatted down next to him and followed his eyes to Malak. "His legs don't look completely right. They don't look strong."

"I know, Maren. His heart isn't good either. Right now I'm trying to decide what to do. He did tell me to ahhh … put him down if it didn't go right. Damn it! All old Malak James ever wanted was to turn back for good. Damn. All because of Jules. He would have changed long ago. All because of Jules."

"Dr. Don. This doesn't sound like you. I know you're upset. Even I can't blame Jules anymore. He has become a better person. Don't you think? And he's here. He's with us all and he's not even a changeling. It takes a strong person like you to do that." Maren put her arm around Dr. Don's shoulder. "What would Jules want for his father? What would Jesse want for his brother?"

Dr. Don's back stiffened. "To let him have his wish. To become a wolf."

Maren nodded and squeezed his shoulder. "What is Malak's wolf name? I didn't remember to ask Jesse or Grandpa."

"Silver Moon. I heard he looked a lot like Big Silver—Sylvester, but a little less black," Dr. Don said, as he dug purposely into the pockets of his medical bag. He pulled out two bottles and syringes. "We're going to keep him alive, Maren. He's going to see himself as a wolf. Even if just for a moment. Help me here, would you? Hold his leg."

Maren leaned over and held Silver Moon's front leg. It felt squishy as if the muscles weren't attached completely. She felt him move—just a little. *Please, oh please don't die yet. Moonbaby will be so sad. Grandpa—Hawk, too.*

"OK. First one is for his heart. He wouldn't make it with just this other one. Probably give him an instant heart attack. The other one is going to kick this process into full gear. It's a tincture of those wolf herbs. I've never used it before. Your father had me keep it. Said you never know. Boy, was he right."

Dr. Don carefully injected the heart medicine into a small vein on Malak's wolf leg. He took a deep breath. "OK, Maren. This next one is critical. I have one more if he goes into cardiac arrest. We ready?"

"Go for it, Doc." Maren held the limp wolf leg with one hand. She stroked his furry face with her other.

"He may jerk a little. Won't necessarily mean something bad." Dr. Don filled the second syringe from the wolf tincture bottle and then got another syringe out of his bag. "Epinephrine. Jump starter. Just in case." He slowly injected the herbs into Malak's vein. Malak's wolfish head bounced up and down on the floor.

Maren pulled a quilt on the floor toward her and tucked it under his head. Dr. Don got out his stethoscope and listened several times as Malak's frail body continued to thrash. "OK. He seems good. Let's give him some room."

Maren and Dr. Don stood up and backed away from Malak's body. He was changing and changing fast. Silver hair pushed its way out. His wolf face fully formed. Even his leg muscles pulsated as more blood flowed through them. He opened and closed his mouth. His eyes opened.

"Oh my god. Look, Don. He's waking up." Maren grabbed Dr. Don's shirt.

"Welcome, Silver Moon," Dr. Don said.

Just then a low growl resonated from the side of the room. Maren jumped. *I know that growl. Moonbaby.* She turned toward him and crouched down on the floor.

"Moonbaby. It's OK. It's me." *Oh my god, he's bigger yet. How is this possible?* Moonbaby hiked himself off the floor onto all four feet. He shook his entire body. Pieces of his longer human hair went flying everywhere. His new wolf coat was thick and shiny. A heavy matt of under hair was a grayish-black color. His coal black outer coat shone as if it had been oiled. The same shining silver streak he had in his human hair now ran down the back of his head and around his neck in a lion-like mane.

He was spellbinding—the most beautiful wolf she had ever seen. Maren whispered hoarsely, "Moonbaby." But he wasn't paying a bit of attention to her. His vivid yellow eyes were fixed on Silver Moon.

"Something's wrong, Don." Maren followed Moonbaby's focus to Silver Moon. He was flailing weakly on the floor.

"Oh, no. Oh, no," Maren gasped. Silver Moon had managed to get the front half of his body into a weak, sitting position. His back legs, although they looked pretty normal, didn't seem to be working right. He was totally silver-gray with just some black on his muzzle and lower legs. *God, I bet he was something when he was young. I bet he was as beautiful and strong as Moonbaby.*

She heard a second noise. This time it was a half growl, half bark. It was Hawk. He was stretched out on the bed, his totally formed wolf head lay on his front paws—he was hanging over the bed to look at Silver Moon on the floor. *He's the smallest of all of them. But he doesn't look sick ... or weak as Silver Moon. Oh please let this work out OK ... .*

"Maren. I think Silver Moon is ahhh ... I think he doesn't have the use of his back legs." Dr. Don knelt down and dug frantically in his medical bag.

Maren put her hand on her forehead and smoothed her hair back. It was obvious that Silver Moon had little strength. He turned his head every which way, straining his neck to do it; he was trying to look at himself. His tongue hung out and he panted heavily.

Moonbaby made a whimpering sound. He walked right past Maren and over to Silver Moon. They touched noses. Then Silver Moon fell down onto the floor. He struggled to pull his upper body back up, but collapsed again.

"Don. Help me get this mirror off the wall." Maren had walked over to an old chest of drawers against the wall. A medium sized, wood-framed mirror hung above it. Dr. Don had a puzzled look on his face. It broke into a look of relief. "Yes, yes," he said.

They got the mirror down and carried it over to Silver Moon, placing one side on the floor. They fiddled around with it trying to get the angle perfect for the wolf.

Moonbaby lifted his head into the air and howled. Then Hawk did the same. Silver Moon looked at his wolf grandson and turned his head to see his old buddy Hawk, still on the bed above him. His tail wagged weakly. Then he gave it everything he had, making strange guttural sounds that made Maren cringe—but he did it. He had pushed his front legs up and was in a half-sitting position, while his back legs and haunches lay in a dormant mass of silver fur.

Silver Moon turned to face the mirror directly. Maren watched his eyes as they scoured the image in the mirror. Moonbaby lay down on the floor, his head on his paws, and watched Silver Moon. Hawk, on the bed, did the same, although he kept whimpering. Then Silver Moon fell flat to the floor. He lifted his head and made a bark sound—more like a dog, but yet not at all. His tail thumped a couple times against the wood floor. He laid his head on the floor and stretched out his front legs. He inhaled and then exhaled, long and peacefully. Maren and Dr. Don moved the mirror aside and continued to kneel where they were. Silver Moon shut his eyes. All was still.

Moonbaby leapt to his feet and slowly walked over to the stilled body of Silver Moon. He looked up at Hawk on the bed, who was now struggling to get his body off over the edge, unable to stand on the soft mattress. Moonbaby tipped his nose to the ceiling and began a repetition of long, mournful howls. Maren shut her eyes. They were bone chilling howls that cried sadness and tragedy only a wolf could feel—or a changeling. Maren leaned forward over her knees, her face in her hands. Her tears dripped against her palms. Dr. Don placed his hand gently on her back.

A loud, pummeling sound on the door made Maren lift her face and wipe away her tears.

"What's happening in there? I know that howl! It's a death howl. God, do I know that howl. Open the door!" Maren could barely recognize Jules's voice. The pounding started again. "Open this goddamn door! God. Jess is out here … he's crying, man. It's been hours out here. Tell me what's going on, dammit!"

Maren beat Dr. Don to the door.

"Jules. Jules. Please. Give us a minute. We're coming out. Please, Jules. Please just sit down. We're coming out." Maren used the calmest, kindest voice she could muster.

"Good job, Maren. You're right. You're the leader here … with these guys." Dr. Don nodded around to the wolves in the room. Hawk was now lying on the floor next to the body of Silver Moon. Moonbaby was standing guard, it seemed.

Maren blinked. The sound of Dr. Don's words sounded preposterous, but it was true. She was Starr. It was time to be the changeling queen Malak James had told her she was. *Malak … Silver Moon. He's gone. So glad he made the change … so glad.*

"OK. Don? Would you go out first and talk to Jules and Jesse? I think you should tell them about Malak. You've known them way longer than I have, and you have their complete trust and respect. Would that be all right with you?"

"Yes, sure. Specially Jess. We go way back. He's taken me home way too many drunken nights … yes. I would like to. Thank you, Maren."

"Sure, Don. I'm going to sit here a minute. Until I see that Moonbaby and Hawk are ready to leave. Then I'll knock on the door so you can open the outside door. I don't want anyone getting claustrophobic. I'm sure they'll be ready to bolt when the time comes."

"You're right, Maren. Absolutely. That's what I'd do." Dr. Don smiled. "How did you know that?"

"I can feel it."

Dr. Don gathered his medical bag and whatever was left lying on the floor from the whole ordeal. He wrapped the bottle of W/H tincture carefully in paper and picked up empty glasses. *He's trying to make the bedroom look normal again … as normal as it can be with three wolves in it—one of them lifeless.* Maren shut the door behind him.

Moonbaby sat on the floor next to Hawk, who was lying next to Silver Moon on the floor.

"Moonbaby. Can you let me know when you and Hawk are ready to go? We'll take care of Silver Moon. I know his brother and son will take real good care of him. I don't know how much Grandpa … I mean Hawk, can understand me in his wolf form. I can see how sad you both are. I'm really sorry. Dr. Don did everything he could. I'm sure you both know that?"

Hawk slowly got to his feet when Maren said "Dr. Don." His head hung down over Silver Moon. He made a deep noise in his throat. Moonbaby did the same. Then Hawk turned and looked Maren directly in the eye. It was the first time since he changed.

"OK," Maren said. She walked to the door and knocked on it. Dr. Don opened it from the living room. "I think they're ready. Is everything OK out there?"

"The best it can be right now. Jesse and Jules are sitting on the sofa. The wolf-guys can linger or head straight out. It's all up to them. Give me one minute and I'll prop open the front door. A little brisk out there."

Maren smiled quickly at Dr. Don and shut the door. She leaned against it with her eyes shut. *God, I'd love to hug my Moonbaby. Kiss him. Love him. But all this happened. So sad. So sad.*

Maren heard the dulled sound of wolf claws tapping against the wood floor, then a thud. A large, warm body collapsed onto her feet. It was Moonbaby.

She slid down with her back against the door, leaned forward and buried her face in Moonbaby's thick neck ruff. She wrapped her arms around him.

"Moonbaby. I love you. Don't forget. Three moons. Three moons."

Moonbaby let her hold him for a few minutes then he licked her face. He turned his head to Hawk, then walked to the door. Hawk followed. Maren stood up, took a deep breath, and opened the door. "We're coming out."

Maren opened the door just enough to peek through. Moonbaby squeezed past her and pushed the door all the way open. He charged out with Hawk right behind him. They went to the middle of the living room and stood. Maren walked out slowly looking for Jules and Jesse. They were on the sofa.

"I'm so sorry. I really am. But Malak—Silver Moon—saw himself as a wolf. He was happy when he died. He went very peacefully." Maren did everything she could to keep her composure and be strong for the two men that had just lost their father and brother.

"Thank you, Maren. That's so good to hear. So good." Jesse stood up. "And look at these two. Wow," he added. Jules said nothing. Maren could see that he was too upset to talk.

"It's OK, Jules. I mean it. He was happy," Maren said. Jules nodded and gave her a small smile. He took a pack of cigarettes off a nearby table and lit one.

"Thanks, Maren. Thank you for everything you did. Both you and Doc."

Dr. Don was standing by the front door shivering, but waiting patiently. Hawk walked ahead of Moonbaby. He was a gray and dark brown color with black streaks around the neck. Smaller and slighter than Moonbaby, but definitely ominous looking. More wildness. More natural wolf. He sniffed the air around him. He took a couple steps, glancing side to side, hunched down in a half crouching position. He stopped by the front door and shook his body.

He's fluffing up his hair. To stay warm. That's what I'd do. I know it. I just feel it.

Jules threw his cigarette on the wood floor and smashed it out with his boot. He looked at both wolves but his eyes fixed on Moonbaby. *He sees Moonbaby's feet.* It was the paws—they were bloody—huge claws with sawed off ends left over from his human trimmed fingernails.

Maren licked her lips. They were completely dry. "Goodbye, Grandpa. Take good care of him, Moonbaby. I love you both."

"Hawk needs to get out of this confined area," Jesse said. He patted Jules's arm.

The cold January air gusted through the cabin. *Ok. Jesse knows. He's the only other human changeling here ... except me. I feel it too. His urgency.*

Hawk took a last look at Jesse and Jules, his ears standing straight up. Then he turned his head to Maren and made a low growling noise in the back of his throat. Maren met the now copper-yellow eyes of her wolf-grandfather with her own. *They told me I'm the queen. Of the changelings. I can't look down. I'm alpha.*

Maren held her gaze. Her knees started to shake. Hawk made another soft rumble in the back of his throat. Then he turned and bounded out the door. Moonbaby gave one short howl, his nose in the air, then shot out after Hawk.

Everyone in the cabin ran to the door. Moonbaby had easily caught up with Hawk. They stopped and tussled in the snow and were off again; Moonbaby running circles around the old wolf. Old Hawk just kept trotting on through the snow, his head in the air, oblivious to the antics of the younger Moonbaby. They disappeared into the tree line.

It was quiet for several minutes.

"I assume, Doc, Maren, we can go in and see my father. He looks OK and everything? Would like to pay my respects," Jules said, wringing his hands in front of him.

"Absolutely," Maren said.

"He looks good." Dr. Don added. "Would have been a damn good-looking wolf with that silver coat and black-tipped tail and feet. And he saw himself. Before he passed. Damn ... he did see himself." Dr. Don pulled a handkerchief out of his pocket and wiped the tears off his face.

"That's so good, Doc. Thanks again," Jules said. He started for the door.

"Would you mind if I joined you, Jules?" I would like to see Malak with you. I would like to pay our respects together. If you don't mind," Jesse said.

"Yes, Yes. Thanks, Uncle Jess." Jules face looked relieved. *God, he looks like he never wants to see a dead wolf again in his life. But this is his father. Damien's family.* Jesse wrapped his arm around Jules' shoulder as they walked into the bedroom and closed the door.

Maren touched Dr. Don's arm. "What do they do with his body in this weather? Frozen ground. Just wondering." She couldn't bear that Old Malak's body, now Silver Moon, would be lying in a pile of whatever in some obscure place.

"We have a nice wooden—well, coffin for him. Malak made it himself a long time ago. I assume it was for his son, Sylvester. It is a changeling's coffin. Special materials and wood. For a large wolf." Dr. Don paused.

"I told him about Silver. That we buried him next to his mother in the cemetery here. I think he was happy about that. He told me about the box today. We'll lay him there and lock everything up in the shed. Then we'll take care of everything in the spring. Already talked to Jesse about it. Don't worry, Maren."

"Thanks, Don." Maren looked around the little cabin. Everything had changed again in one day. She wanted to leave, but was afraid to go home. Back to Blackhawks' place—no, hers and Damien's. But no Damien. No Grandpa. Only, she had promised and her mother was there waiting to hear everything. She still had to help her mother get situated there—before she left. *School. Hard to even think about now. But have to. Have to make plans for the future. Figure things out.*

Maren felt a lump in her throat. It wouldn't go away no matter how much she swallowed.

"Don. Could you follow me back to Grandpa's place? It's almost noon. I just need to sleep for a while. I was wondering if you could explain everything to Mom? I'm just too tired. And I'm sure I would be way too emotional."

"No problem. I'd love to help. You did so much today. It's all good. Better than I thought it would turn out. I'll talk to Laken. You do need some rest."

"Thank you, Don," Maren said, relieved. She found a sheet of paper and pen and wrote a quick note. "I'm leaving this for Jules and Jesse. I don't want to bother them right now. They need their time alone with Malak."

"That's perfectly fine. Go ahead and start the car. I'll be out in a minute and follow you home."

Maren started the old station wagon and cranked up the heat. She squeezed her eyes shut against the bright sun and sat there shivering, waiting for the heater to actually blow warm air.

So much has changed. Grandpa's gone. Probably for good. I won't even know when he dies. Damien—Moonbaby. I miss them both. Who is he for sure? Which one? Changelings. I'm one of them. I'm definitely one of them.

Maren heard Dr. Don start up his truck. She opened her eyes and turned to take one last glance. The outside light was still on although it was the middle of the day. It looked strange. It was the only thing that hadn't changed since they had all come the previous evening. Her eyes searched the fading tree line. Nothing. She leaned back hard on the seat and exhaled. Then she put the car in gear and headed home.

Chapter Twenty Two

Three Moons

Maren threw another log on the fire. She kept forgetting that her mother had lived on the White Earth rez before—that she knew how to start a wood fire, drive in the snow, and live in the wilderness. It was a whole other part of her mother that she hadn't paid attention to.

"Honey, I told you to stretch out on the sofa. I can take care of this."

"Sorry, Mom. It's still hard for me to picture you doing this before. Just a little older than me and living here and teaching school. A red-haired Irish girl in the middle of all those Indians." Maren giggled at the thought of it.

"I was pretty independent. And I loved Native American culture." Laken sat down and patted a spot on the sofa for Maren. "I didn't get to tell you why I decided to come back up here and live for a while."

Maren sat down next to her mother.

"You know? With everything that's been going on I didn't even have time to think about it. But how *did* you retire in the middle of the year? I can't see you leaving all your students like that. I remember I felt they were more important than me sometimes." Maren gave her mother a bump with her elbow.

"Honey. Sometimes it was just my escape. I didn't really know how to deal with your 'specialness.' As much as I loved Jonny ... ." Laken paused. "Your father just wasn't a lot of help in that area. Anyway, I formally retired right after you left in June to come up here. I did some subbing until Christmas. And that's that."

"Wow, Mom. I never thought you would leave teaching."

"It just ran its course. I loved it but now glad to be done. This is a new adventure for me. And that's what I hope this new life will bring you."

"But the house? All our stuff?" Maren paused for a moment before continuing. "Actually, there is nothing there that means more to me than what is here. It seems like a dream—my old life. High school. Always wanting to have surgery on these." Maren held her shirt out and shook it. "Now it's just who I am, period. So done with feeling like a carnival sideshow."

"Oh, Maren. I *am* so sorry about how I handled that. It was ..."

Maren interrupted. "Mom. Quit apologizing. I'm totally over it. Done with it. I want to move on. With Damien. I love him, Mom. I'm so worried about him. He's out there watching over Grandpa. I'm glad he's there for Grandpa, don't get me wrong. But I want him to come back. What if he doesn't? What if he decides to stay wolf?"

"What if *you* decide to stay human? You have to know he's worried about the same things, don't you? You have plenty of time to figure that all out. Don't rush anything. Go to school. Come back. He'll be here. I could see that he loves you."

"That all makes great sense, Mom, but horrible to try and do. I've got a continuous knot in my stomach and feel sick. I'm more worried about losing Damien than going into the change and that's just nuts."

"It's all on you, my girl. It's huge. I know. You'll work it out. Blackhawk told me exactly that. And I believe him with all my heart."

Maren laid her head against her mother's shoulder. They both watched the flames flicker softly and then roar. Flicker and roar.

Maren sat up in her bed. It was so quiet. No Damien next door to play some irritating little prank. No Grandpa to catch watching her and then smile.

Her mother took over Blackhawk's room. She insisted on the feather mattress, but Maren knew her real motive was to keep her and Damien's rooms just as they were—for when they both came back. Meanwhile, her mother insisted on the responsibility of copying some of the old changeling manuscripts. She had real pens with nibs and ink bottles and some beautiful acid free paper. It was a perfect job for her and the only person left other than Damien that Maren trusted with such things.

Maren got out of bed and stared at her duffel bag and small suitcase. The same empty, hollow feeling hung over her. She opened the suitcase for the fourth time just to see again that the jar of herbs was wrapped and secured. She slammed it shut for the fourth time. She brushed out her hair and checked her reflection in the mirror. The silver streaks in her hair ran down both sides of her face. Damien had made her promise to keep it just the way it was.

She turned sideways and pulled her long, flannel over-shirt back. She had carefully done her wraps, making sure the second set of breasts weren't obvious. She was pretty handy with the wraps now. She could do both sets in a few minutes. She was thinking about school—how she'd have to hide this all again. *Oh, well. It would be worth it all. Worth it all to start on her degree and come back to the rez. Maybe spend the summer running in the woods with Moonbaby … .*

Maren leaned in closer to the mirror. *My face has changed. My nose is longer—just a little and my cheekbones more prominent. My eyes! They really have changed color. More copper-yellow. No wonder Grandpa could finally leave—he knew. He just knew.* Maren stared at her reflection.

"Maren. Come here! Donnie's here to see you off."

Maren picked up her suitcase and duffel and walked out into the living room. She dropped them on the floor and ran to Dr. Don, throwing her arms around him.

"I'm so glad you came. I didn't get to say goodbye. I was thinking about stopping at the clinic on the way out."

"No need to do that. I'm here, Maren. It will be OK. I just know it. I do."

"I know, Dr. Don. I know." Maren pulled back and wiped her eyes. She looked directly at Dr. Don.

"I'm coming back right before the Flower Moon on May 4th. I'll be here several days before and I'm making the change. Do you hear me? I'm going to do it. If Damien isn't here, I'll find him myself. I hope you will be here to help me. But no matter what, I'm doing it."

Dr. Don stood silently for a moment while he looked at Maren. His eyes searched her face. He took her hand in his and patted it.

"I was waiting for Starr. And she showed herself at Malak's. Blackhawk told me it was done. I wasn't sure. But darn that old man, anyway. He always knew. He always had the faith. I'll be here for you, Maren. Whatever you need. Don't forget that." He kissed her hand and let it drop.

Maren smiled and glanced at her mother. Laken had her hand over her mouth. Her eyes were watering.

"Will they be OK, Dr. Don?" Maren said. "I know Damien—Moonbaby, will watch over Grandpa, but will they be OK?"

"Yes. Jules and Jesse have been putting meat out for them. They've been taking it. As long as they need it, it will be there. Don't underestimate those two, Maren. Moonbaby and Hawk are tough."

"I know, I know. Just good to hear that." Maren picked up her things and walked toward the door. Laken squeezed around her, beating her to the door.

"Here, honey. Take this." She handed Maren a credit card. "Get yourself some clothes and whatever you need. Remember, you're going to Minneapolis."

Maren looked at the card like it was some foreign object, then put it in her back pocket.

"I suppose you're right, Mom. It's a little different up here. Thanks." She hugged her mother then turned to the door, giving them both one last look. "And don't worry. I'll probably be calling every day." She went quickly out the door so she couldn't hear her mother cry.

Maren got into her little car, throwing the suitcase and duffel in the backseat. She started the engine and sat, waiting for the car to warm up a little. *Sometimes the right decisions are the hardest.* The radio came on to the last station she had listened to. It was way back when she had driven home from Dr. Don's clinic. *So long ago, so long ago.*

She dug in the glove box and pulled out a calendar. It was open to June of the previous year. She had circled the date she left Wisconsin in yellow highlighter and then another circle approximately two weeks later. Maren smiled. *And I was actually only going to be here for two weeks ... how things change. How things change.* She flipped through the months on the calendar to May. Then she circled May 4 with big yellow circles. She laid the calendar on the seat beside her and put the car in gear.

She got halfway down the road when she felt the hair on the back of her neck prickle. It rushed all the way down her back. She slammed on the brakes and cranked the volume off on the radio. *Something ... something's happening.* Then she heard it. People's voices. Yelling. Then a howl. A long, overwhelming howl.

Maren threw open the car door and looked back toward the cabin. She could vaguely make out the figures of her mother and Dr. Don. They were jumping up and down, waving their hands.

Another howl ... . Maren leapt onto the hood of her car like a gazelle then onto the roof of the car in another smooth leap. She stood with her hand up to her forehead to block the sun. There they were. In the tree line. A breathtaking black wolf with a glistening silver ruff, and a smaller gray and brown next to him. Both howling away, their noses to the sky. Maren jumped up and down on the car roof, not giving a damn whether it was denting or not.

"Three moons!" Maren cupped her hands around her mouth and yelled out toward the howling wolves. They both went quiet. The small gray turned and disappeared into the tree line. Maren knelt down on the roof. She stared back at her Moonbaby until he, too, turned and disappeared. She looked back toward the little cabin. She could just make out her mother, her head buried in Dr. Don's chest and him lightly patting her back.

Maren jumped off the roof of the car and got back in. She put the shifter in drive and drove down the gravel road, her hand resting lightly on the calendar in the seat next to her.

Epilogue

Two Months Later

The severe cold was less and less and the days were getting longer. Still, the icy days outnumbered the warmer ones in late March in northern Minnesota. There was two feet of fresh snow on the ground. Although the sun was bright, it did little to warm the older wolf that was huddled in a shallow dug out under a group of heavy, dark green northern pines. Moonbaby sniffed the air. *Another storm coming. More snow. Hard for Hawk.*

The first two months had been a wonder of scents and sensations. Moonbaby felt a joy that he had so missed since he was a baby wolf. *Feel more as a wolf. Smell more. See more.* Even old Hawk kept up with him most of the time. But the smell of sickness was about him, and it was getting stronger. Then things changed. It was after the second moon when Hawk collapsed on the five mile trail to get the meat that brother Jules was putting out.

Moonbaby had to dig out a small hollow in the frozen snow right on their trail. He lay next to Hawk to keep him warm. Hawk was irritable—snapping at him for no reason. *Hawk's angry—angry about being weak.* Moonbaby sensed it from his previous human side, the understanding of reason and why things happen. His wolf side told him only that it was happening and he needed to take action. He even went out to get a fresh kill—a young, tender rabbit. But Hawk wasn't interested. He preferred the human's cow meat over anything Moonbaby brought him, even if it was frozen hard in the snow. *Too long human.*

Five more nights came and went. Moonbaby managed to get Hawk back up to the higher ground where he had made their small den. It had been a slow process with Hawk panting and out of breath. They had to stop several times and Moonbaby waited nervously. Although he felt a sense of relief once Hawk finally crawled into the hollow, it was short-lived. Hawk wasn't moving out of the den anymore. He was eating very little. The snow Moonbaby kicked up over him continuously was not only to keep him warm, but to camouflage his scent. It was useless. His scent and waste were leaving too strong a sign—that of a weakened prey animal.

Moonbaby paced anxiously thirty feet from the den, his nose to the air. He had picked up the scent only a couple days ago. It was a wolf pack. Even though Moonbaby had marked his territory repeatedly, this group was scoping out the situation. They had ignored his markings and were methodically circling Moonbaby's territory. There was danger in the air— an evil. This wasn't an ordinary wolf pack.

Moonbaby could no longer leave Hawk alone while he hunted nor could he make the trek to retrieve the meat left out for them. He spent the days slinking around the borders of his territory, everyday picking up the scents of the wolves that were challenging him. They were bold, pissing right on top of his scent marks. They were moving in faster, smelling the weakened changeling in their reach.

It was on the sixth day that Moonbaby made a kill. One of the pack had arrogantly walked within sight. It was a large grey wolf, probably out of Canada. But he wasn't a normal wolf and he wasn't a changeling. He had burning red eyes and was there for one purpose only. Changeling blood. He was Wendigo.

Moonbaby sat in wait as the grey, eyes glazed over with the kill instinct, moved in. With his nose focused only on the scent that overwhelmed his nostrils, the grey moved too carelessly toward the den where Hawk lay. Moonbaby came from downwind, leapt onto the unsuspecting wolf with his enormous black mass, and quickly tore out his throat. Then he angrily disemboweled him, strewing his entrails along the border of his territory. *Not much time. Not much time until they all come for Hawk. Can't defend him and myself against this pack.*

Moonbaby threw himself tiredly down in the snow next to Hawk. He savagely licked the blood off his black fur as if it were poison. He looked over at Hawk, who was watching him. Hawk's ears were half down as he crawled forward to Moonbaby. He laid his head on Moonbaby's paw and growled softly from the back of his throat. His tail thumped in the snow several times and was quiet. He locked eyes with Moonbaby for several seconds, then licked Moonbaby's jaw as if he needed to taste the blood of the evil Wendigo himself. Then he stretched out in the snow next to him and shut his eyes. His tail thumped again as if he knew they had an understanding.

Hawk sighed and rested. Moonbaby whined, fully understanding what Hawk wanted. *He doesn't want Wendigo to get him—to get his soul. No matter what. Don't let it happen. Don't let it happen. He's happy. He's been happy. Wendigo cannot have him.*

Moonbaby licked Hawk's graying muzzle several times, then he sat up and sniffed the air. It wouldn't be long now. The Wendigo would be too smart to just send in one wolf again. This time it would be the whole pack. Four or five, Moonbaby determined by the scents he picked up. He would wait. He would wait until the last minute. He would lie next to Hawk and remember his days as Damien and Hawk as his mentor and teacher, Blackhawk. Then he would not let Wendigo have him.

It didn't take long. It was dusk. This time the wolf pack was unconcerned with the noise they made, emboldened by rage from the one of their own that was killed.

Moonbaby stood up and shook off the snow. He leaned down to Hawk. Hawk opened his eyes for a moment, then shut them, his tail again thumping against the packed snow. Moonbaby reached down, gingerly opened his jaws, and placed them on Hawk's neck. He positioned the blunt, strong teeth of his back jaw directly over Hawk's carotid artery. Then he squeezed … hard. Hawk's back legs jerked. He was still.

There was a sudden fevered rush from the trees, almost as if the wolves sensed something had been taken from them. Moonbaby bolted. He ran and ran. He paused only to hear the frustrated growling, yelping and fighting noises of the wolf pack when they discovered their prey was already dead.

Moonbaby didn't stop running until he reached "the hook," the place of his birth, over ten miles away. He collapsed on the rocky limestone ridge, panting heavily, every so often growling and biting—angrily—at his feet. It was done. They didn't win. It was a fight for another day. Something else had drawn him … pushed him to run and save his life. He gazed again at the night sky. *One more moon. One more. Maren … Starr.*

Moonbaby exhausted, struggled to stand on all fours, his head drooping for only a minute. Then he stretched his nose to the cold, still, night sky. He howled until his entire body trembled. It was the long, mournful wail of a lone wolf.